Deceiving Ace

Men of Honor Series Book 2

A. C. Gregory

Thomas Publishing

Copyright © 2023 A. C. Gregory

All rights reserved

The characters and events portrayed in this book are fictitious. Any similarity to real persons, living or dead, is coincidental and not intended by the author.

No part of this book may be reproduced, or stored in a retrieval system, or transmitted in any form or by any means, electronic, mechanical, photocopying, recording, or otherwise, without express written permission of the publisher.

ISBN-9798848735598

Cover design by: Art Painter
Library of Congress Control Number: 2018675309
Printed in the United States of America

THIS BOOK IS DEDICATED TO THE MEN AND WOMEN WHO SERVE OUR GLORIOUS COUNTRY. THANK YOU FOR YOUR SERVICE.

Contents

Title Page

Copyright

Dedication

Foreword

Introduction

Deceiving Ace: Men of Honor Series Book 2:

Chapter 1	1
Chapter 2	5
Chapter 3	11
Chapter 4	15
Chapter 5	22
Chapter 6	29
Chapter 7	37
Chapter 8	45
Chapter 9	53
Chapter 10	62
Chapter 11	69
Chapter 12	76
Chapter 13	83
Chapter 14	91

Chapter 15	99
Chapter 16	107
Chapter 17	115
Chapter 18	123
Chapter 19	131
Chapter 20	139
Chapter 21	147
Chapter 22	155
Chapter 23	163
Chapter 24	170
Chapter 25	179
Chapter 26	187
Chapter 27	195
Chapter 28	203
Chapter 29	209
Epilogue: Ace	213
About The Author	215
Books By This Author	217

Foreword

This is the second installment in the Men Of Honor Series. Lot's of action and suspense just waiting for you to delve into.

Ace has his hands full with someone he's spent the last seven years trying to avoid. His mission to rescue Toni leaves him hurt and frustrated. He knew things weren't left on the best of terms, but he was not prepared for a reception like this.

Introduction

Today started out like any other. The team, a target, and a mission. What do you do when the target you've chosen has put a hit out on a family member? You take swift decisive action! The plan is to rescue Toni before the assassins find her. If I fail this mission I will have to face the devil!

Ace:
I have to rescue Chaos' little sister before the assassins get to her. Someone put a hit out on the head of a librarian. The payout is large enough to ensure assassins from all over the globe will be out for Toni's head. There isn't a moment to spare!

Toni knows things about me and the team that she shouldn't know. Lives are at stake. She's keeping more secrets than is healthy. Keeping her alive is my first mission. Finding out what she's hiding and why, is my personal mission. I will get the job done!

Deceiving Ace: Men of Honor Series Book 2:

Chapter 1

Col. Paulson has calls Alpha, Bravo, and Charlie teams to the cave for a 2300hr briefing. A new mission is on the horizon. The Colonel enters the cave looking serious. One can tell by the length of his stride he's not taking prisoners on this one! All the men jump to attention. Locking up tight. They know the drill. The Colonel makes his way to the head of the conference table and says, "*At ease, men.*" A collective sigh is heard around the room as everyone takes their seats. The Colonel doesn't waste time with niceties. He begins the briefing. "*OK, gentlemen, here's what we know. We've received intel that a group of Tibetan monks have been kidnapped. In addition to the monk's untimely removal a few priceless artifacts were also nicked. These are very important cultural artifacts floating in the wind. Artifacts of historical significance and interest to the United States government.*"

"*This isn't a scenario where we can just call the Chinese government and say, "Hey, you know the artifacts we stole from you? The very same artifacts we then lent back to you at a fair price for use in your museums. Well, they've been stolen. Can we have them back, please?*" The artifacts in question became a source of contention when the Chinese government took control of Tibet in 1950. Omega stumbled upon two of the very same artifacts in question up for sale on the dark web. Incidentally, that is also how they came to know the Tibetan monks were kid napped. We've received intel that the Chinese know about the kidnapping, and desires to keep the information contained. They are not aware of our mission, nor will assistance be rendered. So, once again we go in dark.*" Surprise, surprise.

"Omega is working on the location of the monks, and the artifacts. There's going to be an auction held for the most exclusive artifacts. Four of the six pieces stolen will be placed up for auction. One of you will attend that auction. Some of the buyers may be on our most wanted list, so if an opportunity arises to take them out please do so, but our main objective is to acquire the artifacts. If we can save the monks in the process all well and good. If not, we will leave them to the Chinese. The boss has decided we want the artifacts back in our possession. Sooner rather than later, gentlemen. The agreement between both governments was that Tibet would take possession of the artifacts for fifty years. They would pay the US government a possession fee. At the end of the agreement all artifacts would be returned to the United States. Well, it seems they forgot about the last portion of the agreement. Suddenly, they were stolen. Coincidence? I think not. We retrieve what's ours!"

"Just to be clear. This isn't just about a few ancient relics. There are other important pieces on the chess board as well. We will use the artifacts and the kidnapping as an excuse to get us closer to where we need to be! This is how things will break down. Logic, Gator, Coup the Italian Death Dealer was in the states a while back. We lost him, now we have found him again. Chase him down. To the ends of the earth if need be. I will keep you updated en route. Wheels up at 0700 hours. Venom is your base of operations. Gravity, Polar, Chaos, and Thrasher, I need you in Tibet. Like yesterday. Gravity, you take the lead on this one. Polar is your second. Ace is your base of operations. I want you to find the missing artifacts that have not been put up for sale on the dark web.

Omega will pull the thread that leads back to the seller. Updates in progress. I need you men to be aware of the terrain. Your equipment has been loaded on the bird. Double check equipment before wheels up at 0400 hrs. Last I checked it was minus forty degrees in Tibet. Let's not get frostbite, gentlemen. I expect you all to make it back in one piece. You know how pissed-off I get when I don't get what I want. Gravity, some base jumping will be required. Polar *you are the terrain expert. Keep everyone at room temperature will ya! I want you back here thawed and in one piece. I know I don't need to tell you men about how important this mission is. So, let's go out there and kick butts and cross off names! Am I clear?"*

The group responds, *"OORAH!"*

"Razor, Crucible, Reaper, you're on standby for Logic. Anchor, Optic, Sledge, Dome, Pyro, I need you as vapor. I have a mission for you that we will discuss after this briefing. Some of you will be assigned backup for Gravity as well. You choose once you have the details."

"OORAH! The team responds in unison.

The Colonel shouts, *"What's our motto!"* We shout back, *"ONE MAN! ONE MIGHT! ONE MISSION!"* The Colonel says, *"Do what you do best. You're dismissed!"* The Colonel leaves the room with Anchor, Optic, Sledge, Dome, and Pyro on his heels. The rest of the men gather around checking weapons when mayhem ensues. Why don't our weapons checks ever go quietly?

We know it's on when we hear Razor say, *"Yo, Gator, there's a rumor floating around you were recently spotted doing your Spider-Man imitation from the home of a very sexy siren. By way of a second story window. Is that correct?"* Everyone in the room stopped in their tracks. Not a sound can be heard. Gator chuckles and says, *"And who would be responsible for starting such an ugly and vicious rumor? I'm a military man, born and bred. A highly trained covert operative. Why would I need an escape route?"* Razor responds, *"Well, I heard through the grapevine that you took a woman home from the bar, and in the middle of the bump-n-ugly the front door slams open, and her husband makes his presence known. She jumps out of bed like it's on fire. Which let's face it, it may very well have been if you weren't wearing a condom. Sniggering can be heard floating around the room. It's clear the husband was out for blood. Yours! He knows his wife had company and was out for your head. Either head will suffice!"* The men erupt in shouts and guffaws. It's an insane asylum here.

After a short pause Razor continues, "*Any who, your monster truck sitting in the man's driveway was a dead giveaway! She practically pushed you out the window buck naked so as not to get caught. But only you know if that ugly rumor is true or not. Care to share with the group?*" The men are loving every second of it. For the record, this event would not be outside the realm of possibility for someone with Gator's personality. More than a few of his screws are loose. Logic chose him for the team knowing exactly that! Gator stands there with a straight face for a few seconds weighing out his options. All eyes are on him. He loves this stuff! You could hear a pin drop. He grins sheepishly and says, "*I barely had time to grab my boots!*" The men lose it.

The men are laughing so loud it will make your ears bleed. Gator knows how to work a room. After a few minutes pause Gator says, "*Now in my defense, the young lady never stated she was a married woman! Nor was she wearing a wedding ring. I figured it wasn't the husband's fault I was knee deep in his wife, and it wasn't my fault she withheld that pertinent information. There may have been a tan line around her ring finger, but the bar was dark. Mistakes happen. It would have been unfair of me to beat the man down in his own house. You should have seen me squeezing through that small window in nothing but my Stetson and cowboy boots. The young lady was kind enough to chuck the remainder of my clothes out the window down to me. She's such a freakin' lady!*" The men laugh even harder. It's several minutes before any of us can pull ourselves together. This is the tradition. Someone always rips on someone else to get the men out of their own heads right before a mission. It's a great way to decompress. It's one of the best things about being a part of the team. Now, let me introduce you to the men.

Chapter 2

Alpha Team.
Logic: 35-year-old. Alpha team lead. Genius IQ. Married with one kid, and one kid on the way. Ex-navy seal from a small town in Virginia. Six feet eleven inches tall. Hobbies: surfing the dark web, reading, racing fast cars. Has his pilot's license. Good at everything. Birth name is Gabriel Tyler Vazquez. Best to stay on his good side. Fluent in six different languages. Deadly!

Gravity: 34-year-old pilot. Alpha's 2nd in command. Ex-air force fighter. Six feet five inches tall. From Wyoming. Can fly anything. Hobbies: Parachuting, and BASE jumping. He likes killing too. History of cage fighting. Excels at hand-to-hand combat. Likes to observe. Very strategic. Difficult to predict. Birth name Ridge Seales.

Coup: 34-year-old Alpha team member. Ex-special forces. There is no terrain he cannot navigate. Six feet zero inches. From Alaska. Master in Krav Maga, and other forms of martial arts. Hobbies: Running up mountains, ninja throwing stars, love to fight. Birth name is Mason Cooper.

Ace: 33-year-old sniper. Ex-Delta force/MI6. Six feet tall. Can shoot on the run more accurately than most can while stationary. Uses his English accent as a weapon on the ladies. From Liverpool, England. Hobbies: Building his own weapons and ammo. Holds a secret from the team. Thinks he looks like Idris Elba. Birth name is Adam Arthur Prince. Trilingual.

Venom: 33-year-old Medic/Herpetologist. Ex-marine and combat medic. Six feet two inches tall. Has been known to perform an operation with nothing but a hunting knife and snake venom to fight infection. Fluent in seven different languages. From New York City. Hobbies: All things snake related. Expert in poisons and snake venoms. Hyper focused. Birth name is Akito Lee.

Chaos: 32-year-old explosives expert. Ex-marine. Six feet four inches tall. Loves blowing things up. From Chicago, Illinois. Hobbies: Cooking, cage fighting, and explosives. Known for his steady hands. Lost his parents in a motor vehicle accident. Has guardianship of his younger sister. Birth name is Chance Townsend.

Bravo Team:
Gator: 36-years-old. Bravo team lead. Cajun from the Bayou. Ex-Navy seal. Stands six feet seven inches tall. Some say he's psychic. Confers with the dark arts. Knows when Trouble is coming. Hobbies: Professional wrestler. Wrestling alligators. Expert in all types of watercrafts. Mixed martial arts master. Loves the ladies. Birth name is Rene' Andre Xavier.

Razor: 35-year-old. Bravo 2nd in command. Ex-Special Forces with top honors in Sere training. Sniper. Stands six feet four inches. Loves all weaponry. Blades are his thing. From the Appalachian Mountains. Hobbies: blades, throwing stars, razors, knives. Usually walks around with a razor tucked under his tongue. He makes his own weapons. Moves like the wind. Birth name is Raymond Pierce.

Polar: 34-years-old. All terrain expert. Data expert. Ex-Marine. Stands six feet three inches. Excels at hand-to-hand combat. Ready at all times. Born in Iceland. Climbed to the top of Everest and lived to tell the tale. Hobbies: Cold weather sports. High moral compass. Birth name is Jaime Ramos.

Crucible: 36-year-old medic. Ex-Air force. Specializing in Pararescue. Stands six feet four inches. Participated in very dangerous missions. Loves music. Orphaned. No background info. Hobbies: Music, martial arts, and danger. Birth name is Logan Wilde.

Thrasher: 35-year-old Olympic gold medalist in mixed martial arts. Ex-Yakuza member. Stands six feet six inches. The Colonel brought him back to life and added him to the team. Suffered extensive memory loss. Special skill is disappearing, killing and organization. Hobbies: Yoga, Tibetan chanting, cage fighting, and Isolation. Birth name is Chikao Junichiro. He had a sense of humor when choosing his name.

Dolphin: 34-years-old. Ex-Navy seal. Gold Olympic swimmer. Silver medal in Archery. Munitions expert. Judo and Taekwondo expert. From a two-lane Iowan town. Stands six feet two inches. Hobbies: Motorcycles. Swimming. Women. In that order. Can hold his breath for eleven minutes thirty seconds. Birth name is Brandon Fox.

Logic, Gator, Coup, and Ace activate comms waiting to receive updates from Omega. They perform a second weapons check while in transition. They have some of their favorite weapons in tow. They're bringing along a few AR 15s with M4A1s. SIG Sauer P220 10mm Elites. Some Elite tactical carbon fibers G10 retractable blades. M18 white smoke grenades. Pineapple grenades. They throw in a few extras for good measure. A few landmines. M3E1 Super bazookas. RPGs. Just a few toys to ensure mission safety. Locating and gathering intel from the Italian Death Dealer will be no walk in the park. When he goes underground, he goes deep! We must come prepared for every conceivable contingency. Everyone knows one should never arrive at a party empty handed! That's just rude! The guy is slippery! He's managing to become eviler every day! My brain has conjured up quite a few scenarios. Very inventive ways to end this man.

Logic

Leaving Samar and Ty behind hasn't gotten any easier. I doubt it ever will. Knowing my mother will be here to assist gives me comfort. Even still, I can feel the adrenaline spike in my system. I am ready to get this show on the road! My wife, Samar, is very pregnant. I missed the birth of our first child. Reader, you remember the details, don't you. It's a long story. Anyway, only death can keep me from this birth. We've decided to wait to discover the gender of our baby. In my gut I know it's a girl. I hope she looks just like her momma. Venom is our base of operations and will run operations from an undisclosed location close to my private residence. He loves spending time with Ty. Corrupting him is more like it. I feel better knowing my family is in good hands when I'm away. A squawk comes over comms. Then we hear, *"Logic, Gator, Coup, Venom, I have news. It appears the Italian Death Dealer is in Nice, France."*

"From the chatter we're receiving underground he has a very important meeting scheduled. It's unclear with whom he's meeting, but something big is afoot. You can believe he won't be handing out backpacks to underserved youths. This mission has some very confusing moving parts. I will update you as the intel arrives. You can then form your own hypothesis, and plan accordingly. I did pick up a blurb about a safety deposit box possibly in a bank in Italy. It must contain something important. I will notify you once we sort out which bank holds the intel. There is a hive of activity surrounding the Italian Death Dealer and the other person or persons of interest. Enough to make my spidey senses go haywire. Stay tuned men! Omega out!"

Logic says, *"Is it me or is Omega becoming bossy? I may have to add Omega to my kill list. At this point it's a real possibility!"*

We ensure all our gear is loaded on the C20H. We have no idea how long this mission will last, but I pray it's over quickly! Gator says, *"Hey, Logic. I grow more and more curious about what the Death Dealer has up his sleeve. All his evil is done on such a large scale. Him being in the states, and now France seems linked. I'm wondering how the two are connected."*

"As do I, brother. As do I. One thing's for sure, whatever he's up to, we won't like it. Nor will we tolerate it. I missed the opportunity to neutralize the Italian Death Dealer a few months ago. I will not make that same mistake again. Every time his name comes up it's for something worse than the time before it. The world would be a much safer place without him in it. He is number three on my kill list. I have five names left before I can retire. My plan is to grow old and fat watching my children play. Sitting beside Samar on the back porch in our rocking chairs. Learning a few new hobbies. Talking to my neighbors. Working hard to avoid you lunatics! Is that too much to ask?"

Gator replies, *"Well Logic, not to rain on your parade, but the team and I WILL be your neighbors. You should have chosen a better neighborhood! We collectively own two hundred acres of land. You should know. You purchased it. In the line of work you're in, YES that is definitely too much to ask. Let me ask you a question. What were you thinking. Did you imagine you were a regular joe. Working a simple nine to five. Look at you trying to keep hope alive. Isn't that special. Besides, I know you. You would be bored out of your mind! How cute is that. Logic learning how to crochet. Stranger things have been known to happen. But hey, I'm rooting for ya."*

"Gee, thanks! Aren't you cute. You are also so well in tuned to my feelings."

"You said it yourself. We take this job one mission at a time. All we can ask for is to come home safely. Besides, if you retire who will finish raising Coup? I'm not doing it! That's an extremely dangerous mission that will fall to your second in command,

Gravity" Logic chuckles.

"*Roger that!*" Logic totally agrees.

Coup says, "*Logic when you leave, I leave. We ride as one. No need for me to stick around trying to break in a new team lead. I simply don't have the bandwidth for it. Ain't that right, papa bear? Prime. Pops.*"

"*Ha ha. Very funny, baby-bear.*" The group chuckles at that.

Then Logic says, "*On a serious note. Coup, if you were really my son, I would have disciplined you more. It's clear you have no home training. Your head is hard. You don't like to listen, and you never clean your room. Your parents failed you, big time!*"

Coup responds with, "*Well, papa-bear, you may have a point. I will do better going forward. Can I get a raise in my allowance, now?*" All I can do is shake my head at this man. He's not normal, but he's an asset to the team. We disperse for some shut eye. At 0700 hours we are wheels up and on our way to France. Time flies. Oh, happy day!

Chapter 3

Gravity

We have gear to inspect and about two hours to get some shut eye. I am wired for sound and wonder if I'll sleep at all. I get to BASE jump from Mount Everest. Who could sleep knowing that? Thrasher will pilot the aircraft while I jump and find a safe-ish place to land. We need stealth on this mission, but we're not talking about a place the size of Los Angeles. What area isn't covered by mountains and snow, or mountains of snow, has people occupying it trying to eke out a living. Thrasher's job will be a lot more difficult than mine. While mine will be a lot more dangerous than his. Simply put, it's the nature of the beast. Thousands of people have died attempting to climb this mountain. It was on my bucket list. There is no time like the present. Although I won't be climbing the mountain. I will be dropped off somewhere on it and make my way down. I need to see if there's anything up there worth finding. My heart rate spikes just thinking about it.

There is a high margin for error. I double checked my seven-cell ram-air parachute with sliders. My parachute will be required to open quickly. There is an extra one beside it. I triple check this one just in case. My chute is packed in a rig. I am confident the parachutes will perform as expected. There's helmets and body armor. All the equipment is new. Good old Uncle Sam didn't spare any expense. Must be some real pricey relics we're tasked to find. We finish inspecting our gear and huddle up for a last-minute briefing. 0400 hours will be here before you know it. Chaos says, *"Gravity, you and Thrasher never finished your cage match. We won't allow a breach of our compound to rob us all of a conclusion now, will we?"*

Thrasher responds with, *"The breaching of our compound is what saved Gravity's sorry hide. I was knocking the stuffing out of him and enjoying every second of it. He better be thankful Malik Oscega came calling. Otherwise...!"*

"Dude. Please? Stop! Your delusions can't be due to the increase in altitude because we are still on terra firma." We each chuckled at that. *"All I can tell you is anytime, anyplace. All we need is air and opportunity. There's a pile of money waiting to be claimed. I for one am ready to claim it. Wherever. Whenever! You on the other hand not so much. You look like you've been ridden hard and put up wet. What's with you, Thrasher?"*

"Gravity you're just jealous because I'm an Asian Stallion and you're, well...? I'm not entirely sure what the heck you are, besides old and weathered. You're tired. Poor little man. Someone needs a sugar momma. How long has it been since you were intimate with anything besides your right hand? Do share, Gravity?"

Chaos and Ace find the whole exchange hilarious. Sometimes I want to punch each of them in the face. Leave it to Chaos to create chaos. *"Thrasher, why are you all up in my business? You're the Asian Stallion that must settle for my cast offs. You should be very well rested. Even my cast offs aren't interested! Your tattoos scare the women away. Maybe you should do something about that."*

"Believe me when I tell you, the type of women I'm attracted to are not afraid of a little body art! I prefer my women well over the age of consent. Not like the women you prefer. Barely toeing the line of consent. With the smell of fresh milk still tainting their breath!" I even have to laugh at that. Why do I even talk to these people?

"You know what, Thrasher? I prefer my woman matured with

the ability to hold a conversation. But, not to worry, I have plans for you. Don't you worry at all."

"Whatever, old man!"

"I'm going to hunker down. Sweet dreams, misfits." I walk away and can still hear them goofing off. I wouldn't trade these guys for the world.

Omega

"Insipid, we have a huge problem!"

If I had a dollar for every time I've heard or uttered that line I could retire from this job before I go blind. Leave it to Zypher to appoint me 2nd in command and then take a vacation. That should not be allowed! *"What's the problem, Mantra?"*

"You need to notify the Colonel, quick. There's been a hit placed on Antonia Townsend! There's chatter and hitmen from all over the globe locking in to pick up the contract. It's a smorgasbord of accepters. I'm trying to track it down and locate the source of the hit. The signal's a bit little tricky."

"Mantra, pass the data over to my screen. We don't have time to waste! Go ahead and patch me into the Colonel. He won't be happy about this. Someone has a death wish. Who in their right mind would attempt something so reckless? I feel a migraine coming on."

"Insipid, we have the Colonel on line one."

"Did you upgrade the connection to molten lava? We can't afford to have this link hijacked."

"Already done!" I nod at Mantra. This day just turned into two days.

"*Colonel, Insipid. Dark web. Kill order. Antonia Townsend. Ace, nearest to target for extraction. Activated and deployed. Pulling threads for details. Updates pending.*"

"Well done! I was hoping for a quiet evening, Omega. Not possible now, is it?"

I chuckled. "*Good night, Sir.*" I disconnected the feed. Believe me when I say, I get it. I would love a quiet evening by myself. That isn't happening any time soon for any of us, now. The Colonel has to walk a tight rope. For one, Chaos is a lunatic. When dealing with one of the lunatics you deal with the whole team. That means all of Alpha team. Ugh! That man loves his sister. He fights his demons every waking moment. This may just be the thing that pushes him right over the edge. His parents' deaths weren't his fault. Try to convince him that fact isn't happening. Omega will do everything in our considerable power to protect the men! Period.

Chapter 4

ACE

Stealthily, I make my way into the house. Well under the cover of darkness. Using the back door as a point of entry. It took all of four seconds to pick the locks. A toddler could have done it. Not very secure at all! It's a colonial two-story brick-faced structure. Seems a little too large for one person, but what do I know. I have about three minutes to get her out of dodge before she's neutralized. They're professional assassins for hire, and they are coming! They're already enroute. Somehow, they found her. Omega was thorough. Extremely careful! They scrubbed her identity from every database, known and unknown. Eliminated all sources of personal data. They left no electronic footprint behind for anyone to follow. No social media. No bureau of vital statistics. Nothing at all. Not even the IRS could find her, and they manage to find everyone! Then she was given a new identity.

Her new identity came complete with a birth certificate, social security number, passport, school records from preschool to college, and a bogus work history. We falsified tax records, and immunization cards. We were thorough. Thus, this shouldn't be possible, and yet…? There is no way this should be happening! This must involve some pretty powerful players. There was only one other person besides the team who knew her new identity. My mind is blown. I take the stairs two at a time. Careful to avoid the center tread. That's where the weak spots are more likely to be. Don't want to alert her to my presence before I'm in position.

I turn the knob on her bedroom door and ease inside. I stop just inside the room. A silhouette of her sleeping form can be seen wrapped in a thin sheet. Made possible by the sliver of moonlight peeking through her bedroom window. She's sleeping on her back. What I remember of her physical form is stellar. Even back then. I remember every detail. Some things you just don't forget. I burn for her. Missing her is a persistent ache that gnaws at my soul! That is not why I'm here, though. If I don't focus, we're both dead! I swept the room before holstering my Beretta 92X. Then I took up position.

I sit on the edge of her bed, careful to bear the majority of my body weight, clamp my hand down tight over her mouth, to prevent a scream, and give her a few seconds to register my existence. Her eyes shoot open in alarm! I cling to the shadows. I hate scaring her, but my time and my options are limited. I can almost feel the assassins breathing down my neck. They are that close! I've been on edge ever since we received intel that a contract was placed on her head. I was the closest in proximity, so I was given the job. Protect her at all costs. You don't have to tell me twice. I lean over and whisper in her ear. *"Relax Doll. It's me."* I pause, giving her a second to adjust. *"You have fifteen seconds to get dressed. We have to leave. Now! Nod if you understand."*

To her credit she doesn't utter a single sound, she just nods her head. The lack of response catches me off guard. Not sure what I was expecting, but it sure wasn't this. She didn't scream or try to fight. This is not a typical civilian response. I removed my hand from her mouth, stand, and take three steps back. I whisper, *"No light, and no electronics."* She nods again. At least I think she does. She goes into her closet and returns in twelve seconds. Her efficiency is a turn on. *"Let's go!"* She reaches into her nightstand drawer, removes a pill bottle, dumps the contents of the pill bottle into a drawstring bag, and inserts the bag into the pocket of her hoodie. She turns and grabs my hand. I guess that means she's ready to go.

I lead her out the bedroom door keeping to the shadows. The assassins are about two minutes out. I am being fed intel by Omega via a comms unit in my left ear. I hear, *"Ace, they are approaching your location from the east and west. Two vehicles. Four men per vehicle. You have about fifty-two seconds to disappear!"* This limits our choice of escape. I have no desire to engage in combat with a civilian in tow. Normally, I would relish these odds. Eight to one. Not bad! But, not with precious cargo on board. If I'm lucky, I will meet up with these men another time. I hope that day comes real soon. Then we'll see who kills who. My extraction plan is tight. The contract was found on the dark web, and the order was a kill order, not a capture order. That in itself carries all sorts of implications. Someone wants Chaos' little sister dead! Why?

Omega discovered the kill order and informed the Colonel. Then I was activated. Being stateside made me the most logical option. Time is of the essence. This is a prime example of Omega being Omega. We have been in constant three-way communication ever since. Chaos will be notified after the extraction plan is completed. He can't afford any distractions while on the job. People's lives hang in the balance. Withholding this intel will send him right over the moon. There is no doubt in my mind that's true. I'm just glad I don't have to be the one to tell him. This decision was the Colonel's, and his alone. I see his point but would rather have informed Chaos. The Colonel feels it's best to notify him after I've secured the package. For me failure is not even an option! A two-million-dollar bounty was placed on Antonia Townsend's head. Two million dollars for the head of a librarian. Hmmm. Nope! I don't buy it. Something is way off!

Who knows how many assassins will show up to carry out the hit? That's a nice chunk of change. Once she and I slide out the back door, I motion using only hand signals to indicate we are going over the fence. She nods her understanding. I grip her left forearm holding her in place. There's a mean German shepherd a few yards over. An obnoxiously loud German shepherd. I need to time our next move exactly. I hear tires screech to a halt and car doors open. Then the very dog in question starts barking his head off. That's when I hoist her over the fence and follow directly behind her. I couldn't have planned for a better-or well-timed distraction if I tried. It's very effective. My black navigator is parked about a mile south. We have to make it to the safety of that armor plated SUV, before they discover us. My plan is tight, but doable.

It won't take long for the assassins to discover she's not in bed. These people want to get paid! They are highly motivated, well connected, and will continue to search until she's found. These are professionals for hire. In order to collect on the bounty, they have to provide proof of death. Convincing evidence must be handed over to the owner of the contract. The evidence could include a severed head, explicit photos of a deceased body, a finger, or an ear. Things of that nature. The more mangled the better! No one would dare falsely collect on a contract. The entire syndicate would converge on anyone stupid enough to try. While she was in the closet, I arranged the pillows to make it look like someone was in her bed. That will only buy me a few seconds at best. Depending on how sadistic these people are it may not buy me any time at all. They may just go in guns blazing!

They will need time to clear the premises. That's what I'm banking on. That should take about one hundred and twenty seconds. If they're in a hurry to collect, then it won't buy me an extra ten seconds. I don't plan to stick around to find out though. My plan is to be long gone. I won't hold my breath or pray for miracles. We will keep it moving. One thing's for sure, if I fail, we are both dead! Once over the fence, I grab her hand and take off running. Her obnoxiously tall fence will provide ample cover until we clear the next few yards. To her credit she has the foresight to dress in all dark clothing. Yeah, I think I'm in love. We are running as fast as her little legs will carry her. She's five feet four inches tall and weighs about a buck ten. I bench press more than that. She's scrappy, though. I'll give her that!

TONI

One minute I'm sound asleep, and the next minute I feel a hand clamp down tight over my mouth. I'm so frightened I nearly swallow my tongue! The hand over my mouth is so tight I couldn't scream even if I tried. I'm caught completely off guard! What the…? What I don't need to do right now is panic. I feel panic rising up in me like a tidal wave, anyway. Threatening to drag me under. That would be the absolute worst thing to do. It would not help me in the slightest. Panic paralyzes. I need to keep my wits about me. Before my brain can decide on a plan of action I hear, *"Relax, doll."* The desire to fight almost wins out! Through the fog it occurs to me, there is only one arrogant jerk in the whole world who calls me that. Doll. Doll face. I HATE IT! I want to hate him! I honestly never imagined I would hear that nickname again. What is happening?

Why is he sitting on the side of my bed in the middle of the night? He's about to scare me half to death! Every time I think about him, I find myself grinding my molars. His presence is like nails on a chalkboard. Peels the flesh right off me. Given all of that, there is one thing I know for sure, if he's here, this is bad! Like, super bad! I swallow down the panic I feel rising in my chest. I don't bother to ask questions. I will follow his instructions to the letter. If I'm lucky, I'll make it out of this alive. Whatever this is? I honestly have no clue. I can feel my heart thumping trying to escape the confines of my chest. Maybe for more than one reason. There's a proper time and place to deal with my history of pent-up emotions. Maybe, later. Much, much, later! Or never. That works, too. But right now, I will do as I'm told.

I get up, go to my closet, and pull down the first items my hand comes into contact with. I can see the layout of my closet in my mind's eye. I dress in the darkest clothes I can find and go over to my nightstand. I stuff my fear, my heartache, and my confusion way down deep. Hopefully, so far down I'll never find it. Then I grab my sleeping pills and stuff them in my pocket. I grab his hand and wait for further instruction. This is his area of expertise. All I have to do is follow Ace's instructions. We make our way down the stairs and ease out the back door of my house. It feels finite. I'm surer than ever, I will never see this house again. Pity! I like the neighborhood. I won't worry about any of that, right now, though. I'm in survival mode. Fight or flight! We headed out the back door and over to the six-foot-tall white privacy fence.

I had this fence installed three months ago. Its primary function is to obstruct the view of my lecherous neighbor. He likes peaking in while I'm in my backyard enjoying the sunshine. His wife is oblivious to his wandering ways. Her husband is a cheater, and she doesn't have a clue. He's sneaking around with Patty Walthrop. She lives in the beige stucco house on the corner. His wife believes Patty is her friend. So sad! I've lived here for almost three years and have never introduced myself to anyone. I have the vital statistics on everyone in the neighborhood, but I prefer to call my next-door neighbors Mr. Infidel and Mrs. Clueless. Those names are as good as any. Ace pauses. I'm sure he is getting play by play on whatever is going on here. I will wait for his signal.

He indicates we are going over the fence. He takes me by the arm and holds it. Cars pull up, a dog barks, and he takes me by the waist and nearly tosses me over the fence. He follows right on my heels. He's strong and agile, that's for sure. Before his feet touch the ground, he has my hand in his. We take off running as fast as I can manage. More than likely I'm only slowing him down. I am running as fast as I can, and he's barely jogging. His legs are about a mile long. I once found everything about this man attractive. Now, it's just one more thing about him that gets on my last nerve! Oh yeah, I forgot, I stuffed my emotions way deep down. The feelings I'm suppressing are annoyance at his obvious gifts, and my feelings of hurt, abandonment, and betrayal. Nope! Not going there, reader.

We won't go there! Now is not the time. My focus is on surviving. Loathe as I am to admit it, there is no one, other than my brother, who I would trust my life to in a situation like this. Who could keep me as safe as Ace can. He is deadly with weapons. Loyal to the team. Close to my brother. I know he will sacrifice himself for me. That's what they do. The Alpha elite soldiers put themselves in harm's way, so the world can worry about carpooling and live streaming. Most people are oblivious to the sacrifices made by these men. Ace is one of those men. He builds his own guns and ammo for fun. The knowledge that I feel safe with him pisses me off royally! Why should I feel safe with my deserter?! I have to keep in mind Ace is the enemy. He's one of my brother's best friends, but he's still the enemy!

Chapter 5

ACE

I see the navigator parked right where I left it. I hit the key fobs unlock button and hop in the driver's seat. I have all the interior lights disabled. So once the lights flash, the SUV goes dark again. Doll-face doesn't waste a second getting in on the passenger side. She pulls the door closed, careful not to make too much noise, and pulls on her seatbelt. Sound travels farther at night. She is the Bonnie to my Clyde. Then we wait. *"Doll, I need you to slide down in your seat."* She hunkers down in her seat five seconds before we hear a vehicle pass by. According to Omega they have discovered she isn't in bed and is headed in our direction. I parked the navigator in the driveway of a house whose occupants are away on vacation. It's roughly 1:30 a.m. Hopefully there won't be any nosey neighbors lurking about.

The neighborhood is deathly quiet. I do a quick weapons check. My Beretta 92X is locked and loaded. In addition, I have Micro-tech Ultratech S/E tactical blades stashed all over my body. Just in case someone wants to get up close and personal. I never leave home without them. I turn when Toni asks, *"Do you happen to have an extra one of those for me?"* I pull a .380 from my right ankle strap. She's Chaos' sister, so I'm sure he's given her a few lessons on the use of firearms. She hits the button to eject the seven-round magazine. Gives it a once over and reinserts it. Pulls back on the slide to chamber a round and thumbs the safety back on. She does all of this in less than five seconds. I am going to marry this woman!

In her hands she's holding a Sig Sauer P238 380 Extreme with night sights. All I can do is shake my head. Someone's been playing with firearms. I wait ninety seconds before starting the SUV. I navigate the vehicle in the dark, using nothing but the streetlights. Moving in the opposite direction of the would-be assassins. My plan is to avoid a confrontation if at all possible. Not one hair on Chaos' sister's head can be damaged. I would never forgive myself if it did. We have to make it to the exfiltration point. Our ride home will be waiting. I'm certain one of them will be watching the major highway. It's only three clicks away and would be so much more convenient. It would also be more dangerous to use. I'm sure the assassins have eyes on that highway. I will stick to the dirt roads until we are far enough away, and it's safe to hit the highway. My exfil plan was made on the fly.

We are both scanning the roads looking for possible threats. She hasn't said a word, but I can sense she's not happy to see me. I'm not surprised. Not one bit! She has her head turned away from me. Aside from scanning the roads, she is also avoiding eye contact. Toni is using that as an excuse to convince herself that my presence is just a bad dream. I know she is, and I don't blame her. This thing between us is complicated. The last time she saw me was seven years ago. We did not part on favorable terms. My actions were less than honorable. Surely, she hates me. When I allow myself to think back on the events of seven years ago, I hate me, too. Try as I might, I can't seem to forget her. I need desperately to forget her! My life literally depends on my ability to forget her.

I must stay focused. This is the worst possible time to be distracted. We stuck to the backroads, for about ten miles, before hitting the highway. If they decided to double back that would buy us just enough of a head start. I am depending on my engine to do the rest. There is a chopper waiting that will transport us to a safe location. I am on babysitting detail for the duration.

At the very least, until we can resolve this issue. Or until the Colonel states otherwise. This is going to be a very interesting assignment. We drive in complete silence. I almost wish she was one of those females that panicked. One that blabbered when scared or nervous. She is a little too quiet. I want to know what she's thinking. What she's gotten herself into. There will be a debrief once we reach our destination. One of many secure compounds.

TONI

I do everything in my power to avoid looking at *him*. I am scanning the roads for possible threats and pretending this is just a bad dream. Pretending I am not in the confines of an SUV in the middle of the night running for my life. How in the world did this become my existence? I sit behind a computer screen most of the day. Never am I ever evading dangerous criminals. We ride for a while on back roads before hitting the highway. Once on the highway Ace opens her up and is breaking every law in the penal code. If the cops pull us over, he is going to jail. No questions asked. We drive for about an hour before pulling off the road. It's an empty field. Possibly a small airfield. At least I think it's an airfield. The path is rocky and overgrown with tall weeds and brush. I can hear the brush slapping against all sides of the SUV. The ruts in the ground are deep enough to have us rocking from side to side. It's pitch black out here. No streetlights for miles.

Ace cuts the engine and the headlights a split second before I get a brief glimpse of a small plane. I am about to be flown off in the dead of night to who knows where, and I have no idea what's going on. I turn to face Ace. Before I can utter one single word he says, *"Let's go, Doll. Time to move. I will answer all your questions later."* I can feel my blood begin to boil. I don't bother to respond. Just grind my molars. I unlatch my seat belt and open the door. I slide out closing the door gently. Don't want to make any noise. Sound travels farther in the dark. Although, I have to admit slamming it would make me feel better, but only temporarily. Once this issue is resolved, I will never see him again.

My defiant brain chooses the most inopportune time to remind me that that is what I told myself the last time. You will never have to see Ace again! Look how well that worked out for us. Not very helpful brain! Not even a little bit. There are a lot of emotions rolling around inside me. I won't utter a sound until I have them all wrangled in. Not until he tells me that we are safe. I will never let him see how much his departure and reappearance hurt me. Never allow him to see the effects his sudden appearance has on me now. That is privileged information. He is just some stupid guy. No more. No less. Nothing special. Besides, all of that was eons ago. I am so over it! I am over it. Right reader? Of course, I am.

We begin walking towards the plane. He comes over to my side of the vehicle and takes my elbow in hand. I instantly tense up. I'm hit with an overwhelming desire to shake his hand free. His touching me is not ok! He's guiding me over this rough terrain. A death trap is more like it. I refrain from wrenching my arm away! The ground is uneven and wrought with unhappy surprises. The last thing I need is a sprained or broken ankle. Although, a sprained ankle is preferable to his touch. I haven't always felt this way about his touch. I once yearned for his touch. Way back when I was young and foolish. This thing between us is simple really. He regrets ever meeting me. The man has a point!

My time in his presence won't last forever. Once, whatever this is over, I can disappear again. Preferably more successful than I did the last time. Which is what I thought I had accomplished. How on earth did he find me? Just one of the many questions beating a hole in my brain. I climb the stairs of the small plane in silence. When I walk onboard, I'm taken aback. This plane looks like something someone who runs a Fortune 500 company would own. It's sleek and polished. Gleaming sapele wood accents and pristine white marble tabletops. Everything, except the wood on this plane is white. The leather chairs are white. The sofas are white. The carpet is white. I sink onto the leather sofa, and instantly fall in love. This leather is fine grained. Baby bottom smooth. Plush!

I wonder if they'll let me borrow this sofa for my new home. Wherever that's likely to be. At the moment I don't happen to have the answer to that question. My life is normally well organized. These sorts of things never happen to me. I don't happen to like surprises! This aircraft does not strike me as something the United States government would issue its troops. Elite soldiers or not. I can only wonder how they came to fly a plane like this. I'm sure some evil cretin is missing a really nice plane! I needed a distraction. I will use the plane as one. Somehow, my perfectly organized existence life just went off the rails. I need answers. The sooner the better. For a fraction of a second, I allow doubt to creep in. Where is my brother?

A very large man exits the cockpit, gives me a once over, and addresses Ace. *"Strap in. We're wheels up in three!"* Ace nods. Leviathan checks that the cabin door is securely closed, and heads back to the cockpit, closing the door behind him. Effectively shutting us out. The nerve! Not even a hello. I glance around the plane. The plan is to ignore Ace, and pray he disappears in a puff of smoke. Just like he did seven years ago. If I sit here long enough that just may happen. I laid my head back and close my eyes. Now that I'm coming down from my adrenaline high, I feel fatigue setting in. *"Doll, can I get you something to drink?"*

With everything in me I want to ignore this man! Pretend he doesn't exist, but I'm positively parched! There're tufts of cotton floating around in my mouth. That's how it feels anyway. I nod without opening my eyes. There's a shift in the air, so I know he's walking away. I hear him snort. The pilot has started the engines and began to taxi the plane. This is going to be a rough ride. The small plane is bouncing all over the place. The decision to depart from this overgrown weed patch must have been a last-minute decision. I'll be surprised if this hunk of metal makes it up into the air. We are bouncing around like crazy. I hope the pilot knows what he's doing. This has the potential to go very wrong. I may very well be in a death trap. "*Here you go, Doll.*" I open my eyes just as we lift off the ground. Ace has his feet firmly planted shoulder width apart and is barely moving. Ugh! He is so annoying!

I am firmly entrenched in my own thoughts when I hear Ace's voice and open my eyes to see Ace standing over me holding a bottle of water. His sudden nearness disturbs me. I take the bottle from the bottom, careful to avoid skin contact. My actions aren't lost on him. He quirks his right eyebrow and snorts. Again. His face is a mask. I have no way of knowing what he's thinking. Just another thing about him that works my last nerve. He walks over to one of the captain's chairs and straps himself in. I lay my head back again and close my eyes. I can feel him watching me. I really wish *I could* disappear. Why couldn't they have sent someone else? Anyone else! "*Doll, put your seat belt on.*" His voice annoys me. I'm grinding my teeth again. My poor molars!

There won't be any enamel left. They will be ground down to a fine powder well before this ordeal is over. I'll need implants. I refuse to give him the satisfaction of asking him to call me by my name. My name is Antonia Townsend. My friends call me Toni. He very well knows that. He will do just about anything to annoy me. He gets some perverse pleasure from making me want to inflict bodily harm on him. Nothing lethal of course. Just a punch in the throat. A swift kick in the shins.

Whatever. I only ever feel this way around him. This sudden urge to violence. He brings out the worst in me. It's my own stupid fault. I can't spend time in his presence. I pray my brother puts-in-an-appearance. The sooner the better!

Maybe then someone will explain to me what's going on. I'm supposed to be on vacation. I've turned off all my electronics. Maybe that was a mistake. This is supposed to be me disconnecting. Getting some much needed me time. Decompressing. Taking a mental health break. Two weeks. That's all I asked for. A girl just needed a minute. Things at work were hectic. Then I got a promotion. It was a lot. Don't know the last time I took a day off. If this is what happens when I do, I will think twice about trying it again! I'm on day three and managed to be abducted in the middle of the night by the last person I ever expected to see again. Not a good start. Not to mention it does nothing for my mental health. The exact opposite in fact. What is going on? Where is Chaos?

Chapter 6

ACE

Gravity is at the rendezvous point right on time. There is no telling what crazy flying he had to do to get here. He is always dependable! Gravity lands the plane exactly two hours after takeoff. This is one of the many safe compounds our team uses. The three of us deplane. I nod toward a fully armored jeep we'll be using, and Doll-face complies without making a sound. At this point, her compliance should have made me worried. There's a storm brewing, but I'm too preoccupied with saving our lives to notice. I need a word alone with Gravity. Before I open my mouth, Gravity says, *"Ace, you know she's off limits, right?"* Like I need Gravity to remind me of that. Aside from me and Toni, Gravity is the only other person who knows about the events that transpired seven years ago. To my knowledge he hasn't said a word to anyone.

"Dude, I know! Alright? I know!"

"Bro, I really hope you do! Because if you forget, Chaos will remind you. It will be an extremely painful reminder! I wouldn't want that for you! That is exactly what you don't need. Do you need me to take over this babysitting gig?"

"No! I got it."

"You sure?" I simply nod. I'm praying that I'm right.

"Ok. If, you're sure. Keep your comms on at all times. Watch your six. Our plan is to draw everyone connected to this hit out in the open. Shake some things loose. Then we do what we do best.

Execute the long arm of the law. We will wrap things up as quickly as we can. Reunite Chaos with his sister. Hopefully you will stay alive and out of trouble long enough to accomplish that. See you topside." Gravity walks away without another word. Gravity gets straight to the point. I admire that about him. I watch Gravity disappear from view on the other side of the plane. I assume that's where his vehicle is parked. With him you can never be sure. He never takes any unnecessary risks.

I climb into the driver's seat. After the conversation with Gravity, I feel all sorts of things. Tension, anticipation, confusion, anxiety. That old familiar ache is back shouting to be heard over the throng. Normally, I don't do emotion. It clouds your judgement and slows your reflexes. I didn't think seeing Toni would be this difficult. I still yearn for her. This feeling is equal to a punch in the gut. It's been seven years and boy has she matured. She is definitely more beautiful than she was back then. An eighteen-year-old nerd. Already two years into a graduate program. Something to do with cyber security. She was an adorable little nerd. Now she's gorgeous. Her brother will literally kill me if I touch her again!

Not that he's aware I ever touched her in the first place. I have touched her, and very much want to touch her again. She hasn't said a word since finding me at her bedside. I have no idea what she's thinking and that makes me angry. I shake off the nostalgia of the past and start the jeep. The compound is a four-hour drive from our current location. It's late or early depending on how you look at it. I can get the drive done in three. All of a sudden, I feel exhausted. I let my mind go blank. Drawing on the training that has saved my life countless times. I focus on our surroundings. I focus on our mission. I will focus on our goal. We scan as I drive. No one is following us, so that's a good sign. I won't breathe a sigh of relief yet though. In this line of work anything can happen. You learn to expect the unexpected.

GRAVITY

Chaos addresses me, before I come to a complete stop. "Gravity, what's up? You look tense. Is Toni, ok?"

"She's fine. Ace has her covered. Don't worry. We may have a vague idea who put the contract out on Toni. We will redress the situation, and she can go back to her library books. She'll be safe again! We'll make sure of it. She will be safe with Ace at base while we continue on with our current assignment. Operation Paperchase must be completed before we can secure your sister's future." Standing out in a dark empty airfield discussing life and death. How many times have we played out this scenario? Working out the details. Hunting down evil. Making things right. Way too many times to count.

"How in the entire world did they find her? Omega scrubbed her identity from every database in the world. Logic went behind them to double check. You know he never misses anything."

"You're right! I have no idea what happened Chaos, but we will find out. We should be getting back. We have a job to do!"

"Bro, to save time let's sleep on the plane. We can be wheels up at 0430 hours."

"Good idea, Chaos! Let's do it." I know Chaos is worried over the safety of his little sister. He has every right to be. A kill contract is nothing to scoff at. We were enroute to our new mission when I received the order to divert. Ace was the only available option for the extraction of one Antonia Townsend.

It was made clear I would not share this intel. I couldn't follow that order. We ride together, we die together. Chaos is a professional. I trust him with my life, we all do. He will accomplish the mission no matter what! So, I contacted Logic. Then doubled back to exfiltrate Ace and the package. Logic decided it was best to inform Chaos. He is our team leader. We defer to him. He trained us. He knows us best. The Colonel knew the order was a no go. He advised against us informing Chaos citing distractions, but Chaos is the calm in the storm. Keeping this from him would have been a betrayal. It would jeopardize our brotherhood. None of us would stand for that. We trust Chaos to do his job. He always has. He always will!

I decided to pull them out so that he could see Toni is safe, and we can get back to the mission. We are a brotherhood. In truth I was as worried as Chaos was. I groan inside. Ace was the only option for extraction. I get the feeling I will wish more than once for another option. Ace is in love with Chaos' little sister. I'm not sure he's even aware of the fact. I pray this doesn't go south. There are very few brotherhoods rules more tabu than this one. Ace is living on borrowed time. To make matters worse, this could jeopardize the whole Alpha team. Cause a divide. A rift. Logic came up with these by-laws with the team, for the team. They are there for a reason. I have to notify Logic of Ace's history with Antonia Townsend. Hopefully, before this thing implodes. He will not be happy! Sometimes being his second in command is a strain on my sanity. I'm just saying.

ACE

I pulled the jeep into one of the many garages in this compound. I hit the button to close the garage door before exiting the vehicle. I noticed Toni fell asleep about two hours ago. I hate to wake her, but at some point, we have to go inside. I need time to clear the house first, so I will leave her here while I do just that. I take off my seat belt, open the door, and pull my Beretta 92X from my shoulder holster. I came prepared to fight and didn't get a chance to fire one single bullet. I feel frustrated. All dressed up for the party, and no dance partners. What a letdown! I know it's for the best. Wouldn't want to take any chances with the package in tow. If one hair on her head is out of place, Chaos will disappear me. We are that serious about family!

I walk up the three steps to the door that leads to the kitchen. I punch in the twelve-digit code and ease the door open. With my Beretta at the ready I count steps while walking around the rooms. I walk through the kitchen reacquainting myself with the placement of the furniture, and the exits. All our safe houses have the same layout. I know exactly how many steps to each piece of furniture, and where every exit is located. Even the ones not readily visible. I walk into the living room, next. Check closets and behind furniture. I won't leave any stone unturned! Our lives are on the line. Whoever wants Toni dead won't stop sending people until the job is done. Somehow, they found her. My job is to keep her alive until the Alpha team neutralizes the threat!

After systematically clearing every room of the house I walk back to the garage. I cleared the house in ninety-six seconds. Not bad. When I entered the garage I saw Doll-face standing by the Jeep. *"Hey you. You're awake. I was checking the place out before waking you. How do you feel?"*

"Yeah, I figured as much. That's why I'm standing here and not inside. Didn't want to walk up on you from behind, and have you shoot me with your cute little gun. I'm good. What about you?"

That draws a chuckle from me. She's sassy, this one! That's a turn on. *"Thanks, I appreciate that. I'm tiptop, thanks. You ready to go inside?"*

"Sure."

"Follow me." We walk inside, and I lock the door behind us, and press the button to set the alarm. *"Let me give you the nickel tour?"*

"Ok." A woman of a few words. I like that, too. We start in

the kitchen.

TONI

I wake only to find we are parked in a large dark space. I'm alone and it's pitch-black inside. I'm not afraid of the dark but can feel it pressing down all around me. The dark is oppressive. It's complete. I remove my seat belt and get out to stretch my legs. Making sure to cling to the side of the jeep. The smells alone alert me to the fact that we are in a garage. The visibility is poor. My legs are stiff. It may have been scaling a fence, or running full out, or a combination of the two. I go through a few different yoga stretches while I wait. There is no way I'm going inside this building before Ace comes out. He's likely to shoot me or something. I'll stand right here and wait for him. I keep the car door open to cast some light in the dark garage. After a few minutes, I heard Ace coming down the steps.

For the record, he is more gorgeous than he was seven years ago. How is that even possible? I had a huge crush on my brother's friend. My brother is nine years my senior. I was a surprise birth to both my parents. Definitely not planned! My brother Chance (Chaos) became my guardian when my parents died. Before their deaths, I saw my brother a couple times a year. He left for the marines when I was about nine years old. My parents died when I was eighteen. We had already moved, and I was already enrolled at Princeton by that time. I had been attending Princeton for two years when my parents died. My parents made a lot of sacrifices for me. They were wonderful parents. Loving and attentive. Always encouraging me to pursue my dreams.

They sold our house in Florida and moved to New Jersey when I got accepted on a full ride. They knew I was likely to refuse the scholarship feeling nervous and uncertain about being alone. So, they decided to sell our house and moved to New Jersey to be closer to me. Their one caveat was that I stayed in the college dorm and not at home. They were trying to encourage me to make friends. To come out of my shell. Eventually I agreed. They were only a forty-minute drive away. That fact was very reassuring. I was such a computer nerd back then. But my parents loved me. After their deaths, I came to see how fiercely my brother loved me too. We emailed often. He checks in and I shared with him how excited I was to be in college. Some of the things I was working on. Stuff like that.

After my parents died, my brother and I became very close. We have no other family members. I never told my brother Ace, and I hooked up. He would kill us both. Ace has kept his distance all this time. That's the excuse he used for not dating me. Something about violating a bro code. My heart was officially and completely broken. After the funeral I went back to school and tried to delve into my studies to get over my heart break. I am officially over him! I won't admit it even to myself that he is standing here looking all kinds of yummy! That was the past. Best to let sleeping dogs' lie. We are totally different people now. Besides, I have a secret I keep even from my brother. It's for the best. I will keep my distance from Ace. Whatever vestige of emotion still circulating in my blood stream is an inconvenience. I will not allow nostalgia to weaken me. No matter how handsome he is. I can't afford to have Chaos, Ace, or any other Alpha team member discover this secret. Not ever! Lives could be at stake! Namely mine.

Ace gives me a tour of the place and leads me to the final bedroom door on the second floor. He opens the door with a flourish to reveal a huge bedroom. It looks like the master suite. He says, *"This is home for the time being. Make yourself comfortable. The bathroom is through that door over there."* I walked by him into the room. It's a beautiful room. Decorated in cream and different shades of blue. With a king sized, four poster, canopy bed dominating the center of the room. Two nightstands, one on each side of the bed. A dresser and chest of drawers all occupy the room. All beautiful cherrywood pieces. I will take this bed with me when I leave. I'm in love with his bed. Who did they take this house from? Heaven only knows.

    The bed has sheer white curtains surrounding it. The curtains are pulled back and secured to the bedpost. It's my dream bed. I walk over to it, and plop down on the mattress. I give it a few bounces testing the mattress. A very comfortable mattress indeed. Not too soft and not too firm. If I had to guess, I would say it was top of the line. Someone paid a fortune for this mansion. This is lovely. I like it here, although I have no idea where here is. I should sleep like a baby. Something about this house makes me feel safe, or is it being in Ace's company? Either way, I know I am physically protected. Emotional protection will be mine to secure. I'll keep everything else buried deep. That has worked for me so far. *"Thanks, Ace. It's a nice room."*

"I'm glad you like it. Meet me in the kitchen in five?"

"Sure." Ace leaves the room, closing the door softly behind himself.

Chapter 7

ACE

I walk out of the bedroom, closing the door behind me, and nearly double over. She's said my name for the first time since this adventure began. For the first time in seven years. The way she says my name weakens me. I need a nap. I go down to the kitchen to wait. Three minutes later Toni appears. *"Take a seat. Let's talk."* She sits in the chair farthest from where I am standing. The implications of her actions aren't lost on me. She wants space. That I can do. I have to remember space is best for both of us. It's counterintuitive to what I'm feeling though. I want to explore the curves I see hiding beneath her hoodie and yoga pants. I give myself a mental shake. There will be no exploring anything. Unless of course I have a death wish. Chaos would kill me! Besides, I am on a mission. That comes before everything else. Always! Stay focused man!

I take a seat at the other end of the table. I notice she won't look directly at me. She has gotten good at hiding her thoughts and feelings. I wonder what that's all about. Is she dating someone? Having sex with someone? That thought makes me roar in my own head. She's mine! Only she isn't. I gave up the right to call her mine when I walked out on her. I take a deep breath. Stay focused. *"So, here's what we know. Someone placed a two-million-dollar bounty on your head. We don't know who yet. We believe it's connected to the hit and run accident your parents suffered seven years ago. Your testimony put some heavy hitters behind bars. They've been looking for you ever since. We were sure we neutralized them, but somehow here we are."*

"There is no other reason to want to harm a librarian. Can you think of anyone that would want to cause you harm? A relationship gone bad. A jealous roommate. An ex-boyfriend perhaps?" I nearly choked on those words.

"No." She says this without making eye contact. Something is definitely off here.

"You don't know why someone would put out a hit on a computer nerd like yourself?" I ask this last question to get a rise from her.

"No. No idea. Sorry."

She didn't take the bait. All types of warning bells are ringing in my head. She is hiding something. She is compliant, evasive, and quiet. She is definitely hiding something. On her best day, she would try to decapitate me. Right now, she's sitting here all meek and cooperative. Yeah. I ain't buying it!

Antonia Townsend is hiding something big. Something that could be important to saving her life. Important to concluding this mission. I have to find out what that secret is. She knows better than to keep secrets from me. From us. What is going on here? I walk over to where she's sitting and bend over to whisper in her ear, *"Doll, whatever you're hiding from me, I will pull it out of you inch by delectable inch. You know that right?"* She jumps out of her seat like it's on fire, and all but runs to stand on the other side of the room. Effectively putting an entire kitchen island between us. That was quite an overreaction. She is hiding more than one secret it seems. Let the games begin.

"It's late. You should get some rest." She leaves the room in a hurry. I need Toni to think I've fallen for her little ruse. Once she lets her guard down, oh it's on. She thinks she's home free. I laugh just thinking about it. Let her think whatever she wants. The more relaxed she becomes the better. I am working against

the clock. Time is not on our side. I need to encourage her to share her little secrets, and I don't have a lot of time to do it in. If she were anyone else, I would seduce her to get what I wanted. I wish! That option isn't available to me. Mores the pity. I have other ways to extract information from an unwilling subject. Toni is about to be declared an enemy combatant, but only in the gentlest sense of the word.

TONI

The last thing I need is Ace all up in my personal space. All up in my face. He is too observant for his own good! He has no idea the effect he has on me. If I have my way, he never will. UGH! It just isn't fair. Why him? Why now? Why me? He is everything I ever wanted in a partner. Why do my heart and body betray me? I hate this! Ace is more than a pretty face. He's very clever. I need to stay alert. Stay on my toes. People's lives depend on my ability to keep secrets. There are things he, Chaos, and the other elite team members can never discover. Deception is my only option. I literally have no other choice. How did we get here? I need to check in. I need answers. I must find a way to get to some form of communication. It isn't like I can waltz up to Ace and say, "Hey, can I use your phone?"

I was forced to leave my phone and my laptop at home. So, without those items I am literally flying blind. I'll have to figure something out though. Quick, fast, and in a hurry! I need a sit-rep in the worst way imaginable! I walk back to the bedroom trying to think of a plan. I know there has to be some form of communication somewhere in this compound. I will wait until Ace falls asleep and do some digging. Time is of the essence. I walk back to my room with my mind whirring 1k bpm. My brain functions like a modem. Filtering information in and out so fast it will make your head spin. I'm discarding a lot of different ideas on how to establish a link between me and my boss. His identity must be guarded at all costs. I can't imagine what would happen if it were discovered. I don't need that type of headache in my life. Not now! Not ever!

My job entails top level security. The library is a very effective cover. What I do in the bowels of that library is something else altogether. Above top secret and classified information flows through monitors in what I like to refer to as the underbelly of society. Information on anyone in the world is at my fingertips. I lay back on one of the fluffy pillows working on a plan. It's thin at best. I could simply ask Ace for the use of a communication device. A SAT phone or secure video link. I could convince him I needed to speak to my brother. I wonder if he'd buy that. I could cry and act all distraught. No one likes to see a woman in tears. It pulls on their heart strings. I will tuck that one away in my back pocket. I may get desperate enough to try it.

I can't wait for Ace to fall asleep, so I can snoop around this compound. I will be looking for his cell phone. Anything that will allow me to contact someone on the outside. I feel desperation creeping in. There has to be some sort of communication device in this monstrosity. There is no way Ace would bring us here blind. He has a mode of communication, and I mean to find it. I will lay here and wait for him out. At some point the man has to sleep. He does sleep, right? I mean, do they sleep? Everyone sleeps. Surely the man sleeps! I will just wait a sufficient amount of time and then go in search of what I'm looking for. How hard can it be? I wouldn't put it past him to stay away just to annoy me!

ACE

I need to check in. Get the latest sit-rep. I walk down the basement steps. Automatic motion lights illuminate the way. This is no ordinary basement. Hidden behind a stack of paint cans and a large gray tarp is a hidden room. Completely hidden from the naked eye. I place my left thumb three inches from the top of the door on the right side. The biometric scanner lights up. Unless you know the door is there you will never find it. It was designed expressly for that purpose. It is the exact opposite of a panic room. In fact, if the enemy saw the cache of weapons, we have stored on hand they would be very afraid. We never leave anything to chance. Logic is a stickler for details. We are all paranoid!

The door slides open noiselessly. Everything is in working order. I step into the room and wait for the door to close before turning on the lights. Once the door is closed, I flip a switch and the room lights up. The room is chock full of digital equipment. Everything we need to run ops from this very location. Behind a panel on the far wall is a cache of weapons. Again, everything we need to run a mission from this location. I sit before a bank of computer monitors and begin to punch in a series of keystrokes. The keystrokes are today's security code. A new security code comes in early every morning. We get them every morning at 0600. Same time same bat station, no deviations. Ever!

The codes come via a secured cell that has more encryption software on it than a NASA spacecraft. You get ten seconds to memorize the code before it disappears. If you miss the day's codes, there will be the devil himself to pay. That devil has a name. We affectionately refer to him as the Colonel. I was one month into my newly appointed position with Alpha team when it happened to me. I was under a buxom brunette and didn't get to my pants in time. If I'm being honest, I had no idea where my pants were located. She took them off in a hurry and threw them somewhere. I was in just as much of a hurry to discard them as she was to get me out of them and didn't bother to track where they landed.

She was on her knees in front of me when the undressing began. It's safe to say I was distracted. After missing the daily code, I had to call the Colonel for a new set. I'm pretty sure the hearing in my right ear is a fraction of what it used to be. My hearing will never fully recover. He chewed me out so badly I wanted to shoot *myself* in the head! He threatened to have the team take me out into the desert and put me out of my misery. He was not very subtle about it. He even went so far as to insult the legitimacy of my birth. His butt chewing was good enough to ensure I never miss the daily codes again! Not ever. The only way I will ever miss the daily codes is if I'm in a coma, or dead. Lesson learned. The Colonel does not take prisoners.

The moment I connect with the team Chaos' face pops up on the screen. I can see some of the other team members gathered behind him. Gravity and Thrasher and Polar. Logic is off sight working on a mission that requires a finesse only he can bring. Chaos doesn't waste time. He has members from Bravo and Charlie team also present.

"How is she, Ace?"

"Surprisingly calm, all things considered. She is definitely your sister. No hysterics. No drama. If I didn't know better, I would think she was one of us. You know, instead of a librarian. She's upstairs resting. It's late."

"Thanks Bro. I appreciate you keeping her safe. I owe you one."

"We believe one or two maggots squirmed away during the Crash and Burn op."

"You still believe this is connected to your parent's car accident?"

"That is the only thing that makes sense. My sister has her nose buried in books all day. She isn't dating anyone. She has no friends. No known enemies. What else could it be?"

"I'll trust the intel. For now, at least. The sooner we put an end to this, the sooner she can get back to her books."

"True dat!"

"Unless something else comes down the pike we are pulling this *thread. Please keep her safe, Ace? I really do owe you one."*

"Nah, bro. She's family. I got you."

"Thanks." I disconnected the feed. Having a family member targeted is a first. We will put an end to this quickly!

I log off and shut down the equipment. I leave shutting off the lights. I need a shower, and some shut eye. I climb the stairs and open the basement door. Only to find a dark silhouette sitting in a kitchen chair. I put my hand on my beretta seconds before realizing its Doll-face. Why is she sitting here in the dark? I flip the light switch on. Then I snap, *"What are you doing? Why are you sitting in the dark? I thought you were in bed. Fast asleep. Don't ever make me pull my weapon on you. You know better than that!"*

"I can't sleep, so I thought I could ask you a few questions. I went through the house and couldn't find you anywhere. I assumed you wouldn't leave without at least speaking to me first. Not at all like the last time I saw you." Yeah, I know. Cheap shot. He winces at my comment but doesn't speak. *"Anyway, I figured you were hiding somewhere close by. That is why I'm sitting here. It didn't occur to me to turn the lights on. I prefer the darkness. It's soothing."*

I lean against the island, crossing my arms and my ankles waiting for her to ask her questions. What I want more than anything in this world is to go to bed. I have been awake for about forty-eight hours. I'm starting to feel it. *"What's on your mind, Doll?"*

"For starters, you can call me Toni. Please! I insist. I would like to know why you kidnapped me from my bed in the dead of night. What is going on?" I knew this question was coming. This conversation was inevitable. Here goes everything. *"We received intel that led us to believe someone associated with the situation seven years ago is looking to neutralize you. That is the scenario we are going with at the moment. Unless of course you know why*

someone would put a bounty out on your head? Did you charge an exorbitant late fee on an overdue library book or something?"

"Give it a rest, Prince!" My hearing must be faulty. What did she just call me? There is no way Antonia Townsend just called me by my government name. That is not at all possible. There are only a few people on the planet who know my name and Antonia Townsend should not be one of them. And yet she just addressed me as such. What in the blue blazes is going on!? I can feel my blood run cold. The implications of Toni knowing my birth name are staggering. How did she come by this information? This is no mere coincidence. This has the potential to be catastrophic! An error that could cost several people their lives. The desire to shake the information from her is killing me. I close my eyes and take a long deep breath. I need calm. My brain is fully awake, now!

Chapter 8

TONI

I freeze in place. The entire atmosphere in the room shifts. It feels like someone is dragging me under water. I can scarcely breathe. I dare to scarcely breathe. My brain must be shutting down because I can't believe I just slipped up and called Ace by his birth name! There are less than ten people on the planet who know his birth name. To make matters worse, I don't know how to recover from my faux pas. I can feel cold dread seeping in. All my blood draining away! Why didn't I stay in bed? My brain is way too foggy for effective subterfuge. His presence throws me off my game. Stupid! Stupid! Stupid! Now what? How do I recover from this? Maybe I can just go back to bed and get a do over.

Ace stalks toward me like a giant menacing predatory cat. My heart is in my throat. My brain completely stutters and then shuts down all together! Even my brain knows to get out of dodge. There is no getting around this! I moved abruptly looking to escape. He's advancing stealthily and quickly. I am backing up trying to put as much distance between us as humanly possible. My back hits a wall, and I'm brought up short. Looks like it's the end of the road for me! I can almost imagine Ace as an evil villain rubbing his hands together when he says, *"It's the end of the road for you, my pretty!"* I have nowhere left to run. He stops directly in front of me. He's standing so close I can feel his breath moving the hairs at the nape of my neck. He leans in even closer.

Violating all my personal space.

In my ear he whispers, *"What did you just call me?"* He sounds menacing. CRAP! CRAP! CRAP! Why does he never miss anything? Honestly, that's so annoying! For once could he let this one thing slide? Stupid! Stupid! Stupid! I used his government name. We both know there is no way in this world or any other world I should have his personal data! Only, I do have it. I know his full name! I know everything about him! How, you ask? Well, I'll tell you. Seven years ago, I hacked a top-secret government database to gather intel on the man that broke my heart. I had a vague idea of the work my brother was involved in. He was a part of my brother's team. So, I put two and two together. What I came up with was an ocean of hot water.

That explains why I hold my current position. I accepted the offer extended to me in lieu of federal prison time. Yes, reader, I got cold busted! It was all laid out very neatly for me. Work for us as a data specialist or go to jail. It wasn't that hard to decide. Not really. After Ace took my virginity and disappeared, I needed answers. I was hurt. I was angry. I wanted revenge. So, I went looking. Data collecting is my specialty. I eventually found more information than was safe for me to possess. But here. Now. As it stands, I have no viable answers to give him for any of that. He wants to know how I know his name. I am so screwed! I can't tell him that without revealing the truth.

"You have three seconds to answer my question, Doll. It's simple really!" Not simple at all, reader!

LOGIC

We're in a small villa in France, where we've been hold up for the better part of a week. This is no sightseeing tour. If that were the case, I would be here with my wife and son. I am so ready to go back home. I hate leaving them alone. My mom has been a great help. Samar's belly grows larger by the day, and I'm missing it. I also miss her and Ty like crazy. I sleep better knowing Venom is on babysitting duty while maintaining our base of operations. He is linked into comms and hears everything we hear. He won't let anything happen to my family. I will be happier when I am home with them, though. Maybe, it's time to think about retiring. Maybe?

I'll gather as much intel as I can, then we will neutralize the targets. Turns out the Italian Death Dealer was not in the states for great tasting pasta or a family reunion. His plans were a lot more nefarious than that. I fully intended to take him out while he was on my turf, but things rarely work out the way we wish them to. Why is that? My plan was to rid the world of one more bad element. The team showed up at the restaurant Samar and I went to celebrate our wedding anniversary. We intended to have dinner, but when we arrived, I spotted the Italian death dealer. The team began the surveillance. I mean, I knew having him in the United States would not be good, but I had no idea just how not good!

In the last week, I have trailed this man through three different continents. One would think he'd grow tired. I know I am! His bad is worse than most. You would think selling illegal arms, a little drug smuggling, some sex trafficking of underage children would be horrific enough. Apparently not enough for this guy. The Italian Death Dealer likes to believe he's an artist. He murders people in inventive ways. He makes it an art form. Yet and still, he grows bored. He usually flies under the radar. Keeping to the shadows. The way I figure it, for him to come out of hiding it must be for something huge. He never does anything by half measure. Ugh! For the record, I really hate it when I'm right!

I activate my comms unit. *"Gator, Coup, Razor, Crucible, Reaper, I have good news and bad news. Which do you prefer first?"* I hear a chuckle over comms. Yep, it's Gator. That Cajun is itching to kill some people and get back to his gators. He raises them for pets.

Crucible says, *"I'm tired. Hit me with the bad news first. Then, maybe once I hear the good news, I won't have nightmares when I close my eyes."* Even I have to agree with that logic. This job ensures you *will* have nightmares.

"Well, fellas, the good news is we've found the intel we've been searching for. I will give you ten seconds to celebrate. Commence." I wait a few seconds and say, *"Time's up."*

The bad news is our Italian friend found a way to procure uranium." Coup lets off a string of expletives so forcefully they scorch my ear drums. Reaper and Razor are instantly mute.

Then Gator says, *"Logic, tell me this is some sort of horrific joke. Go ahead. I'll wait!"*

"I wish I could, bro. I wish I could."

Reaper asks, "If Salvatore Parisi (Italian Death Dealer) was in the process of buying uranium, why would he be in the United States? There is NO uranium for sale in the United States. If there was uranium for sale in the United States, we would know about it. Wouldn't we know about it, Logic? We would have been read in and sent out to neutralize all the parties involved. Why didn't we read it? Can any of you answer that questions for me. What would the Death Dealer need with a nuclear bomb anyway?" I get the feeling my nightmares just went nuclear. What is wrong with the world?

I say, *"Reaper, that is the trillion-dollar question? But more importantly, does he have the capability to fashion a bomb or is he going to sell the uranium to an enemy of the United States? Our first objective is to find out who has the uranium. Who is selling it to the Italian Death Dealer? Where is it being stored? Then we need to devise a plan that will get it out of their hands and into ours. It's a good thing my wife is pregnant, I may not be able to perform that particular function again after handling uranium. We are on our way back to the van. Our work is cut out for us, gentlemen. Which* one of you wants to inform the Colonel of this latest development? We can draw straws." I hear nothing but silence over the comms link.

Gator says, "As team lead that is technically your area of responsibility. But since Razor has been reasonably quiet on this op, I will nominate him. Does anyone want to second my nomination?"

I hear Razor chuckle. Then says, "Boss, if you want me to tell the Colonel, I will. I don't mind. While I'm at it, I have a few other items on my list to share with the Colonel. Such as you jumping out of windows naked. You're not always setting a proper example for Bravo team to follow. Always coloring outside the lines. These types of things. I would not hesitate to share them with the Colonel."

Gator roars with laughter. The men of Bravo and Charlie teams are as close to each other as we are on Alpha team. There is no way any of them would betray the other. Gator is a madman. He was my obvious choice for team lead. Because he colors outside the lines. Him jumping out of windows is entirely possible. I wouldn't doubt it. Who knows what he gets up to? I can only imagine.

Once Gator pulls himself together, he says, "Dude, you are not being a good team player. When this is over, I want you on the mat."

Razor responds, "Boss, are you threatening me? I only want to share with the Colonel all the wonderful things you do as Bravo team lead. You foster such a warm and wonderful nurturing environment for the team." The group is cracking up.

Gator shouts, "Hey, Razor, suck it! You're carrying the uranium. All your future children will glow in the dark. I ain't kidding." These two are insane. Razor is crying and laughing.

Once Gator, Razor, and I make it back to the van, Coup takes off. I have a very important phone call to make. In my mind I can hear the Colonel screaming already. He is going to have a conniption fit over this one! I can scarcely believe it myself. Nuclear arms are banned by NATO. That is why Iraq happened in the first place. Well, not really, but that's the excuse given to the masses by POTUS. Anyway, Italy is a part of NATO. When the Italian Death Dealer gets caught purchasing uranium, and believe me he will, I will make sure of it, his government will not be pleased. The Colonel will use this as leverage. The Italian government will want to keep this quiet. We will make all their problems go away, and in return they will owe the Colonel a huge favor.

This is politics at its worst. Were we to notify the Italian government in advance of the uranium deal on the horizon they would interfere with our mission. They would attempt to send a team to France to extract it before we could get there. We are ghosts on this mission. Even more so now that uranium is in play. I will devise a plan that secures the uranium, raises the Italian Death dealer's head on a pike, and get us home in one piece. I can only imagine how pissed the Italian government is going to be when they get wind of this. Let's pray the French government remains in the dark! An op of this magnitude on French soil could get tempers flaring. This could start a war between both countries.

Anything that threatens a country's stance with NATO is a threat to their national security. The very last thing any country wants is to be without allies. Or to have sanctions placed on them by the United States. The Italian government should have kept a closer eye on him. They should never have let their dog off the leash. Salvatore Parisi (Death Dealer) is an Italian citizen and mob boss. He is technically their problem. Unfortunately for him, I've had him on my personal hit list for a while now. I will neutralize him, and the Italian government will thank us for it. None the wiser as to my personal goals. I consider myself a Good Samaritan.

On the drive back I work on the details of a plan to find

and extract the uranium. Once we unload our gear, we meet up in the master suite walk in closet. It is the size of an entire apartment. We have all our equipment set up here. There are no windows in this room. We have noise canceling equipment set up. A signal blocker making the entire villa invisible to anyone hoping to listen in. Cameras are set up both inside and outside the building. In a five-mile radius. A bank of monitors being watched by Omega. They are also using satellites. I activate comms and speak into it. *"I need a secure channel to the Colonel."* Seconds later I hear a squawking sound. Then I hear the Colonel's voice.

"What have you got for me? It's only ever bad news when it's delivered before five a.m."

"You got that right, Sir! Uranium."

"Logic. Before you continue with the rest of your sentence just know I am too old for this crap! Ok. Got that off my chest. Go ahead."

"The Italian Death Dealer was linking up with someone in the United States to set up a deal to purchase uranium. Can you tell me how it's possible there's uranium for sale in the U.S.?"

The Colonel is silent for so long I am beginning to believe he fell asleep. When he finally speaks, it makes me glad I'm sitting down. I feel my whole body go weak. *"The information I'm about to share with you men goes way above your pay grade. It is shared on a need-to-know basis only!"*

"The U.S. government intercepted a supply of uranium on its way to a country that should never have it. That shipment was held in a site considered so safe its mind boggling. One of the three scientists stationed at the secure facility managed to disappear. Oddly enough so did a portion of the uranium."

I interrupt with, *"Who is running point on the mission to find the missing scientist and the uranium? Alpha, Bravo, and Charlie teams are tasked out. Who else is qualified for a mission like this?"*

I hear dead silence. I look over at Gator and the rest of the team to find we are all waiting with bated breath. I realize there is no answer the Colonel can give me that will be acceptable. I can think of no one else that is qualified! That thought makes the small hairs on the back of my neck stand on end.

Why isn't the Colonel answering my question? All the hair on my body stands up. *"Sir?! I asked you a question."* I can feel heat suffuse my entire being. There are things the Colonel can't share with us because of his new title as Head of National Security. That we understand. But what is this? What is happening here? Now.

"Logic. I wish I knew. I've been told it's handled. I have a million more questions rattling around in my brain. This goes to the top, and he is being very dodgy with his intel. So, we focus on our end of the mission. Salvatore Parisi, his handler, and his portion of the uranium. There is no need for us to worry about that portion of this op. I need you to devise a plan to get your hands on the missing uranium and to get the Italian Death Dealer off the chess board! Can you manage that?"

"I want everyone responsible for the theft taken out of play. I will handle the rest. We need to make sure this is the same uranium in question? I will provide you with batch numbers once they are secured. Again, I have all sorts of questions. Discover how the Death Dealer even knows about the uranium? Find out if he had direct contact with the scientist? There are a whole host of loose ends, Logic. I am depending on your teams to tie them all off for me." Gator and I exchanged a quick glance. Yes. He is thinking exactly what I'm thinking. If all three elite teams are tasked out who else is qualified for a job of this magnitude? *"Let me know when you have them."* The line goes dead. We each sit here in stunned silence.

Chapter 9

There are so many thoughts running around in my head I feel dizzy. Every bit of information I've gathered this last year runs through my mind. Pieces of conversation I found odd. Things that didn't add up. This thing with Chaos' sister. Yeah, something isn't right. Razor is the first to speak. *"Logic, you know I have always trusted the Colonel. There are things we can't know, I accept that. Can anyone tell me what this is? I don't like the way it makes me feel."*

Gator says, *"We trust him till he gives us a solid reason not to trust him. My Cajun senses are red hot on this one. Logic, it's your call. What's our next step?"* I wish I knew!

"Waiting is always the worst part. I guess I'm going to shut it down for a few hours, Logic. I suggest you do the same."

"That's the plan. I'm setting up a search algorithm with specific words to help find our target. Omega has scanners running from satellites to find the Italian Death Dealer using cell phone signals. Facial recognition has been activated on every cell phone in the world, so when he surfaces, I will be pinged. While that is happening, I will get some shut eye too. I need operation Paperchase sewn up with a quickness. The sooner I get home to Samar the better. I don't like the fact that NATO is using uranium as a bargaining chip. This whole thing was bound to go sideways. I would love to know whose idea this was and put a bullet in their brain."

"Yeah. I hear you on that. The games that are played in politics are frightening. There will always be jobs for men like us. As long as

there are people who live and feed off power. Who feeds off control. Who feeds off other people. We will always have work to do."

"You've got that right, Gator! It's one big sordid mess. There are never any good guys. There are bad guys and worse guys. Once the public figures that out there will be mayhem. The good versus evil narrative sells newspapers. There is no good. There is bad and worse. Our job is to clean up behind all of them."

"Yep. See you later." I'll hopefully manage to get a few hours of sleep.

"It's four o'clock in the morning. Why are you up, Gator?"

"A better question is had you slept at all?"

"Yeah. I took a catnap."

"That's what I figured. Are you any closer to finding the Italian Death Dealer?"

"I think I may have found something."

"Care to share?"

"I will soon. I'll go lay down while my computer runs the search. Hopefully either we'll have found him, or Omega will have found him. We need to get to him before he buys and sells the uranium. I don't want to go chasing my tail on this. This needs to be done in order. Besides, I need to get home to my family."

"Roger, that. Go. I got this. I'll keep an eye out and call you if anything pops up."

"Thanks." I walk down the hall to the room I'm using. I'll need a solid ten to twelve hours of rem sleep in the very near future before I feel anything like me again. My brain feels boggy. These catnaps only help temporarily. I can feel the fatigue way down deep, and it's rising to the surface. I can't keep running off coffee and adrenaline. That's not healthy. I lay down on the pillow and tried to wind my brain down. I need to shore up our exfil plan. It doesn't need to happen at this very moment though. I take a few deep breaths.

Before I pass out our comms activate. We hear, *"Hello, fellas. Long time no hears."* Yeah, it's Omega. Turns up like a bad penny every time! Omega is just who I needed to speak to. Gator enters my sleeping quarters.

"Omega, you know you're on my personal hit list, don't you?"

"Of course, boy wonder! It's a love, hate relationship we got going here. You love to hate us. No idea why. I contacted you out of the goodness of my heart. I am here because you have questions, and I have answers. I will give you what I can. Let me start by saying, you can trust the Colonel."

"Who says we don't trust the Colonel?" I dart a quick glance in Gator's direction.

"Your skeptical tone suggests you may have doubts. You, boy genius, question everything. That is what makes you so formidable! If it were me, my brainiac compadre, I would have questions too."

"Knowing the way your computer brain works tells me you have doubts. The Colonel is not in the habit of explaining himself. He is used to his men following orders. It doesn't occur to him that sometimes we humans need an explanation. But this stays here. Am I clear?" I am practically barking down the line when I say, *"Go!"*

Omegas' chuckles come back at me. I still need to kill these people. I've just been too busy. *"Fine! This particular uranium was going to be used as part of a NATO arms deal. The deal was so secretive only two other people knew of it besides the President."*

"Then how do you know about it?"

"I read minds, high IQ! Just like I'm doing right at this moment. You my trusty inquisitor are wishing you had your hands around my throat." I have to laugh at that. Omega is spot on!

I needed that laugh. I am strung tight. *"We are on the same side, by the way."*

"Uh, huh. Do you know who was sent to find the missing scientist and his cache of uranium?"

"That I don't know. I will dig around to see what I can shake loose. This really isn't a job for the CIA (Crooks in Action), so I doubt they were read in on this situation. I will let you know what I find out. In the meantime, oh wise one, there are hazmat suits, Geiger counters, and everything else you will need for this portion of the mission. Those items are already stashed in the basement of that monstrosity you're holed up in. I took the liberty of having it delivered while you were out. I hope you don't mind. If I've missed anything don't hesitate to give me a jingle. I will be running point for this op with one other Omega. This op is officially titled Operation Glow Worm. Get home safe, gentlemen!" Those are the last words we hear before comms go silent.

Can I shoot Omega now? All of them. Pretty please? How on earth did they organize all the equipment, and had it delivered so quickly? How do they know about an above top-secret NATO arms deal? How are they one step ahead on this mission? I come away with more questions than answers. I hope Omega doesn't think for one second, I believe they don't know who is securing the missing scientist, or the other uranium. Only a small portion of uranium was removed when the scientist went missing. Which means there is more where that came from. You can't know about an above top-secret NATO arms deal, but not know who will run point on securing for the missing scientist. They must think we're stupid. Someone knows more than they are letting on. Before it's all said and done, I will know what they know. It looks like I will have to crack a few skulls! Challenge accepted!

OMEGA

I hate lying to Logic. There is just nothing to be done about it. He already wants to kill us. Even though he has no idea who we are. He's deadly. It's not because he dislikes us. It's because we sometimes know things he doesn't. He hates that! I chuckle just thinking about it. Logic is a solid team leader. His priority is always his men. During operation Thistle he nearly died trying to protect those men. He got tired of the enemy chasing them and decided to take the fight to the enemy. Single handedly. He's a real nutjob, that one. A few of the men were injured during that mission. He himself was running around with a bullet in his gut. Then add in the rescue of the Colonel and a coup d'état. There were a lot of moving parts. It was a logistical nightmare. Alpha team excels at logistical nightmares.

Logic's brain is a phenomenon. He has an eidetic memory. Which makes him a whiz at his job. He will always take the hardest assignments and the most risks. I don't think his brain could handle it if something were to happen to one of the men, he's responsible for. Alpha, Bravo, and Charlie teams have kept this country safe for a very long time. He is tasked with finding the Death Dealer and a tiny portion of the uranium for sale. The people responsible for locating the scientist and the uranium the scientist took, well, let's just say they don't exist. Not really. They don't exist for a reason. Zypher stumbled across a bit of data that suggests…. Well, if I'm being honest what the data suggests is really hard to believe. We haven't shared our find with ANYONE! Not even the Colonel. Together we've been quietly putting the pieces together. Some initials are what we found. What we are quickly discovering is those initials spell trouble. Alpha, Bravo, and Charlie teams may not be the only lions in the jungle! Whatever this is can never go public!

TONI

I need to come up with an answer quick as to how I know his name. *"I... uhm."* My brain has stuttered to a complete stop. I have two PhDs and can't come up with one single solitary lie. Just great! Usually, I function pretty well under pressure. Why are my abilities failing me at the very moment I need them most? Time is ticking. Feeling more and more like a gravitational ticking time bomb every second. I feel my armpits begin to moisten. My comeback is weak at best. *"I'm sure I've heard my brother call your name a time or two. You thought you would take my virginity, flee the country, and I wouldn't find out who you were?"* Will he fall for it? Please fall for it!

"Nice try, Doll. I know for a fact your brother did NOT tell you, my name. BUT, if you insist that he did, well, we can just give him a call and find out. It won't take but a second. You can stand right here while I verify the information, you're giving me."

Nope, it didn't work. At this rate I'm not sure which of the Alpha team members I'm more afraid of. Ace or my brother Chaos. *"No! Don't. Please?"* Let the groveling begin.

"You care to tell me the truth this time, Doll?"

"I can't."

"What do you mean you can't?! You can, and you will." When he's like this he can be so intimidating.

"I mean, I can't! Ok? You don't have to worry about me repeating it. I have no desire to ever say your name again. Just drop it?" I know I sound whiny and wounded. My plan is to guilt him into dropping the subject. I attempted to sail past him headed for the stairs. He ain't buying it. He takes my arm effectively halting my progress.

"Not so fast, Doll. I asked you a question, and I want an answer!"

"If I tell you, you have to promise never to repeat it. You know, keep your word. Better than you did the last time." I shoot those words at him like poisonous darts. He flinches and looks away. I don't want to hurt him, but I have to throw him off the scent. He can never know anything! Not really.

"Look, Toni. I'm sorry about that night seven years ago. I never should have touched you. It's forbidden. I messed up, ok? I should have guessed you were a virgin. This thing between us, it was…"

In my head I'm screaming, STOP! STOP TALKING! Each word he utters cuts deep into my very soul. HE'S SORRY? He looks like he really means it. I feel the tears clogging my throat. I feel worse than I did seven years ago. I would never have guessed that was a possibility. I whisper, *"Don't, say another word! You are a real douchebag, you know that?!"* I ran right past him, right up the stairs to my bedroom. He lets me go. He does not have the power to stop me. He does not have the power to hurt me. I won't let him!

Whatever vestiges of emotion I still carried for him died in the kitchen. Adam Arthur Prince is now dead to me. Just another awful memory regarding that fateful night seven years ago. A night that nearly changed the trajectory of my life. I learned to cope. I learned to function. It wasn't instantaneous. It took a while after my parent's death and Ace's departure. I know I can do the same again. I am a lot stronger now. I haven't just survived over the last seven years; I have thrived over the last seven years. I am someone I can be proud of. I will not allow old memories, ancient demons, or someone else's regret to change how I feel about me. He is right. He never should have touched me. He doesn't deserve me. If I'm lucky, he never will again! Some people!

I slam the door so hard the roof rattles. Then I collapsed on the bed. The twenty-five-year-old me is not crying. I am weeping for the eighteen-year-old me. The me that fell in love and gave her virginity to a heartless douchebag. Who now regrets that night. How poetic. I shed a tear for the younger version of myself that believed in love at first sight. That naïve girl that wanted two-point-five children. I wanted all our children to look like Ace. I wanted a ring and a white picket fence. I held a wake and a funeral for that girl. She is long gone. Why does it have to be him on this particular babysitting detail? Couldn't they have sent anyone else? Anyone but him?! Or just let the assassins kill me. It must be less painful than this.

I promise myself; this will be my last cry. Ace really isn't worth the tears. Seven years ago, after the death of my parents and his abandonment, I spent a lot of time in therapy. My brother was worried. I was losing weight. I couldn't focus on my studies. I was a hot mess. I took a sabbatical from school. By sabbatical I mean one entire semester. Nothing too drastic. I needed time to get my head on straight. My brother assumed I was taking the death of my parents harder than was healthy. He suggested therapy. I fought it at first, tooth and nail, but then I caved. It wasn't just my parents' death. It felt as if everything was pressing down on me. Suffocating me. It was a combination of their death and Ace's abandonment that threw my life into a tailspin. I thought about ending it all.

Chapter 10

I am no longer the eighteen-year-old kid I was back then. I was insecure and naïve. Lonely and hopeless. I didn't have any friends because I spent all my free time writing and running code. Snooping in places I had no business being. The death of my parents scared me. They were my support system. My brother and I are so far apart in age I felt like an only child. I withdrew into myself even more. Became more introverted. I nearly became a recluse. When Ace came to the funeral and started talking to me, that's when things changed. It felt like he really saw me. He was gentle, patient, and sweet. He was attentive and kind. Now I realize he was all those things because he and my brother are close. He's eight years older than me, but I didn't think that mattered.

I'm sure I misinterpreted his kindness to mean something else. My brother and all his buddies were up late drinking one night. I decided in my brain it would be a good idea to seduce Ace. Not much of a plan was put in play. I think back on that time with shame. My whole body heats up. I imagined we would marry and have babies someday. He rejected my advances. I was so humiliated I ran away crying. The irony is I ran up to my old tree house. The same treehouse I used to play in when I was a kid. My version of a security blanket. I cried until I was exhausted. It felt like my whole heart was breaking. A few hours later, Ace found me in that tree house. He came to apologize, but I was so angry with him. I was very nearly hysterical. Having him so close was fogging my brain. I went to rush past him and tripped over something on the floor. He caught me. His reflexes are amazing. I plastered my lips to his. I was acting purely on instinct. He hesitated, and then, before you knew it, he had his tongue in my mouth. I had no idea what I was doing. It was my first kiss.

It was glorious! One thing led to another and before you knew it, we were undressing each other. The second he entered me I cried out in pain. He froze! He looked down on me in abject horror. *"You're a virgin?"* I can still hear the shock in his voice. Or was that disgust? I tried to pretend his impaling me didn't hurt, but he knew it did. The fact of the matter was written clearly across my face.

"Toni?! You're a virgin? Why didn't you tell me?" Whatever else he was going to say got lost in his throat when we heard my brother calling his name. The look on his face was almost comical. He was terrified. He placed his hand over my mouth, not unlike what he did tonight. I laid there blinking up at him. There was no way I wanted my brother to find either of us naked. Ace is still hard inside me. I stayed perfectly still for what felt like hours. I was mortified!

Once the coast was clear, Ace stood up and started looking for his clothes. I found my shirt and jacket and used them to cover my nakedness. Once Ace was dressed, he looked down at me and said, *"Doll, we have to go."* His tone was so impersonal. It nearly killed me. *"You should go first; I will wait a while then come down."*

"Are you sure?"

"Yes."

"Toni, I'm sorry. This should never have happened. There is no excuse. I'm sorry."

Every word he uttered went straight through me like a warm serrated blade to butter. I heard myself say, *"Don't worry about it. It's no big deal."* A small part of me believed every word because I was already dead inside. When he descended the ladder, he took what was left of my heart with him.

Once I was sure he was long gone, I let the tears flow. I cried for hours. I was sure I cried out all my heartbreak. I cried myself right into dehydration. I certainly cried myself to sleep. When I finally got the nerve to come down from the treehouse, Ace was long gone. I never saw or heard from him again. The months that followed tested and tried me to my very core. Eventually I took my brother's advice and went to therapy. Once I began to feel better, I then went back to school. The rest, as they say, is history. That should be the end, right? Fast forward to the present. I am back in my memories crying over a man I was sure I had exorcised from my system. This is too much!

ACE

At this point I don't know whether to go after her or stay put. She knows my name. That should not be a thing. This situation is made even more complicated by our shared past. At some point the past is going to come to the surface. It will present a huge problem when it does. I shudder to think. Toni is hiding something. What? Why? Something that would make her lie to me. Lie to her brother. I scarcely believe it. Even knowing she's lying I have an overwhelming desire to protect her. I have to find out what she's hiding before I check in at 0900. Somehow, I find myself standing outside her bedroom door. She's crying. Again! Not unlike that cold night seven years ago. My heart breaks.

I remember standing in the shadows at the base of that treehouse listening to her cry for hours. Every part of me wanted to go to her. Just as I'd made up my mind to do so and was on the verge of going back up that ladder, Gravity stepped out of the shadows. He said, *"Bro, don't!"* Those two words stopped me dead in my tracks! I turned to stare at him. I was so torn. I didn't know what to do. I was falling for her and knew I shouldn't. She was off limits. Big time! OFF LIMITS! A neon flashing sign couldn't have been clearer. She had just lost her parents, and I took her virginity. I screwed up big time. All of that was running through my mind in a continuous loop. Gravity says, *"Before you climb that ladder know this. You can never come back down. This brotherhood will be no more. Chaos will kill you, and I will be forced to assist in your death as per the bro code. You have three other brothers that will have to choose sides. Can you look Chaos in the eye and tell him you are throwing our brotherhood away over a woman?"*

I had no answers to give Gravity seven years ago, and I have no answer for myself now. I still dream of Antonia Townsend. I have slept with more women than I can count since then. Trying to erase her from my mind. It hasn't worked. Maybe I should have relented when Gravity asked to take over this detail. I have a feeling I'm in way over my head. I can't think clearly with her being so close. There is one pervasive thought drilling a hole in my brain, and that is the idea of being with her again. It is inescapable. I'm sure she hates me, but after this is over, I am going to speak to Chaos about dating his sister. I've had enough! Enough of listening to her cry. Enough of forcing myself to stay away. Enough of watching her from the shadows. Enough of pretending I don't love her. Some rules were made to be broken. I walk away from her bedroom door without making my presence known. If I enter her bedroom in this frame of mind, I am making her mine. Period!

I head down to the gym to work off some steam. I'm frustrated, restless, anxious, and angry. Angry with myself mostly. At any rate, I am much to wound up to sleep. I hit the treadmill for a ten-mile run. I ran full out. I run so fast it feels like my lungs will explode. I accomplished ten miles in sixty-two minutes. That's two minutes off my time. I'm not exhausted enough to sleep yet, so I go over to the punching bag. Maybe pounding the bag will make me feel better. I beat that bag for an hour, and all I accomplish are bloody knuckles. None of it helps. The only thought on my mind is *her. Toni.* I shake my head. It occurs to me that I smell like a pack mule. Time for a shower. I chose the first room on the second floor for myself, and the last room on this floor for Doll-face. Anyone trying to get to her has to go through me first. Good luck with that.

I turn on the shower and strip off my sopping wet clothes. I place my beretta on the ledge in the shower. The ledge is strategically placed far enough from the spray of the shower to keep from getting the weapon wet, but close enough at hand should I need it. I designed this ledge myself. I have one in every compound. I don't take chances with our safety! Not ever. We each bring something unique to the team. That is one of the reasons we were chosen. Our individual skill set as a whole makes us a formidable weapon to be used against the enemy. Logic was very precise and strategic when assembling the units. He had a picture in mind and set about bringing it all together. The Colonel gave him complete autonomy over who was chosen and why. The Colonel trusts Logic that much.

When my head finally hits the pillow, I know it will be short lived. Only for a ninety-minute cat nap. After my shower I go back to check on Toni. I slipped into her bedroom unnoticed. She has fallen asleep with all her clothes on. Her scrunchy came undone and her hair is fanned out on her pillow. I couldn't resist touching it. Even in her sleep she looks troubled. Tossing and turning. Whimpering. I want to stretch out beside her. I'm guilty of creeping into her dorm room once or twice just to watch her breathe. Believe me, I know how creepy that sounds. Doll-face thinks I completely abandoned her. In truth I was skulking about way more than I should have. A time or two I nearly lost it when I couldn't find her. Chaos was always in contact with her. That info came to me via Gravity. Who seems to know more than he's letting on.

I set my alarm for 0555. Then send out a text to a local expat for groceries. Lizard used to be one of us. He's gone into retirement but will lend a hand when the situation calls for it. We have a few retired expats all over the country that we call for things like this. I can't very well march Toni to a grocery store now, can I? I set the alarm so as not to chance oversleeping and missing my 0600 security codes. I don't need any other complications in my life. I toss and turn thinking about doll-face. I made her cry. Again! That fact is beating a hole in my skull. At some point, I must have drifted off to sleep. The little bit of sleep I managed to carve out for myself did me a little good. When I wake, I am more tired than before I went to bed. I woke up fully alert. I sit up on the side of the bed and take my cellphone in hand. I don't hear any movement in the house. Toni must still be asleep. I'm glad. She needs it. She and I have a lot to talk about this morning. I want her to be well rested. I allowed her to believe her ruse worked. That her distraction technique was successful. She has no idea. I will uncover the secret or secrets she's hiding if it's the last thing I do.

Her knowing my name could put so many people's lives in jeopardy. There's a reason our identities are nonexistent. There's a reason we use call sighs. We protect ourselves at all costs! What's worse is I'm sure Chaos has no idea Toni knows my true identity either. How many other team member identities does she have? Toni is brilliant. Started college at about sixteen. Was a whiz with computers, but if she's hacking the level of security that holds my identity, that could put the team in danger and land her in Gitmo. There are very few people on the planet that hold the level of security clearance that would allow them access to this type of information. Hourly scans are run to erase our likeness and personal data from every database around the world.

We don't do social media of any kind. There is a team

of people dedicated to working on scrubbing our likeness and personal data twenty-four hours a day. How is it possible Toni hacked a system as sophisticated as that one would have had to be? If she's that good she should be working for the government. Her talent is wasted at the library. She could be working for the FBI or the CIA. What a waste! I memorized today's security codes and set my phone back on the nightstand. There are riddles to be solved. Puzzle pieces to be put in place. I better get started so that I will have some information for the team when we communicate next. I won't go easy on Antonia Townsend.

Chapter 11

Toni makes for one cute librarian. She stands about 5'4" and weighs 110 pounds soaking wet. Curves in all the right places. With a smooth buttered toffee complexion. Almond shaped milk chocolate brown eyes. All these years later those memories never left me. I have to stay focused to keep her alive. If I fail, my mission all I'll have left will be memories. Because If I fail either the enemy will kill me, or Chaos will kill me. I take my job seriously. Putting all nostalgia and personal feelings aside I must treat Toni like I would anyone keeping secrets that could jeopardize the mission and the safety of the men. She can be no different. I won't go so far as to waterboard her for the information, but I will treat her as a hostile combatant. Especially if she isn't forth coming with the intel. She's an adult. I would never harm her, but this isn't a game we are playing either.

Whatever she's hiding could be the missing piece we need to solve quite a few puzzles. If she's hacking top secret government data stores, what else is she up to? Maybe she's into more than assessing penalties for overdue library books. I have to admit aside from knowing she's a librarian in Washington, I know little else about her job or her hobbies. I know even less about her extracurricular activities. Given what I know now it is a very real possibility that Antonia Townsend is more than a computer specialist in the library. It makes absolutely no sense a contract would be placed on her head if she were. Once we figure out who put the hit in place, we will find out what Miss

Townsend has got herself mixed up in. When I allow myself to consider the possibilities then it makes sense as to why she's been so calm throughout this entire ordeal. The questions are endless!

A thought just occurred to me that shook me to my core. Can we trust Antonia Townsend? Why is she working so hard to keep her secrets? I know for a fact she loves her brother. I can't imagine her deliberately doing anything that would put us in danger. What do I know for sure? I know she has information she is deliberately hiding from us. I know someone wants her dead because the contract is real. I know if I fail my mission, we may never get the answers we need. The team is depending on me. My personal feelings have me torn. More than anything I have to be able to trust her. She must be able to trust me too. Our lives depend on it. Maybe that is the way to get her to open up. Make her feel safe. Make her feel like she can trust me. I need answers and am running out of time. Danger is lurking around every corner.

The monsters we face don't go bump in the night. There are no sounds of any kind. They are silent assassins. By the time you hear them you are well on your way to being dead. Any sound means it is well past too late. If I could just get Toni to understand the severity of our situation maybe she would be forthcoming with her intelligence. Make her understand her brother's life and the lives of the brotherhood are in danger. I am working under the assumption that she would never do anything to hurt Chaos or the other team members. There is no room for error in my judgment. I have to lock this down. Lock it down tight before my entire plan goes off the rails!

Maybe the best option is to help her understand why I left seven years ago. Get that out of the way. explain my departure to her. It's what's standing between us. It's the elephant in the room. It's what's keeping her at bay. If I'm honest I don't want to be apart from her anymore. I will wrap up this mission then I will convince Doll-face we belong together. Then I will convince Chaos Toni and I belong together or die trying. The latter is more likely to happen. Once his mind is made up about something, forget it! He's an expert at blowing things up. I sure hope he doesn't include my name on his hit list. My decision has been made. I am willing to suffer the consequences. Now all I have to do is get Toni to fess up. Get her to trust me. Reveal her secrets. In my gut I feel I can trust her. I will go with that assumption until she gives me a reason not to. If this situation is related to her parents' death, then that will answer quite a few questions. I will have no reason to be suspicious.

TONI

I wake up to wonderful warm sunlight streaming through my bedroom window. It looks like it's going to be a beautiful day. From the looks of it you wouldn't know I was in protective custody. Nothing about the morning says people are out to kill me. Once my brain kicks in the prospect of seeing Ace this morning fills me with cold dread. I can feel the dread as it spreads through my limbs. Making me feel sluggish. After last night, I'm not sure I have the heart to converse with him again so soon. Listening to him apologize for taking my virginity nearly crippled me. I thought I was stronger than that. Knowing he's filled with regret is even for soul crushing. A few words should not affect me this way! On top of that, I've given him a reason not to trust me. Not an ideal situation.

I can't imagine what he must be thinking. I made the biggest mistake of my life when I slipped up and called him by his birth name. This situation went from bad to it can't get any worse. I knew I would see him again, one day. I foolishly assumed when I did, I would be ready. Needless to say, I was not ready! Not only was I not ready but I severely underestimated the man Ace has become. He's even more hyper-focused than he was seven years ago. To have all that laser focus directed at me is a little disconcerting. I mean a lot disconcerting. Extracting information from people is their specialty. If I'm being honest, I really don't stand a chance against him. I spend most of my time with my own thoughts. Looking at a computer screen. Doing what I love. That really does not include other humans. So, the art of being mysterious is completely lost to me. I don't lie as a rule.

Maybe I can hide in this room all day. Avoid him. Maybe he will forget I exist. What are my chances? Zero! I shake my head resignedly. Might as well shower and brush my teeth. I walk over to the dresser and fish around for something to put on. In the top drawers there are a variety of undergarments available. Some for men and women. I find undergarments with the tags still on them. This is awesome! In the drawers below I find a pair of jean shorts that look like they will fit, and a large black T-shirt. I will tie it up in a knot. I can make this work. I go into the bathroom and start the shower. While the water is heating up, I root around looking for a new toothbrush. Bingo. I found a stack of new toothbrushes. All-in-store-bought packages. It feels like Christmas.

I step into the shower and adjust the temp. I prefer the water more on the cool side. This is a walk-in shower with shower heads pointing at me from every direction. I am taking the bed and the shower with me when I leave. I'm racking my brain trying to come up with a plan. I can't afford to make Ace any more suspicious of me than he is already. All I need is a logical explanation that will throw him off the scent of something bigger. Why is this so hard? Because subterfuge doesn't come naturally to me. I am a rule follower. Never had to lie to my parents about where I'd been. I was always at a library or museum. Never snuck out during late nights with friends. Didn't have time for friends. Never went to meet a boy. Couldn't care less about boys. All that changed when I met Ace. Not going there!

I spent thirty glorious minutes in the shower. My hair has curled up to its natural S-shaped spring curls. The day before yesterday I spent two hours straightening it with a flat iron. Oh well, curls it is. I wear it curly ninety-nine percent of the time anyway. I work in a dungeon where there is no one to impress. The cabinet is stocked with all sorts of lotions, potions, deodorants, and all sorts of moisturizers. I have a field day trying out different products. Some I like, some I don't. I know I'm just stalling for time. Attempting to postpone the inevitable. Sue me! When I hear my stomach start to grumble, I know play time is over. I need food so I can't stay up here all day. Which means I have to face *him.* Ace. My tormentor. I will go down to the kitchen for food. Then hide out in my room afterwards. Sounds like a great plan. That's all I've got, reader.

Needless to say, I fell asleep before I could even look for a way to communicate with my boss. Being on the run is exhausting. All the stress of the day put me in a sleep coma. So, I am exactly where I was yesterday. Nowhere. No plan and no way to communicate. I feel desperation seeping in. The smell of coffee hits me before I hit the last step. I'm propelled forward into the kitchen. I don't normally drink the stuff, but these are exigent circumstances. Besides that, it feels like I haven't eaten in a week. My nerves are strung tight. I have no idea what I'm doing. My emotions are all over the place. It just feels as if I've lost complete control over my life. That is causing my anxiety to rear its ugly head. Did my left eye just twitch? I groan inside.

Ace is standing over a frying pan scrambling eggs when I enter the kitchen. My stomach growls in acknowledgement. Not too subtle at all. I wonder if he heard that. I stand in the center of the kitchen, torn. Do I stay or do I leave? Why is being in his company this difficult? It was a long time ago. It only feels like yesterday. I am a grown woman! Get a grip Antonia Townsend

He watches me in silence for a few seconds before saying, "*Breakfast is ready. There's fresh coffee if you're interested.*"

"*Thanks.*" With my decision made I make my way over to the cabinets. I take down a coffee mug from the cabinet to the left of the kitchen sink. "*Can I pour you a cup?*"

"*Sure. Thanks.*" I take down another mug and fill them both.

"*What do you take in yours?*"

"*Black for me.*" I pour a few drops of milk in my cup and take both mugs to the kitchen table.

I placed his mug in front of the seat he occupied during our talk last night. I am stationed at the other end of the table. I heard him snort again. I ignore him. He walks over to my end of the table, places a plate with a few slices of buttered toast in front of me, then reaches for an empty plate and scoops eggs onto it. He walks down to the end of the table and scoops eggs on his plate. Then place the empty frying pan in the sink. He then walks back to my end of the table, picks up two slices of toast, and walks back to his seat. Yeah, it looks more ridiculous than it sounds. I tasted the eggs. Not bad. I am very hungry!

We eat in silence for a bit. That works for me. Well, he's eating. I've lost my appetite. I know what's coming and a large knot has formed in the pit of my stomach. Mainly from the fact that I still don't have a plausible excuse to give him for how I know his name. I am reduced to pushing the eggs around on my plate, and barely nibbling on the toast. I know the hammer is about to fall. It will land squarely on my unprepared brain. Mores the pity.

"*What's wrong, Doll? You don't like the eggs?*"

I respond without lifting my head. "*The eggs are fine. Thanks.*"

"Why aren't you eating them?" I need fresh air. I stand abruptly.

"Can I go outback? Just for a bit of fresh air. Please?"

"Sure."

"Thanks." I all but ran from the room. The walls feel like they are closing in on me. There is an exit to the backyard off the kitchen. Once outside I notice the walls are twelve feet high enclosures. Concrete. The nearest neighbor is probably miles away. Other than birds chirping there is no other sound. The only people looking over these walls have helicopters. I am locked in a gilded cage. I guess I'm as safe as I'll ever be. From the looks of it no one is getting in here.

Chapter 12

I didn't bother to ask where we were, but it doesn't mean that I'm not curious. I figure the less I say the better. My mouth seems to have a mind of its own. Spouting off and getting me into a world of trouble. Yeah, I will remain mute. That is all I can handle at the moment. I sit down on a swing and gently rock back and forth. This swing set is meant for children, but they have one here out in the middle of nowhere. Hmmm.

"*Doll, are you ok?*" I nearly jumped out of my skin. He snuck up on me. Gah! I am up off the swing before I register movement. "*Whoa, there. I didn't mean to sneak up on you. I called your name, but you didn't answer. I came to ask if you want to speak to your brother?*"

"*Yes, please.*" I feel my eyes grow moist. I have to pull myself together.

"*Follow me.*"

I followed Ace back into the kitchen. I'm skittish because my nerves are frayed. He pulls a burner phone from a kitchen drawer and punches in a long series of numbers. I recognize the numbers by the sound of the buttons. I memorize those numbers, sixteen in all. More than likely a code that will bounce the signal all around the world. Making it impossible to establish the location of the caller. It never occurred to me to look in the kitchen drawer for a phone. Ugh! Ace hesitates a few seconds then says, "*Roger. Affirmative.*" He hands me the phone and disappears while I'm talking.

"Hey, kiddo. You good?" The sound of my brother's voice is reassuring,

"Yes."

"Don't be scared. Ace has your back. You can trust him."

"I know."

"Once this is over, we are going on vacation. You in?"

I have to smile at my brother, he still thinks a trip to Disneyland will make it all better. "Somewhere tropical would be nice."

"You got it! Love you. We will get this mess sorted, and then you can get back to your job. We will have to discuss living arrangements, but…"

"Yeah, I figured."

"Your new residence will be amazing. Don't worry. Put Ace back on."

I yell out, "Ace!?" He reappears as if by magic. He couldn't have been too far away. He takes the phone and says, "What?"

Sounds like someone woke up on the wrong side of the bed this morning. He looks tired. "She sounds lonely and scared. Make it better. You copy?"

"You sure?"

"Yes."

"Roger, that." The line goes dead. I am stuck on stupid. Never in a million years!

Chaos just gave me the green light to date his sister. My entire being lights up. Someone up there loves me. I remove the chip from the phone, drop it in the garbage disposal, and turn it on. I break the phone in half and drop it in the trash can. I stand here and take ten deep breaths. Then I turn off the garbage disposal. I look around at an empty kitchen. Toni is nowhere in sight. I didn't even notice she left. I have to put my head back on straight. I am going upstairs to claim my woman. Nothing or no one will keep us apart any longer. I take my time walking up the stairs. I need time to reign in my emotions. I tap on the door and wait a few seconds. I opened the door without warning. Just in time to see Toni wipe her tears away.

Seeing her cry kills me inside. I walk over to sit beside her on the bed. *"Talk to me, Doll. Tell me what's on your mind."* She won't even look at me. *"At least tell me why you're crying?"*

"No reason."

She moves to get up off the bed. I trap her body between mine and the headboard. The desire to crush her lustrous curls in my fists while plastering my lips to hers has me in a strangle hold. *"There must be a reason you're crying. Please tell me what has you so upset?"* Without looking at me she says, *"Is there any way someone else can be put on my babysitting detail? Anyone else. Please?"*

ACE

Her desperate plea effectively snuffs the lights out that had me lit up from within mere moments ago. She wants nothing more to do with me. She would rather be here with anyone else than me! I am staring out the window and can scarcely breathe. She hates me. How do I come back from that? There is no coming back from that. My shoulders slump. I'm defeated. *"I can put in a few calls if that's what you want. What do I tell them is the reason for the sudden change?"* I drop my eyes. I don't bother to look at her. I will only see the pain and confusion that is sure to be on her face. That would be my undoing. She doesn't answer. *"Fine. I will figure something out. I will let you know the outcome."* I leave the room the same way I entered it, in silence.

I head down to the basement. I need to pummel something hard and unyielding. Work off some of the hurt. A red mist has enveloped me. Maybe it's for the best. I'll just keep telling myself that. I am at a loss. I need to extract information from Toni and can't seem to keep my head on straight. She is distracting me from my mission. Right when time is of the essence. All I can think of is the fact that I've lost her. I lost her before I even had her. She wants nothing to do with me. Would rather be here with anyone else but me. What do I do about that? How do I process that? My head is spinning, and my heart is breaking. I've hurt her this badly. I'm dying inside. This is the worst possible outcome. I have got to come up with a plan. Less feeling and more thinking.

I punch and kick the bag so hard, for so long, it feels as if my lungs will explode. I collapsed in a heap on the gym floor. I'm sure I've sweated out all the liquids in my body. I feel dehydrated. My knuckles are bleeding profusely. There are blood spatters on the floors and walls. I feel nothing. I feel numb. I feel empty inside. I wish I could say I was closer to a plan of action. The truth is I'm not. I'm functioning on autopilot.

"Why are you doing this?" I whip my head around to see Toni standing by the door. I didn't hear her enter the gym. I get up off the floor on wobbly legs. I need a shower. I can't breathe with her so close. Now I'm the one running away. I make it to the door when I feel her small hand on my arm. My very sweaty arm. I stop dead in my tracks.

"Adam?"

WTF! What is happening? Why is she calling me by name? I am powerless at this point. *"Antonia. Don't! Go back upstairs."*

"You're bleeding!" I close my eyes and count to ten. I count again. Then again. She has no idea how close I am to my breaking

point. In my head, on a loop, going around and around, like a merry-go-round, is an incessant chant. You've hurt her. She doesn't want you! She doesn't want you! She doesn't want you!

"*Please Adam? Let me tend to your wounds?*"

"Don't call me that. If that slips out at the wrong time someone could die!"

"*Ok.*" She sighs, and asks, "*Will you come to the kitchen table and let me wrap your hands?*"

"I need to shower. I will tend to them in the shower, Doll... I mean Toni. It's no big deal." I am moving as we speak. I have to get away from her. "*Adam Arthur Prince, you are bleeding all over the floor! It is a very big deal! Sit in that chair and don't move! I will be right back with the first aid kit. I'm sure you have one. Somewhere around here. Where is it?*"

"Over there under the kitchen sink." I sit and stay seated. It's obvious she has made up her mind. For a second there she sounded like my mom, calling me by my full name. That is how I knew I was in trouble when I was a kid. This time is no different. I sit in silence, waiting for her to return with the first aid kit. I will grit my teeth and bear it. This shouldn't take long. Toni sits in the chair next to mine and turns her body to face me. Our knees are touching. I like it.

"*Let me see your hands please?*" I extend both of my hands out, palms down. My knuckles are dripping with blood. I pulled them back in time for the blood to hit my sweatpants and not her bare thighs.

Toni gets up, grabs a dish towel, and folds it in half. She lays it on the table and instructs me to place both hands on the towel. I do as instructed. She removes gauze from the kit, opens a bottle of hydrogen peroxide and pours some on my knuckles. The peroxide mixes with the blood and starts bubbling. The blood splashes on the towel. What a mess. I am numb inside and don't feel a thing. I sit in silence with my eyes closed waiting for her to finish. I lose all track of time when I hear her nearly whisper, "*Being here with you, like this, is too painful for me. That is why I requested another detail. I thought I was over you, but hearing you apologize for what happened back then brings it all back. It's more than I can handle.*" it's clear she totally misunderstood me.

"*Doll, I'm not apologizing for making love to you. I apologize for not finishing what we started. I'm apologizing for leaving you. I should have stayed! I wanted to stay. I shouldn't have made love to you if I couldn't stay. This life comes with a very complex set of rules. Rules I can't explain. Just know that I wanted to be with you then, and I want to be with you now. If you will have me.*"

She regards me in silence. I'm not sure what I expected after my little speech, but it wasn't silent. It's obvious she's at a loss for words. I didn't mean to put her on the spot. My needs are clearer to me now than they have ever been. I want this woman! Chaos has given me the green light. I am going to put everything I have into pursuing Antonia Townsend. I will give her time to digest all that I have just revealed to her. Once a sufficient amount of time has elapsed, I am going all in. I won't stop until Toni and I are in a fully committed relationship. That is the only acceptable outcome. "*I'll go take that shower now. See you a little later.*" Toni is chewing on her bottom lip in that special way she does when she is trying to put the puzzle pieces together. That must be a good sign. Mustn't it?

Toni absently mutters, "*Ok.*" It's clear she's distracted. At least she's thinking over what we discussed. I walk out of the kitchen leaving Toni to her thoughts. It's the second longest walk I've ever taken. The first was walking away from her that cold winter night seven years ago. I hurt her worse than I thought. I trudge up the stairs heavy hearted. Maybe I didn't make the best choices back then. I must keep in mind that hindsight is 20/20. I chose my job over her. That just tells me

I don't deserve her. She should be first. Always! I strip off my clothes and jump in the shower. I got out of the shower before realizing I was really in the shower. My mind is in shambles. This is the last thing I need right now. To be emotional. To be distracted. I must focus, or someone will die.

Chapter 13

TONI

Watching Ace pulverize that punching bag was ripping my insides to shreds. I know my requesting another detail hurt him, but I'm in self-preservation mode. I was honest about my feelings. This wouldn't be so hard if I was here with someone else. Anyone else will do. Being this close to him has skeletons falling out of closets I thought were sealed shut. I'm tripping all types of bones. It took years of therapy to get this far, and in one fell swoop all those years of therapy amount to absolutely nothing. I still care deeply for Adam Prince aka Ace. Is it because he was my first? In truth he's my only. I can't see myself with anyone else. How pathetic is that? It's not like I had a ton of offers. I was wrapped up in my studies. I never had time for frat parties or sorority functions. I was busy working on the details of my life. Yeah, at this rate I will die a lonely old maid. The hours slip past with no other Ace sitting. He has gone off the grid. So, I go up to my room.

I'm not sure what time it is, but I feel exhausted. I'm bone weary. I turn on the TV and begin flipping through channels. I'm not watching anything in particular. I just have it on for background noise. Trying to sort through the tattered pieces of my emotions. I let my mind wander. Thinking over all Ace revealed to me in the kitchen. It's a lot to process. At some point I must have dozed off. I must be dreaming or having a sense of déjà vu. Someone has their hand clamped tightly over my mouth. Yes. Again! In my dream I'm kicking and punching. Fighting for all I'm worth. When I hear him whisper, *"Relax Doll. It's me and we've been breached. Time to go!"*

I hate doing this to her again. I don't have time to check the surveillance cameras. But once the boots hit the ground the silent alarm was triggered. I have just enough time to get Toni out of here. I hit the self-destruct mode button on my phone. We need to get a move on! Time is of the essence.

Wait! This is no dream. Ace is bending over me with a sense of urgency. *"We have to go! Now! Nod if you understand. The backup team is fifteen minutes out. We don't have fifteen minutes. Let's go!"* Ace grabs my hand and pulls me over to the fireplace. I just barely have enough time to slip my tennis shoes on. He reaches under the mantle and presses a button. I hear a soft snick. One that sounds way too loud in the stillness of the room. He pushes on the fireplace and the wall slides back soundlessly. We step into the dark space. *"Don't move, Doll."* He tells me. He then turns and pushes the fireplace back into position. It's pitch black in here. He flips a switch, and a red-light bulb comes to life. Once the fireplace is back in place he pushes a button, and a faint popping and hissing sound reaches my ears. *"Watch your step. Listen closely. There are ten sets of ten steps. Count as you go. I will be right behind you. Use the wall to guide you. Ten sets of ten. Are you ready?"* I nod.

He whispers, *"Let's get out of here. I've activated the fireplace in your bedroom. That should buy us a few minutes. They will clear the house first. Once that's done, they will check all escape routes. They may end up finding this one. We need to be a mile away from this location before the building blows."* Wait, what did he say? Before the building blows! What the freak?! I am flying down the stairs as fast as my legs will carry me. Running for all I'm worth. The steps aren't too steep or slippery so that's something. We reached the bottom quick enough and headed through an underground tunnel. It's dark, wet, and cold down here. All I have on is a T-shirt, sweat pants, socks, and tennis shoes. Definitely not dressed for this weather. I barely had time to slide my feet into my shoes, there was definitely no time to grab a jacket.

After about two minutes we exit the tunnel and went out into even colder weather. We are on a beach just past the exit to the tunnel. I have no idea where we are going, but Ace seems to know exactly where we are headed. I trust him. After another minute of inching along he stops so abruptly I slam into his back. He turns to steady me. We are in deep shadow. I can't see much of anything. He points toward the ocean. I can barely make out the two men patrolling the beach. It looks like they have weapons. Ace seems to see them just fine. He motions for me to stay silent and crabwalk to the men patrolling the beach. He slips up behind the first guy. He yanks his head back and slits his throat. He doesn't make a sound. I feel my body shiver all over. Ace was deathly accurate. His efficiency should frighten me. For some reason it doesn't.

The second guy is walking with purpose. He's carrying an automatic rifle. His back is now facing away from us, and he is moving in the opposite direction. Faster than I've ever seen anyone move Ace races up behind the assassin. Over the crashing of waves, it's hard to hear anything. Something makes the assassin turn around. Before he can fire Ace sweeps his arm up sending the rifle up in the air. The assassin loses control of his weapon. A fight ensues. I see slivers of light reflecting off metal. I find myself inching closer. I don't want to lose sight of Ace. Punches and kicks are being thrown so quickly it's hard to determine who's doing what to whom. It's all a blur. They are both in all black attire. Almost identical. Black fitted shirts, cargo pants, and boots. Maybe they buy this stuff at assassins-r-us. The surplus store must have had a clearance sale.

Ace manages to get the guy in a choke hold. The assassin is trying to get his hands on his rifle. I can hear the man gasping for air. Fighting to get Ace's arms from around his throat. Ace doesn't let up. I don't know how much time passes before the guy finally goes limp in his arms. Ace twists his neck and gently lays him on the beach. He tosses the rifle into the ocean. To be swept out to sea. I stand here in stunned silence. I don't know how to feel. Happy. Sad. Relieved. I know Ace risked his life to save mine. I am grateful. I find myself shaking. Unable to control myself. Unable to move. Were it not for his hands on my shoulders I wouldn't know he was directly in front of me. Clouds pass over the moon blocking any sliver of light. Ace says, *"Are you alright, Doll?"*

 I nod my head. Of course, he can't see me. So, I say, *"Yes."* I notice a quiver in my voice. It could be from the shock of witnessing two men die or the cold. I'm not sure which at this point.

 Ace says, *"Up ahead tucked away in a little cove west of where we are standing is a speed boat. I need to check it out to make sure it hasn't been discovered and tampered with. Take this flashlight. I am going to check it out. You stay here. When you hear a hoot, like the sound of an owl, turn this flashlight on and run like your life depends on it! You got me?"*

 "Yes."

 "Good. Ninety seconds, Doll. Keep your ears open." I have a death grip on the front of his shirt. I have to force my fingers to release him. He places a kiss on my forehead and begins to pry my fingers loose from his shirt. *"I promise I will keep you safe."* I nod. He turns away and is swallowed up by the darkness. One thousand one. One thousand two. One thousand three. I continue to count until I hear a loud boom. Sparks of fire shower the night sky. Illuminating the velvety darkness. A few seconds later I heard the signal. I turn on the flashlight and run like the hounds of hell are chasing me!

I don't bother turning around but the explosions come one after the other. Leveling all in its wake. The ground shakes hard under my feet. I barely managed to stay upright. No one could have survived that. I make it to the side of the boat and Ace hauls me up and deposits me in a seat. The boat shoots off like a rocket. I am trembling. Both from the cold and the adrenaline. He grabs a thin shiny blanket and hands it to me. I wrap it around my shoulders. I don't expect something that feels like cheap aluminum foil to be of any use. But it's quite warm. I strap myself in. We are going really, really fast! I can't see a thing, but Ace is navigating at this speed in the dark like it's daylight out. He doesn't seem worried. I'm sure he's driving in the dark so as not to give our position away. On the off chance someone survived the explosion. We sped through the surf for close to two hours before we stop. I unsnap my seatbelt with shaky hands. It's even colder on the water. Ace lifts me and hands me over the side of the boat into a pair of waiting arms.

"Hey you. How is it going?"

"Chance. Is that you?"

"Yeah, it's me kiddo. You, ok?"

"I think so."

"Let's get you inside." It's too dark to see clearly, but it looks like a log cabin of sorts.

"I can walk, Chance."

"*It's faster this way.*" I snort at him. We enter a brightly lit large room in what looks like a log cabin. A fire is crackling in the fireplace that takes up one whole wall. It's warm and cozy here. Ace comes in and positions himself nearby. Hovering. There are a lot of men in this compound. I'm not sure what I was expecting, but it wasn't this. I guess this is the equivalent of a welcome party. My brother finally sees fit to set me down on my own two feet, and Ace comes to stand behind me. His hand resting on my hip. All eyes are on him. No one speaks. I can sense tension in the air. There is a lot being communicated, but no words are spoken. My brother discreetly nods in Aces direction and a collective exhale is felt around the room. The tension deflates like a popped balloon. I wonder what that was all about. There are roughly seven very tall rugged looking men standing in this building. All this testosterone is making my throat itch.

My brother says, *"Toni, let me introduce you to everyone?"*

"Ok."

"You remember Ace?" The guys find that particularly funny.

"Yes." I find myself blushing and staring at the floor. Everyone pretends not to notice.

"This huge bear of a man is our second in command, Gravity." I extend my right hand.

"Nice to meet you, Gravity." I pretend not to remember him. *"You're the pilot, right?"*

"That's correct. Nice to see you again Antonia." Gravity walks away and another takes his place. *"This is Dome. He's on loan from Charlie squad. This is his teammate Pyro"* I extend my hand, again, and shake theirs. One after the other they step forward. Then Polar steps up, he takes my tiny hand in his, bends over it, and places a kiss on my knuckles. All the while staring at Ace. The room erupts in laughter. I pull my hand away and took an involuntary step back, bumping right into Ace. Ace growls at Polar.

Chaos says *"Dude, stop slobbering on my sister. Hands off!"* Polar is a jokester. It's written all over him.

"Nice to meet you beautiful."

"Nice to meet you too."

Ace growls, *"You know she's only saying that to be polite, right?"* The guys laugh at that. The next man steps forward. I extend my hand, and Ace reaches forward to pull my arm back. *"No one else touches her. Doll, ignore them. Everyone this is Toni. Now go away, everyone. Enough with the introductions."* Polar shrugs and walks away. These guys are a hoot. *"Logic and a few of the others are off site. I'm sure you'll see them again, one day soon. You must be tired. Let me show you to your room?"* He has no idea how tired I am. Once the adrenaline starts to wear off, I can feel my energy levels plummet. I could sleep for a week.

Ace and Chance (Chaos) share more silent communication. They think I don't notice, but I do. *"Toni, let Ace know if you get hungry. I will whip you up something tasty."*

"Will do. Thanks."

"Toni, follow me. It's down the hall and to the right." I follow Ace down the hall away from prying eyes. Way too much testosterone in that one room. *"Doll, are you ok?"*

"I'm ok. Thanks, Ace. Thank you for putting your life on the line for me. Thank you for keeping me safe. I'm sorry every time you see me, I seem to cause you nothing but trouble."

He stops inches from me. *"Don't. This isn't your fault. Someone is out to hurt you. I won't allow that to happen. We won't allow that to happen! We'll find out who's behind this and put them out of their misery. We'll give you your life back."* I turn away to hide the tears. I'm only this weepy because I'm tired.

I'm emotionally exhausted. He steps up behind me and wraps his arms around my waist. He plants a kiss in my hair. *"Doll, you don't have to hide from me. You've been very brave. I understand how scary this must be."* We entered a bedroom. *"This is where you'll sleep for the time being. I'm here if you need me. I'll be sleeping in that chair right between you and the door. I wish someone would! Try and get some rest."*

"Wait. What? You're sleeping in here with me? You mean just the two of us?"

"Yes. In that chair over there by the door. Don't worry, you will be safe. We will keep you safe. All you have to do is rest. Try not to worry."

In my head everything he's saying makes sense. My heart is thumping to the beat of a different drum. An emotional drum, not a logical drum. The two of us alone together may not be the wisest choice to make. Ugh!

Chapter 14

He can't mean it. I can't sleep in here alone with him. He is out of his mind. My brother is nearby. The chemistry between us sizzles. I'm sure people noticed. My emotions are all over the place. He says he wants a chance. I wish I could say the words he said back at the safe house didn't matter. That they had no effect on me. But they do. Boy, do I wish they didn't! His words went straight to my heart and began to unthaw it. Stupid, traitorous heart. My feelings for him have persisted despite the pain. It isn't fair. I needed to hate him. I wrapped myself up in my anger, so I wouldn't focus on the pain. He wants to be with me. I wish I could say I didn't want to be with him too. But boy, do I ever! He put his life on the line for me. Standing here looking all lethal. Who could resist that? I certainly can't!

"What's wrong, Doll? Don't you trust me?"

"That's not it."

"Then what is it?" He steps into my personal space to ask his last question. He's fingering my hair. He seems mesmerized by the strands. I'm sure my head resembles a bird's nest. *"You have soft beautiful hair, Doll."* I nod. My voice escapes me. I'm saved by a knock on the door.

Ace says, *"Come in."* I can tell this intrusion annoys him. The door opens. It's Chance. Ace doesn't move an inch. I am forced to step around him to speak to my brother. My brother quips, *"Just checking to make sure you're ok."* He glances in Ace's direction. "Everything ok in here?"

"Yeah. Thanks. Just tired. I can't wait to go to bed! Wait! That

didn't come out right." I don't want my big brother thinking I mean with Ace. So, I stammer and say, *"Ace is sleeping in that chair over there."* Chaos glances at Ace, his expression never changing. My brother tilts his head and says, *"Is that right? Well, on that note, I will see you later this morning. Get some rest."* He's laughing as he exits the room. He finds this situation particularly amusing.

"Ace, what's going on between you and my brother? Don't think I haven't noticed the side eye the two of you slip each other over my head."

"What do you mean, Doll?"

"Please, don't do that? Don't treat me like I'm some dumb kid. I'm all grown up in case you haven't noticed. I've noticed the secret looks you and he share when you think I'm not paying attention. What is going on?"

"Believe me when I say I've noticed. You've grown up quite nicely!" Cue the warm flush! *"Your brother seems to have worked out that I'm staking my claim on you. He has given me the green light."*

"Huh? Excuse me! Say again? You're staking what? You are kidding me, right? What is this the sixteenth century? You and my idiot brother have worked it all out, have you? Well, la-dee-dah. Why don't you go discuss your claim with him? Please, leave my room Adam. I am not a piece of furniture you can lay claim to! Thanks for giving me options. You are a piece of work. Get thee gone!"

Ut oh! That didn't go over well. *"Doll, it's not like that! That's not what I meant. I didn't mean it how it sounded."* She looks ticked off. *"I am giving you all of three seconds to leave my room. If you're not gone in three seconds, I will scream my head off!"*

"Come on, Toni? Don't be like that. You misunderstood. Hear me out. Besides, there is nowhere else to sleep. All the other bedrooms are taken. Don't I get a break for saving your life?" At this point I

will try anything. She doesn't look the least bit fazed.

"Thank you for saving me from the bad guys. Now get out! I'm sure you'll manage. A big strong strapping tough guy like yourself. Securing sleeping arrangements shouldn't be a difficult task for a man with your many talents. You got this. Surely! Goodnight Adam."

I turn my back on him and cross my arms. Now I'm just mad! Out of nervous habit I begin tapping my foot. After a few seconds of silence, I hear the door close softly behind me. He has some colossal nerves! About five seconds after he leaves, I hear raucous laughter. The laughter is so loud it sounds like it's in the same room as me. It doesn't take a rocket scientist to work out why they are laughing. It serves him right! Making assumptions. He's a piece of work. I haven't seen him in seven years. The nerve of that guy, and my brother, too. Who do they think they are? They have decided?! I shake my head in total disbelief. It's all I can do to keep from screaming. I don't know who I want to punch harder, the arrogant jerk or my idiot brother.

My brother and I are having some serious words sometime in the near future. Men! Why are they so clueless? I have to admit the very last thing I thought was possible is now a possibility. I never imagined my brother would be okay with the idea of Ace dating his kid sister. He is overprotective to say the least! The world must be coming to an end. We have never discussed dating or having boyfriends. Mostly since I have never dated or had boyfriends. He never pried or asked embarrassing questions about my sex life. I thought it was because he respected my boundaries. What a joke. He believes he is the boss of me. He has no idea! Ace is actually the closest thing I've ever had to either of those things. I just assumed my brother thought I wasn't ready. Maybe he knows more than I thought. I'm so confused. I'll leave these thoughts for another day. Can't afford brain overload.

My heart rate has finally returned to normal. I'm glad it was too dark to see either of the dead bodies Ace left behind. I don't need those pictures stuck in my head. Giving me nightmares. More importantly, I need to come up with a plan. A plan to get out of this compound and away from my brother. Ace discovered I know his real name, and so the team will know too, sooner than I would like. They don't hide things or keep secrets from each other. That's the way the brotherhood functions. One for all and all for one. No, that's the three musketeers. Never mind. The team calls him Ace. In my heart he is Adam. He will always be Adam. My Adam. Well, maybe not *my* Adam. He does not belong to me. There was a time when I dreamt, he would. I dreamed of being Mrs. Adam Arthur Prince. Make that Townsend-Prince. That's more like it. I'm a modern woman. I realize those were the desperate musings of a naïve and foolish child. That was the past. This is the present.

I'm all grown up now. I have a very grown-up job, and I have moved on! I need to remember that. Remind myself of that every time Adam looks at me with those puppy dog brown eyes. He's staked a claim on me indeed. I. HAVE. MOVED. ON! My first thought has to be what to tell Chance (Chaos), when he asks how I know Ace's government name. I'm sure Ace is obligated to notify the team. I need to be ready. I don't see how putting a contracted hit out on me is connected to my job. What I do is done on the fringes of society. Unless I can find a way to communicate, I won't know whether withholding information is causing more harm than good. Or if I'm jeopardizing more lives.

What would the boss want me to say? Share or not to share. That is the question. I don't want the men to risk injury following a false narrative. Ugh! Knowing the right thing to do is nearly impossible. I need to find a way to make contact with my boss. Check in. Get read in on the current situation. Finding out who wants to kill me is the second thing on my list. I need to get some pieces in motion. It would be great if I could get my hands on a computer. I could accomplish all of that in record time. I would love to go up to my brother and ask politely for computer equipment. That would raise all kinds of red flags. He will then ask about one million questions.

I spend most of the early morning hours tossing and turning. I'm desperate to come up with a solid plan. I'll just get up and take a shower. Maybe then I can organize my rattled thoughts. I do my best thinking in the shower. Besides, it's early morning now. Maybe around five a.m. I'm wide awake. I'm also feeling desperate. For the record, this is the worst vacation ever! I might as well start my day. After about fifteen minutes I step out of the shower with a towel wrapped around me. I wipe the steam from the mirror and take a look at my reflection. My hair is wet and dripping water onto my shoulders. I have dark circles under my eyes. I may have lost a few pounds after my last assignment. It was a very tense and stressful time at work.

That was months ago though. The weight hasn't returned. My life is just starting to return to normal, and here I find myself on the run. Not just on the run but running from assassins. Stuck with the same man who broke my heart. Who took my virginity and then took off. You can't make this stuff up! My brother is going to kill me when he finds out I've not been forthcoming with him. A lie by omission is still a lie. My brother is no dummy. He will start adding things up. If I'm not careful he will know things he shouldn't know. If Ace tells him I know his true identity, I will have a lot of questions to answer. Answers I am not at liberty to share with anyone. Not even my brother or Ace.

I am no closer to a plan than I was thirty-six hours ago. I hate lying to my brother, but what else can I do. I also hate lying to Ace. If they find out about my lies, it could jeopardize our relationship. My brother and I have grown close since the loss of my parents. The only thing I can think of doing is to find a computer and sneak off to send a message out to my boss. I can't very well waltz up to my brother, and say, "Hey. You'll never guess what I did. Seven years ago, I hacked into a secure database and stole top secret information. Why, you ask? Because my heart was broken. I now know the official names of all your team members. Reader, how do you imagine that conversation would go over? On top of that, the hit out on my head may not have anything to do with the death of our parents.

The hole I'm digging keeps getting deeper and deeper! It seems to have no bottom. Because if it turns out the people that put a hit out on my head have nothing to do with the death of my parents, and everything to do with my current job, my brother and Ace will string me up by my ankles! Not to mention this puts the entire team in even more danger because they don't have all the information required to neutralize the threat. My boss will be in trouble too when my brother gets wind of it. I need a computer in the worst way! Why is life so complicated?

The best scenario I can think of would be to leave this compound. Far away from my brother and his team. All it will take would be one thread for them to pull on. Then the whole thing comes undone. Alpha team is the best! To add insult to injury, some of Bravo and Charlie team members are in attendance. That Gator guy is scary! Getting out won't be easy. My brother will go loco trying to find me. Ace will blow a gasket. The entire team will shoot and kill whoever they must; to find me. This is tricky. I have to thread this needle carefully. It's almost comical. I can't even find a way to communicate, but I am planning to escape the compound. I have big dreams. My being here is not a good option. My hands are tied here. I need answers, and I can't get them being watched twenty-four-seven.

The question is who placed the hit on the dark web? If I can talk to my boss maybe, he could line up the events that lead me here. That may give me a clue as to who the players are. Then I could decide my next move. I know for a fact there is no way my brother is letting me out of his sight. Nor Ace. Mister, I staked my claim on you. Every time I think about it my insides get all fired up. The feminist in me could spit fire about now. I finish tying my shoelaces when I hear a knock on the door. I stand and say, *"Come in."*

The door opens and Ace pops his head in. He steps into the room when he sees I'm dressed. *"Good morning, doll. You're up early. How did you sleep?"*

For the record he looks way too good this early in the morning. I was expecting my brother, not him. I can feel my heart rate increase. This is not what I need. *"Good morning. I slept, ok. You?"* Ace need not know I haven't slept a wink. This is all smoke and mirrors. *"How did you sleep?"*

His eyes are boring a hole in my face. *"Do you really want to know?"* I glance away. I hear him chuckle. He says, *"You must be hungry by now. Breakfast is almost ready. Let's eat."*

"Ok."

"I figure while we're at breakfast you can explain to the team how you know my birth name. That should make for an interesting breakfast time conversation. Don't you think? You might as well lay it all out on the line. This way you only have to tell your story once. You are keeping secrets. I want to know what, and I want to know why."

"Please, Adam. I mean Ace." He gives me the side eye, *"Please, don't tell my brother I know your birth name. I can't explain any of that to any of you."*

"So, what I hear you say is there's a whole lot that needs explaining. You can either explain it to them or you can explain it to me. What's it going to be Doll?"

"I need you to trust me. Just like I've trusted you." Before he can respond there's another knock on the door. *"Come in."* I am grateful for the distraction. The door opens and Polar sticks his head in. He looks from Ace to me and back again.

Then Polar says, *"Good morning, beautiful. You are a sight for sore eyes. Breakfast is ready. I thought I'd come to escort you to the kitchen. It's a large compound, I wouldn't want you to get lost."*

He is doing this just to annoy Ace. A little jealousy goes a long way. It's working. Ace has a vein throbbing in his forehead. I used to think a little jealousy never hurt anyone. That's about to change judging by the look on Ace's face. Serves him right, though! Take Ace down right off his high horse. Staking a claim. Who even says that? I smile at Polar and say, *"Thank you, Polar."*

Ace is actually growling when he says, *"You know I'm here to take Toni to breakfast, right? There is absolutely no reason for you to be here though. Keep it up Polar. I went out on an extraction and have yet to discharge my weapon. Don't make me shoot you!"*

Chapter 15

Polar looks at me and says, *"Toni, when you get tired of Mr. Personality, you know where to find me."* Then he leaves, closing the door on his way out. I can't help but laugh. I wait a few seconds, rush to the door, open it, and say, *"Polar! Wait up."* Of course, he's nowhere to be seen. He's already gone.

Ace looks annoyed when he says, *"You step one foot out that door without me, and I will spend all night making you pay, and then I will shoot him! Your choice Doll."*

I can't help but throw my head back and laugh. Ace is not amused. Is this really jealousy? It looks like jealousy to me. Why do my insides warm up at the notion? Ace is being very territorial. I should not be pleased about it, and yet I am. That must mean something. Doesn't it? I wait for him by the door.

He steps up to me and looks me dead in the eye. *"You are mine! I am yours. There is no room for anything extra. Please don't make me hurt anyone."* He looks serious. My eyes are huge. I swallow and nod my head. That was the sexiest thing I ever heard. My whole body responds to him. This scarcely seems fair. He lifts my chin and presses his lips to mine. I am frozen in place. He takes his time exploring my mouth. Like he can't get enough. My whole world falls away.

Until I hear, *"Ahem."* When I looked up, I saw it was my brother. I jumped back so fast, I nearly fell. Ace wraps his arm around my waist before I land on my butt. My brother's face is blank. And, yet I feel so guilty. I'm a full-grown woman. Why do I feel guilty? Chaos says, *"You guys coming to breakfast? The food is disappearing fast."*

Ace says, *"Yep. On our way."* My brother leaves without saying another word.

I glance up at Ace. He is strung tight, and his nostrils are flaring. *"Are you ok, Ace?"*

"Yep. I'm fine. Can I sleep in here with you tonight? I promise to behave."

"Will you keep my secret?"

"No. We don't keep secrets on this team."

"So, my brother knows you took my virginity seven years ago?"

"No."

"Then that's a secret. All I'm asking for is six hours and a computer."

"Toni!"

"Ace please. I am counting on you."
"Six hours?"

"Yes."

"Fine. Six hours. After that you tell me everything."

"Deal." I extend my hand to shake on our deal, but Ace pulls me into his arms to seal the deal another way. He plants a kiss on me that's so hot, I forget my own name. When he pulls back, we are both panting. He is putting all sorts of ideas in my head.

He whispers in my ear, *"I know I don't have the right to ask, but I'm asking. Please give me a chance to fix what I broke. That's all I need."* Wow. He has no idea how big his request is. I barely managed to mend the pieces of my broken heart seven years ago. There will be nothing, but fragments left if he walks away this time. And when he finds out what I've been keeping from them, he is definitely going to walk away! Or kill me. Looking over his right shoulder, I nod, as if in agreement. I don't have the heart to look him in the eyes and lie. The look on his face tells me he's offering me everything I always dreamed of, but things are different now. I'm different now. I can only hope this gets cleared up quickly. I would rather die than hurt my brother or Ace.

There is no clear path forward. My only hope is to check in. Get a sit-rep and go from there. For the first time in forever, I don't have a plan and that drives me insane. It's not hard to find the kitchen. We follow the noise. The noise level is unbelievable. Then you add in silverware clanking against plates, some very deep voices, and compliments to the chef, raucous laughter, and viola'. We are in the kitchen. A blind person could find this kitchen. There are two empty seats available at the end of the table. They are next to Polar. I take a quick glance in Ace's direction. I saw a severe scowl on his face. I look at Polar's face and it's clear this was a strategic maneuver. Not because he's attracted to me. Not in the slightest, but because he knows his flirting with me is getting under Ace's skin.

He is doing this on purpose. He's a big kid this one. I'm not convinced Ace won't shoot Polar. Ace asks, *"What would you like? I'll bring you a plate."*

"Surprise me." I'm about to take the seat next to Polar when something makes me glance in Ace's direction. He is watching me with a neutral expression on his face. I strategically slide over one spot and sit at the end. Ace goes back to fixing my plate like nothing happened. I can hear Polar chuckling under his breath. Troublemaker! From the looks of it everyone at the table is trying to hide their smiles in one way or another. Someone coughs. Another hides his smile behind a paper napkin. I see my brother watching from the corner of his eye. From the looks of it he's about to lose it. Barely controlling his laughter. I know Ace is well aware of what everyone is doing at the table. He is ignoring everyone but me.

He brings me a plate, silverware, and a glass of orange juice. He walks to the counter and grabs me a mug for coffee, complete with cream and sugar. He sets it all in front of me. I look up at him and say, *"Thanks, babe. Umm, I mean Adam. Ace. I mean Ace."* The entire room stops breathing. I can feel my face heat up. I am sure my heart is no longer beating. This is all Ace's fault. He is distracting me with his kisses and chivalry.

In a tone I don't think I've ever heard before, I hear my brother say, *"Give me the room!"* Several overly grown men grab their plates and their drinks and file out of the kitchen. Like marionettes on a string. The move is so well executed you'd think it was choreographed. I see Ace take a deep breath. The implications of my error just went nuclear. I have three seconds to come up with something quick. If I don't things will go from bad to worse. The need to look at Ace is almost overwhelming. I'm not sure even he can help me at this point.

LOGIC

After meticulously going through all the gear Omega dumped in the basement, we are satisfied we have all we need. We've determined Coup will be the one in the monkey suit attending the online auction. Initially the auction was going to be held with the prospective buyers in attendance at a super secure location. A location that only invited guests would be given access to and with only a few hours to arrive. At the last minute someone got spooked and changed it to an online auction. I'm sure the live feed will be just as secure. Hopefully Omega can get a bead of the original feed before the purchases are made. Otherwise, we will have to chase down each artifact one by one. More than likely, they will be scattered all over the globe.

Since no one volunteered to attend the online auction, we

drew straws. Coup drew the short straw. Oh well. He's been grumbling about it ever since. Gator has been ribbing him endlessly. Even though the auction is online it's still a black-tie affair. No jeans or sweatpants allowed. I can't wait to see Coup all dolled up. He'll be so cute in his little tux! Omega was kind enough to have one sent over. It seems Omega knows all our measurements. Imagine that. I'm starting to wonder at what they don't know. They may not know everything because they also sent one for Razor. Just in case, I guess. By the way Coup's acting one would think he was being asked to donate a lung. Omega was able to add a bogus name to the guest list complete with bogus background and banking information.

The powers that be wanting to make sure the people bidding on the stolen artifacts can actually afford them. It appears Coup, or Mr. Fredrick Dirk as he is not so lovingly referred to, is worth an estimated one billion dollars. The people that attend these auctions are so rich they've run out of things to buy. They are bored with their ostentatious wealth. This purchase gives you bragging rights, nothing more. I don't see there being a large commercial market for ancient Tibetan artifacts. Not even to the Chinese. It seems Coup would rather be shot at than attend this online auction. The man is just hard wired all wrong. He's happiest in cargo pants, black tees, and combat boots. Add on his accessories, throwing stars, AR's, sharp blades, and he's already to party. He is all about the hunt.

There's a squawk in my left ear. It's Omega on the line. *"We have a status update for you. We were hoping to pull the data we needed from the satellite on the feed from the location of the auction. As it happens, they are not going live until seconds before the actual auction is set to begin. I don't know in which order the items will be auctioned off in, so tell Mr. Dirk he will have to stay until he wins the bid on all four pieces or until we scout out the location. Tell him to go crazy with the bidding because it's cryptocurrency. It will be erased from their accounts as soon as the artifacts are in his possession. No one will ever be paid. Once I ascertain where the artifacts are being stored, I will let you know. I was hoping for the intel so we could have a backup team breach the facility to retrieve the artifacts while you handle Salvator Parisi and his handler. But because we don't know where in this world the artifacts are stored, we think it's best that all sleeper cells be activated.*

We will use local law enforcement as a distraction should a diversion be necessary. Everyone is on standby and can mobilize at a moment's notice. Because of the sheer number of moving parts in the game we will be multitasking. We now have intel that suggests the Italian Death Dealer will make contact with his handler at a renovated warehouse. We believe the uranium will be transported in some of the crates with the artifacts. Once the Italian Death Dealer is identified a sleeper cell will tail him until you arrive. They are not to engage. The Colonel doesn't trust anyone else to deal with Parisi. He only wants your hands on this. I don't need to tell you how badly the boss wants this thing contained. I will keep you apprised. Omega out."

I call Gator, Razor, Crucible, and Reaper into the closet for an update. While Coup is sitting in front of a computer screen getting the same update over comms, the rest of us will be mobilized and ready to move out. Wherever the Italian Death Dealer is I can't wait to get my hands on him. I get the feeling he's closer than I think. Once Omega sends out his location, we will track him down. The goal is to get him, the uranium, and the artifacts all at once. As bad as I want to get my hands on the uranium, I want to get my hands on Salvator Parisi even more. I trust Omega to find both. This is a dangerous situation with a lot of moving parts and very little time to prepare. There will be no advanced recon. I will be planning on the fly. I don't even know how much security he's traveling with. The most I can do is make sure my team is ready for almost anything. "Ok. So, this is what we know. *The Italian Death Dealer was scheduled to make* contact with his handler at the live auction.

"Omega found intel to suggest the ancient Tibetan artifacts is what was used to transport the uranium. Now that the auction has been moved to a live feed, we still expect Salvator to make contact with his handler at the actual auction. There is no time for the auction master to move all the objects in question. The decision to go viral with the auction is just an extra security measure. Because we don't know the exact location of the uranium and/or the artifact everyone in covert ops has been activated. Sleeper cells from all over the world. Past and present members. We are casting a very wide net. Local law enforcement will also be in play. Try not to kill any of them. They are inept at the best of times. Once the Death Dealer is located a tracker will be attached to him and satellite imaging will be used to keep tabs until we arrive. The Colonel has made it clear our team does the capture."

"He knows we are set to receive the uranium. We are the only team prepared as such. Our goal is to minimize casualties. Uranium is deadly as you well know. So, this is the breakdown. Dolphin you're on me. We will handle the uranium and the artifacts. Gator, you take Razor, Crucible, and Reaper to lock down the Death Dealer and his handler. Once the uranium is secured for transport, we will rendezvous, and I will escort Mr. Parisi to a gravesite near you. We have no way of knowing what his security forces will be. So, if it looks like he can't be contained I want him neutralized. Under no circumstances does Salvator Paris live to fight another day. Are we clear?"

The group answers, "*Oorah!*"

"That is the plan. Keep in mind it will be influx depending on what active updates we're fed by Omega. Are there any questions?"

Gator says, "*Not on my end. Sounds like a solid plan.*" The rest of the team remained silent.

"Ok Dolphin, we gather the Haz-mat suits and coordinated

accessories and load up the van. Gator you guys gather up Haz-mat suits and coordinated accessories and load up the bird. We want to be prepared for every eventuality. Since we don't know where they are located, we prepare both. We load up the weapons along with the any other materials. Let's get a move on. We have no idea how much time we have since everything will be done on the fly."

Chapter 16

TONI

My brother looks at me and says, *"Start talking."* He is deceptively calm. He's looking at me, but his attention is on both of us. Ace takes the seat beside mine and reaches over to place his hand on my thigh. I would love to sit in his lap right now. Use him as a human shield to hide from my brother. I'm terrified! He's still staring at me when he addresses Ace. *"Did you tell Toni your birth name?"*

I can tell he is loath to get me in even more trouble, but he can't lie either. Then he says the very last thing I ever expected him to say, *"I'm in love with your sister. She and I have been intimate. It only makes sense she should know my name."* I feel all the color drain from my face. Not because he told my brother we made love, but because he just threw himself in front of a runaway freight train to save me. He is putting himself between my brother and me. My brother may very well kill him.

My brother is completely still when he asks, *"How long?"* I go to speak when I feel Ace squeeze my thigh. I look at him and he gives me a brief head shake. He wants me to stay silent, but if I do, he is a dead man. He can't make my brother think he took advantage of me. My brother will assume I was vulnerable after my parent's death and Ace took advantage of me. There will be nothing standing between Ace and certain death. Not one single thing.

I blurt out, *"Since the safe house."* My brother looks over at

Ace and quirks his brow.

Ace says, "*I made love to Toni seven years ago.*" All the air is sucked right out of the room! In my mind I'm screaming *NOOOOOO!* After that everything is a blur. Everything stops and explodes into motion at the same time. My brother has Ace choked up against the kitchen cabinets. His hand is on his weapon. Ace has his hands up in surrender. He isn't even attempting to fight back. His nose may be broken and by morning he will have a black eye. I don't know how my brother got to Ace without moving one hair on my head. I was sitting between the two of them. Ace's jaw may also be dislocated. It's hard to tell. Out of nowhere Gravity comes into the kitchen. He whispers something in my brother's ear that has him releasing Ace. My brother is furious. He's breathing like he can't get enough air into his lungs. I have never seen him this angry.

This is all my fault. He is glaring at Ace so hard that if looks could kill, Ace would be dead already. My brother says, "*We follow the code. We take this to the mat.*" I attempt to speak to my brother. I am not sure he is even aware of my presence. A red mist is hanging over him. He is going to kill Ace. I can tell by the look on Ace's face he doesn't plan to fight back. He's resigned. He feels guilty for what occurred between us seven years ago. He will let my brother kill him to protect me.

Tears are streaming down my face. I choke out over the lump in my throat, "*Chance. Please. I'm begging you. Just listen to me for a second. Please.*"

He doesn't even acknowledge me. He glares at Ace and says, "*Five minutes.*" He stalks away. Leaving me in shock and the room in complete silence. Gravity throws his hands up in the air. Even he's at a loss for words. This is all my doing and I have no way of undoing it. The man I love is about to die at the hands of the other man that I love. How is this even a thing?

Ace goes to leave the room and I grab his arm. I have to

talk some sense into at least one of these Neanderthal's. *"Please, Adam. Don't go in that rink with him. He's angry. Just give him time to cool off."*

"That isn't how this works, Doll. There are strict bylaws in place. I violated a major rule. I have to suffer the consequences of my actions. I made a decision that day that led me here."

"Well at least tell me you will fight back. You must protect yourself."

"Toni, what I did was wrong. Per the code, I don't have the right to fight back. You are family. Its hands off! Period. What I did required a green light. One I never sought. I didn't have the go ahead to be with you. Tell me you understand that." I can see her whole heart breaking. Again! Because of me. Maybe my death will spare her future pain. I love her and I keep hurting her. If I hurt Chaos, she will never forgive me. So, I lose her either way. Chaos and I are evenly matched. But since I forfeited my right to protect myself, this is just going to end up being one big bloody mess. Mostly my blood. Maybe a little blood from Chaos' bloody knuckles added in for good measure.

Gravity looks at Toni and says, *"Toni, only you can end this. Tell your brother the whole story. Tell him what happened seven years ago and tell him what you are hiding from him currently. That is the only way Ace lives. It's up to you."* Gravity walks away. He's a man of few words. He has a point, but it isn't that simple. The stuff from seven years ago I don't mind explaining. That's simple. I wanted that with Adam. The other stuff I can't ever share. Lives hang in the balance. He has a team to protect. I get it. My life is a little more complicated than he realizes. They think they have it all figured out. They don't! Nothing is ever as simple as it seems. This situation has so many layers it will make your head spin. I'll be honest, I don't know where to turn. I can't let Ace die at the hands of my overprotective brother. I won't stay and be a part of this fiasco, and I can't confess. My hands are literally tied!

Both Gravity and Ace leave the kitchen. I am stuck on stupid. I am looking around searching for answers when I see Ace's phone on the table. He walked away and left his phone behind. This is the only way I know to put an end to this madness. I snatched it up and stuff it in my back pocket. While everyone is making their way to the rink, I make my way to my bedroom. I don't have the heart to watch my brother kill Ace. I quickly override Ace's security code and send a message. I wait mere seconds for a response. I send out a ping for my location and pace the floor. I have to figure out a way to get out of here while they're all distracted with blood sport. My window of opportunity won't stay open forever. Help is a little more than an hour out.

I have to hole up until then. I found the control room and set about disabling the outer perimeter scanners. Then I set up a relay to this very phone. I initiate an automatic lockdown sequence that will commence the moment the outer door closes. It is set so that lockdown mode lasts four hours. I disable the override. I pray my brother doesn't blast his way out. I grab a piece of paper and a pen. I'm leaving a note. I placed the note on the kitchen table on my way out. With Ace's phone in hand, I slipped out of the back exit. Clinging to the shadows. Praying this works before I'm discovered. Praying this works before Chaos kills Ace. Once the team discovered I am gone they will be both parts worried and angry with me. I would rather they were angry with me than with each other. That is all that I can give them.

I make my way to the woods surrounding the compound. Once lockdown mode is initiated, the internal alarm starts blaring. Hopefully the noise will stop Chaos from killing Ace. That is really the only thing that will stop my brother in his tracks. The possibility the compound has been breached. I pray Ace is still alive. I can hear the alarm so clearly out here which means it must be deafening in there. My escape plan took all of four minutes. That's not terrible I think to myself. Hopefully, Ace is still in one piece and both he and my brother will forgive me. The entire team will respond to the alarm, thus ending the massacre. I realize I still love Ace and that does not make me feel any better. One thing's for sure, now my brother is going to kill me, too.

I hope they find the note I left on the kitchen table. I won't make them worry needlessly. They need to know I left of my own accord. I remove the SIM card and use a rock to smash the phone once I'm about a mile away. I throw the pieces in two different directions. I know they will find them eventually. I just need to contact the boss and come up with a plan before that happens. Simple right? It should be, but nothing in my life is ever simple. Once my transport arrives, I will use a secure network to call my boss and find out what my next move will be. My boss will know what to do. I can imagine the team running around like chickens without heads. By this time, they are looking for me and have discovered I am not where I should be. Yeah, I'm scared. My brother is going to kill me!

Off in the distance I can still faintly hear the alarm blaring. They will silence the alarm soon enough. The lockdown sequence, well, there is nothing to be done for that. They are staying put for a few hours. I can only image it must be total chaos in there. No pun intended. Once Chaos discovers that I'm gone, he will go ballistic! I am well aware my actions will cause them to have even more questions, but desperate times being what they are. I love my brother and I love Ace. I need them not to kill each other. I need them to get along. If they can't do that, then I can't be near either of them. There is no negotiating that point. The wait seems to last forever but alas. My transport arrives, and the extraction goes off without a hitch. I breathe a sigh of relief once we're in the air. I grab a SAT phone and call the boss. I breathe another sigh of relief. I spent most of the ride working out different scenarios in my own head. A few hours later, I am sitting in my boss's office with my feet up.

From the look on the boss' face, it's easy to see he's not pleased. He tells me when my brother and Ace realized I was gone they nearly had a stroke. He is urging me to call Chaos to ease his mind, but I'm a scaredy cat. He already has a cover story in play for me. It isn't fair for me to worry him this way, so I grab a secure burner to take to my quarters. My plan is to place the call that might end my life from the comfort of a hot bathtub. I make my way to my temporary home and place a call to my brother. I am literally shaking in my boots. I dial his number.

He answers on the first ring. *"Hello!"*

"Chance it's me, Toni?!"

"Where are you?! Are you safe? Were you kidnapped?! Where are you?!"

"I'm fine. No, I wasn't kidnapped. How is Ace?"

"Toni, I am going out of my mind with worry, and the first question you ask me is, how is Ace? Your little boyfriend is still breathing! All things considered. I consider that progress. Now tell me where you are!" I hear a muffled argument in the background. It's probably Ace. I hear my brother say, *"Fine!"*

Then Ace comes on the line. *"Doll, where are you? I am dying inside with worry. Tell me where you are so we can come to get you. Please, Toni."* I can tell Ace is in a lot of pain. His speech is altered. From the sounds of it he was beat up pretty bad. Poor baby. My brother can be so vicious at times. I'm not a little kid anymore.

"Ace, I need you to trust me. I'm sorry I slipped away. I'm sorry I locked you in, but this thing is more complicated than you realize. I promise to call you soon. Please put my brother back on."

"Toni." He sounds grieved. My heart is breaking.

Chaos comes back on. *"Where are you, squirt? I promise, I won't be mad. I promise not to kill your boyfriend either. I was just caught off guard. I may have overreacted! I'm sorry. Now tell me you are safe, and where you are, so I can come get you."*

"Chance, please don't hurt Adam. This isn't his fault. I seduced him. I wanted him. I kissed him. He tried so hard to let me down easily. He was a gentleman. But my feelings were hurt, and I ran away crying. He came after me in concern. Then I threw myself at him. Everything that happened that night is what I wanted to happen. I care for him, Chance. I want to be with him. But I won't if you don't give us you're blessing. You're the best big brother ever. I'm so sorry I disappointed you and made you worry. I'm sorry I ran away. I panicked!"

"I am not disappointed in you, squirt. I was disappointed in myself. I didn't protect you. Like I couldn't protect mom and dad. Something in me snapped. I don't know what came over me. I know Ace would never force himself on you. He's one of ours! I have come to my senses. Now, tell me where you are! People are out to kill you, squirt. Very dangerous people. If they find you, they won't go easy on you!"

"I can't tell you where I am just yet, but I promise I will call you every day. Ok. I'm safe. I need you to trust me."

"I do trust you, but no one can keep you safer than the team."

That's what he thinks. I'll just let him believe that's true. We'll go with that for now. *"I can't, big brother. I will call you tomorrow. I love you."* I end the call before I cave. I can't tell him where I am. But I am safer here, than anywhere else on the planet. I'm surrounded by "C.E.N.T.A.U.R" Enigma came and extracted me personally. That's a big deal. I'm honored. Enigma laughed really hard at the fact that I locked the teams in their little bunker. What a sense of humor Enigma has.

I destroyed the burner and head back to the bathroom.

I need a bath in the worse way. I pad to the bathroom on silent feet. I plug the drain and begin to fill the bathtub. I add all the items I can. Epsom salt, bath bombs, fragrant oils, you name it I add it. While the bathtub is filling up, I pour myself a glass of wine. I undress and walk to the sink. I look in the mirror and don't recognize the face staring back at me. It's been a rough few day. These are the luxuries you take for granted. I'm at a safe undisclosed location. Suspended up in the clouds. This place costs a small fortune. It belongs to a very capable group of people. I designed the security system myself. With code written and created just for them. I never registered for a patent, and there are no schematics for this system anywhere in the world. It's all in my cloud. My brain. I will stay here until the threat has been neutralized. My brother believes the hit is due to our parent's death. It's not!

Chapter 17

My boss tells me the hit is the final desperate act of someone who is dead already and doesn't even know it. There are things that lurk in the night that if the world at large knew about them they would never close their eyes again. Things that are scarier than the things that go bump in the night. These things don't make a sound and believe me that is terrifying. We are working on a plan to explain my slip up. Devising a rescue that will put a period at the end of the sentence. The last thing we need is for any of the team members to come away with more questions once this thing has been put to bed. Logic always has more questions. He is scary smart. With an IQ even I envy. I know for a fact the Colonel has no idea just how brilliant and deadly Logic is. Logic holds all his cards close to the vest. Let's not fail to mention Gator. He can smell a lie from a mile away. I am starting to believe he's psychic. Sometimes Gator freaks even me out!

I relax in the bathtub and sip on my white wine. I allow my mind to wander back to Ace. I have to deal with these feelings now before they spiral out of control. Number one, I realize I have been in love with him this entire time. Crud! If I weren't already sitting down, that knowledge would send me to my knees. Instead of dealing with the pain and anguish from seven years ago, I pushed it away and dove into anger and my studies. After graduation, I dove into my work. My therapist would be so disappointed in me if she knew. There are things I could never admit to myself, let alone my therapist. I have to figure out a way to wrangle these feelings in. It's not like he and I can have a marriage, two point five children, and a two-story colonial with a white picket fence. Our jobs are dangerous. The secrets I am forced to keep could destroy us. That is a pipe dream for people like us. This knowledge also explains why I never dated. Well, aside from being hung up on Ace that is. No one else compares.

I thought it was because my heart was broken, but even more than that, it was the sense of betrayal I felt just thinking about the possibility of being with another man. Nope. Ace is it for me. This is one big sordid mess. Because I ache for him. And when he kissed me back at the compound, I wanted to throw myself at his feet. The only thing that prevented me from giving myself to him was knowing my brother was close by. I couldn't engage in those types of activities with my brother so close. Gross! That's just wrong. Even thinking about Ace does things to me. It's so frustrating. Once he finds out I've lied and kept secrets from him, that will kill any and all feelings he has for me anyway! I want to cry just thinking about it. It's worth noting that my mood has not improved.

ACE

"Let me talk to her again. What's she saying?"

Chaos just looks at me and shakes his head. "*She hung up. She hung up on me. She hung up without telling me where she was or how I could reach her. I don't like this one bit. I'm going to put a call in to the Colonel. Ask Omega for help. He can have Omega use the satellites to search for her.*"

"She hung up. Why did she leave in the first place? Her note doesn't say much."

"She left because I couldn't control my temper. She actually believed I would kill you. Well, I may still kill you. But I know you love her, and she loves you, so… Maybe I won't kill you. I guess. I don't know. Who knows?"

I'm in so much pain I feel half dead already. Chaos is being more gracious than I expected him to be. The thing that hurts me most is knowing I violated his trust. It's burning a hole in the lining of my stomach. "Chaos. I'm sorry. I never meant to deceive you. Or go behind your back. It was never planned. I never meant to hurt Toni. I fell for her so quickly I didn't even realize it. I tried to walk away. This brotherhood means everything to me. You know that. You also know this is the only family I have. If you tell me to walk away from the brotherhood, I would. But please don't ask me to walk away from Toni. I don't think I can. Not again. I love her. I tried to fight it. I tried to stay away. Give her space to grow up and date other guys. Toni is the one. I will stay out of your sight. Please don't take her away from me."

"So, you're saying you would leave the brotherhood over a woman."

"Toni isn't just any woman." Gravity says, "I told you he had it bad! Now do you believe me, bro? Over the years he has taken bullets for us, but now he is willing to walk away to be with your sister." Gravity shakes his head as if the idea of what I'm suggesting is the craziest thing he's ever heard. I don't know. Maybe he has a point. None of it matters if we don't find her before the assassins do. Gravity asks, "So, what's it going to be Chaos? Do we kill him now or let him live? Either way I'm fine with it." Gravity looks at me. He is dead serious. The shock on my face makes him and Chaos laugh. They are only joking. I hope. Neither have confirmed they are joking. No idea at this point!

"Nah. Just kidding, bro. We won't kill you. You are one of us now. And besides, I get the feeling Chaos knew something went down between the two of you seven years ago. Would that be about right, Chaos?"

"Well, they were both acting weird. When I spoke to Toni, she'd ask about you Ace. And you'd subtly ask questions about Toni. It doesn't take a rocket scientist to figure it out. I never imagined it would go that far though. I figured an innocent kiss. Ok! Enough! My brain is starting to bleed. I will say this, and this is the last time I will speak on the subject. If you hurt my sister, I will not forgive you. Are we clear?"

"Yes. Very."

"Good."

"Hey. Thanks."

"Uh huh."

I walk away with a little pep in my step. For a bunch of reasons. One being, I am still alive. Two, I have Chaos' blessing. Well maybe not his blessing, but he has agreed to let me live. That's something anyway. Three, Toni says she loves me. That releases the vice grip that has been wrapped around my heart for the last seven years. Now I have to find her. Her life is in danger. What does she mean traipsing off into the unknown without protection? I'm furious with her. A few self-defense classes will not protect her from what's coming. I must find her. Quick. When I get my hands on her she's in deep doo-doo.

LOGIC

Our comms unit squawks. Yep, it's Omega. *"Logic, I just sent a set of coordinates to your phones. Please check they've been received."*

"Copy. Received."

"It took a while, but we finally got a read on the Tibetan ancient artifacts. You are never going to believe where they are stored."

"The coordinates read latitude 48.859961 longitude 2.326561. Isn't that Paris, France? If I had to guess, I would say that *puts the coordinates around the Seine."*

"*Bingo. Logic you are more than just a pretty face. That puts you square in the middle of the Musee d'orsay. According to the schematics the artifacts are located in a warehouse attached to the museum. I don't have all the pieces, but it looks like a security guard has been bribed to open the Musee d'orsay after hours. That is where the auction is also taking place. It seems you got lucky. If it all goes to plan you can have the Italian Death Dealer, the uranium, and the Tibetan artifacts all in your hands by morning."*

"*Nothing ever goes as planned, but that does explain why Salvator showed up in France. I hope to get my hands on him very soon."*

"*Happy hunting, boy wonder!"*

"*If I were you Omega, I'd watch my back."* Nothing but silence follows. I have to admit having Omega on our side does come in handy. I would die before admitting that to anyone. "*Ok, team. Mount up. We are wheels up in two minutes.*" Gator says, "*Paris, France here we come.*"

We can make it to Paris in sixty-two minutes. We know the participants are on standby and will be given a moment's notice to log in for their attendance for the auction. I hate the fact I will miss seeing Coup in a tux with my very own eyes. That would be comedy gold. I so wanted a photo to share with all the teams. We can always use a good laugh. Everyone hops on the bird while I go through my pre-flight check. I'll be flying low to avoid radar detection. Because the distance is so short, I won't worry about visual detection. I specifically chose this aircraft because it blends in with a lot of privately owned aircraft in the surrounding area. The people that might notice from the ground won't think twice about it. What I don't need is the aviation department asking for identifiers. I have them, of course, but they are bogus.

We don't need the smoke. We are up off the ground in the

time it takes you to tie your shoelaces. I am running through different scenarios in my head. More than likely the rest of the team is sleeping. I don't hear any chatter so that is a real possibility. We are trained to fall asleep in seconds. Getting some shut eye where and when we can. You never know when the next time the opportunity for sleep will present itself. So, you take advantage when you can.

Gator is my co-pilot. He says, *"Why do you think they chose the Musee d'art to move stolen artifacts?"*

"I suspect this isn't a one off. The section of the warehouse where the auction is taking place is closed for a facelift. It only makes sense if you're working for pennies on the dollar and an opportunity for additional cash presents itself some might take it. This portion of the warehouse does not in any way lead to the museum itself. I'm sure all the art was removed for the repairs. It's a low-risk venture for the security guard. Small chance of being caught. But a safe risk for criminals. No construction is being done on the building at night. So why not? Keep in mind using the museum adds an air of legitimacy to the stolen artifacts. Having them tied to a reputable establishment like the museum whose reputation is above reproach is a brilliant plan."

"Yeah, that makes sense. Evil has no conscious." If it were to be revealed that the museum was connected to stolen artifacts it would ruin their reputation. A reputation crafted over hundreds of years. Why would criminals care about that?"

Once we land Dolphin drives the van off the plane. All our gear is ready, so we make our way over to the coordinates provided to us by Omega. According to our latest update the auction has not yet been announced. There is still no starting time. We make our way to the Musee d'art. Dolphin parks the van in an area with no streetlights. We have a clear view of the warehouse because it's lit up like Christmas. We are in a flat black van. You wouldn't see us unless you bumped into the side of the vehicle. The paint is designed to absorb light not refract it. I go silent and still. I am excited to finally get my hands on the Italian Death Dealer. He needs to be forced out of business. That is where I come in. Once he takes possession of the uranium, we will swoop in and relieve him and his contact of the package. Salvator and whomever he's buying the uranium from will be in my custody. I am also hoping the funds are untraceable so we can relieve them of that too. To the victor go the spoils.

We scanned the area. It appears that the Italian Death Dealer is traveling with a small army. I say over comms, "*I count ten men on the north side of the building.*"

Razor says, "*Roger that. From my position in the sky, I count four on the roof of the warehouse.*"

Gator says, "*We have seven on the south side of the warehouse and a driver. By my count that's twenty-two soon to be deceased enemy combatants.*"

I say, "*Salvator is traveling with twelve additional organ donors. How many does that put us at Dolphin?*"

"*I don't know, team lead. I would have to pull off my socks and shoes to count that high.*" Everyone finds that amusing. I wonder if any of these men ever take themselves seriously.

"*Once the handler shows up and is in position, we start removing pieces from the chess board. Razor, I will leave you to the pieces on the roof. Dolphin, you and I will neutralize the pieces on the north side of the building along with the driver. Gator, you, Crucible, and Reaper will handle the pieces on the south side and as many as you can of the security escorting the handler. Once we have cleared our respective areas we will swing around for strays and back up. Any questions?*" All I hear is, "*Roger that.*" Now we wait.

Our comms unit's squawks. "*Omega here. Our latest intel says the auction is set to begin in thirty minutes. We will begin scanning signals in and out of the warehouse to track down all the players on the chess board. Anyone attending the virtual auction will be apprehended. For your part I will only relay the exact coordinates for the uranium and those attached to it. All other players will be accounted for by the sleeper cells. Any questions."*

"None."

"Happy hunting, gentlemen."

Chapter 18

ACE

We've been on an active hunt for Toni for days. It's like she's disappeared from the face of the earth. I am trying to remain optimistic. It's tough. We only know she's alive because she calls us daily. She refuses to tell us her whereabouts and her signal can't be tracked. Chaos isn't faring well either. He hasn't killed me, so he is staying true to his word. That's something anyway. Maybe if Chaos found out seven years ago that I slept with his sister, he wouldn't be able to forgive me. There was just too much going on back then. The loss of his parents. Becoming his sister's sole support system. There is an age gap. Toni is quiet. Reserved. They didn't spend a lot of time together because Chaos was always away. According to Chaos, his parents doted on Toni. She is quite brilliant. A lot like Logic. I wouldn't be surprised if her IQ wasn't just as high as Logic's. Gravity will have the pleasure of filling him in when he returns. I don't envy Gravity his position. No. Not one bit.

I want what Logic has. I think back on the events of a couple days ago. I was never so relieved in all my life than I was when I heard the alarm screeching. It stopped Chaos in mid-swing. I was bleeding profusely, barely standing, but still alive. He didn't kill me, but he made me pay for touching his kid sister without permission. Sure, she was eighteen, but she was not worldly like other eighteen-year-olds. I wasn't fighting back and that seemed to piss Chaos off even more. He understands why I wouldn't. The rules are clear, but still it would have been more of a fight if I could have at least thrown a punch or two. Beating me to a pulp isn't nearly as rewarding for him if I'm only going to take it. Once we heard the alarm we took off in different directions. We ran for weapons and monitors. Well, my run was more like a limp. I needed to see what was coming. Or better yet, what was already here. It was our internal alarms blaring. That meant someone had breached the compound. I had to get to Toni. I searched for the last place I'd left her first. Which was in the kitchen. Gravity is yelling out orders. It's controlled chaos here. Everyone knows exactly what needs to be done. I make my way to the kitchen. Toni isn't here.

I run out the room and almost slam into Chaos. "*Whoa!*"

"Ace, where is Toni? I just checked her room, she isn't there."

"I just checked the kitchen she isn't there either."

Gravity comes over comms. "*I am on the monitors and there is no breach. I repeat, there is no breach. Stand down!*" That makes zero sense. The alarm that was triggered tells a different story. What the heck is going on, and where is Toni? I hit the comms button and say, "*I want everyone to scour this facility looking for Toni! Now!*" I hear, "Roger that" from a few different voices. Then I hear boots slapping against concrete. I'm pretty sure I stopped breathing. Chaos is barely maintaining control. He takes off in search of his sister. I want to punch something!

We finally silenced the alarm. I now have a splitting headache. I have a headache for a myriad of reasons. One being from Chaos' knuckles. Another being at a loss for where Toni is. Why are the internal alarms sounding and there is no breach? Why can't we find her inside the compound? Someone rendered the cameras useless. They are completely offline. We are stuck inside. Chaos is threatening to blow the doors off. It doesn't take long to perform a thorough search. My heart sinks! Toni is gone. We've searched every inch of this compound. Where is she? The implication of her absence is suspicious. If we were breached, we would be in a firefight with the intruders. So how is it possible for a librarian to hack into our security system, override our failed safes, initiate a lockdown sequence, disable our cameras, and disappear into thin air? Without so much as a sound. When I get my hands on her, she has some explaining to do.

If she can do all of this, then I have to wonder what else she's capable of. I'm going over the calculations in my head and the math ain't mathing! Nothing about Antonia Townsend adds up. I've noticed during this entire rescue attempt she didn't seem scared much at all. There are people out to kill her, and she does not seem fazed in the slightest. How is that possible? There are only a handful of options on why she wouldn't be. Neither of those options are a possibility, and yet. We will peel back the layers of this onion one ring at a time. Gravity, Chaos, and I put in a call to the Colonel. We have to explain to him how she managed to escape and lock us in our own compound. The embarrassment of it all is more than we can handle. This is going to be one very long night. Chaos is acting like a berserker. I am staying well out of his way.

There is nothing to be done about it. Some very bad people are out to hurt my sister. I have to put my pride aside and get outside help. I can't believe I allowed her to slip through my fingers. Some very well-trained elite operatives can't keep an eye on one tiny female. How can we ever hold our heads up again? She used her PH. Ds against us. She hacked our server. Used our technology against us. Locked us in our own compound. For four freaking hours! The counter is ticking down across the monitors like a death knell. After escaping our very own compound we spent hours combing the grounds for Toni. We found remnants of my destroyed cellphone. But little else.

The grass was bent in a way that suggests she was airlifted out. But by whom? We have way more questions than we have answers. If there weren't assassins out to kill her this would be funny. A fantastic riddle to solve. She escaped without a trace.

There is no way a librarian should know how to do half of the things Toni has done to escape this compound. At this point I am at a loss. I have no idea what to think! Toni has some splaining to do. I don't know what's going on, but I know it's big. Worrying for my sister is burning a hole in my gut. The Colonel takes his sweet time answering the phone. What the heck is he doing?

"*Speak!*" He barks. He is out of breath. I can feel his annoyance coming down through the connection. I don't think I want to know what he's doing!

Gravity says, "*Sir. We have a situation.*"

"What?!"

"Antonia Townsend has gone AWOL. She hacked our server and escaped the compound."

"*Pray tell, what were my elite forces doing while the little librarian was doing all of that?*" There is no way I am telling the Colonel Chaos was in the process of rearranging Ace's entire body. Where is Logic? Keeping his eye on this incorrigible group of misfits is his job. At this point, I don't happen to currently want to be his second in command. Me wondering if I can quit.

The Colonel doesn't wait for a response. He says, "*Let me shake some trees.*" He ends the call after giving me an earful. He is not pleased but agreed to tug on a few strings and get back to us as soon as he can. Chaos is on the verge of losing his mind. Ace is primed and ready to explode. What I can't figure out is who helped Toni escape. Once the timer hit zero, we scoured the surrounding area for hours. If she was out there, we would have found her. It's now going on forty-eight hours since her disappearance. Someone evacuated her from the island. Something is definitely up with Chaos' sister. She is not an ordinary librarian! We must find her to find out what she's hiding. From the very beginning something seemed off. She was entirely too calm. From the moment I showed up in her bedroom in the dead of night she's been almost stoic.

A typical civilian would be hysterical. Go into shock with the prospect of assassins beating down their door. But not Toni. Why? What don't I see? She lives modestly. Her house was more than affordable on her salary. She has no outstanding debt. No overdue credit cards. Her car is modest and paid off. Everything about Toni's life seems bland. Maybe it's all too perfect. There is no social media of course, but also no dating history. We created her history, but it seems too sterile even for me. I would find it impossible to believe if there was no dating at all. She's gorgeous. No red-blooded male would pass up the chance to get Toni in bed. She's the type you bring home to mother. The type you put a ring on. This whole situation gets curiouser and curiouser.

Chaos walks into the room. *"Gravity, Ace, what's the plan?"*

Gravity answers, *"While we wait for the Colonel to pulls a few strings and get back to us with some answers, we will continue to shake a few trees of our own."*

I tell them, *"Nothing about this case makes sense. Am I the only one seeing it?"*

"No."

"Nope!"

"We see it, and we have just as many questions as you have," Gravity quips.

Chaos says, *"Someone took my sister off this island. There is no indication she was taken by force. There is no evidence of a struggle. There other set are no other footprints besides Toni's. She doesn't have a pilot's license. Who does she know with the resources to pull off an extraction like the one we see here? My sister is holding out on me. I am less than pleased. When I spoke to her earlier, she didn't sound scared. She wasn't begging me to come save her. She was almost in control of the situation. That makes no sense. It tells me she has connections. Very good connections. It also tells me, being a librarian may only be a front for her real job."*

Gravity says, *"Yeah. Little miss Toni is holding out on us."*

Ace grunts his approval and says, *"I went ahead and investigated her finances. There are no red flags. My gut is twisted in knots with worry that the assassins will find her before we do. I can't believe she says she loves me, then disappears like this."*

"I hear you, bro. We will find her. I will not allow anything bad to happen to my sister. My heart couldn't take it. Wherever she is, she believes she's safe. My sister is smart. I have to believe she's safe too. That is our only other option, Ace. That is what keeps me from turning into a berserker."

Three days go by. Toni calls me once a day. Every day she insists she's safe. She refuses to tell us where she is, and we are all going a little stir crazy. We were supposed to be in Tibet. That mission has been sidelined. Toni disconnects her calls before we can get a lock on her location. It's frustrating to say the least. The good news is the assassins don't know either or she would be dead already. We are on the clock and time is running out. The assassins won't give up looking. When they find her, they will kill her. Omega is keeping an eye on the dark web. The kill order has not been rescinded. Nor has anyone claimed the kill. When I hear her voice, I know she's alive. But the time in between her calls has me wracked with worry.

Omega has been searching, but it's like Toni has disappeared off the face of the earth. Not one clue as to her whereabouts has surfaced. The fact that Omega hasn't come up with anything doesn't make this any easier. I feel useless. How is it possible for Toni to vanish into thin air? I haven't eaten much or slept much in the last three days. I am down to my wits end. The team has split up. Pyro and Dome went to an undisclosed location to do a bit of recon. Logic is still away. Me, Gravity, and Chaos are looking for Toni. Our nerves are frayed, but Chaos is an explosion waiting to happen. He needs no additional proof that

I'm in love with his sister. I have given it in spades. I am out of my mind with worry. We have to get her back in one! That is the only acceptable option.

Our comms unit buzzes. The team always keeps their comms in. I know it's either the Colonel or Omega. I hope this has something to do with Toni. My nerves can't take another minute of not knowing. I want to find her so I can tell her how much I love her. Not knowing is torture. I raise my right hand to activate my comms unit.

I hear Gravity speak, *"What you got for me?"*

"We finally cracked the code on who put the hit out on Townsend." Yep, you guessed it. It's Omega. I have never been happier to hear a voice in all my life. Even a disembodied voice like the one Omega uses. The Colonel did some digging. Called in a few favors. *"It seems the former Head of National Security's top aide, Alexei Petrenko's wife Arlene Petrenko bought the hit. You remember Alexei Petrenko, don't you? The nasty piece of work who decided to try and overthrow the government. Well, his wife Arlene Petrenko is up in her feelings. Apparently, she's still alive and salty about her current marital status. I don't have all the details yet, but it seems his brother Victor Petrenko used his Omega connections to do a deep dive on one Antonia Townsend.*

He figured out her connection to the team. We found some documents which have now been recovered listing her as Chaos' emergency contact. Arlene Petrenko wants revenge for what was done to her husband and brother-in-law (lover). It gets even stickier. Alexei's wow Arlene has a baby by his brother, Victor. Alexei is not the father of their five-year-old son. Victor Petrenko is the father. Talk about keeping it in the family. Arlene Petrenko is more than a grieving widow. She is an angry wealthy woman with a wealth of secrets. Gravity, your team has been given the green light to talk to Arlene Petrenko and convince her to rescind the kill order. I am reading Anchor and Optic in on this operation. You guys will rendezvous on a select set of coordinates. You have NOT been given a green light to kill Arlene Petrenko. Are we clear? Repeat the order!"

"Why the distinction? Who's protecting Arlene Petrenko?"

"I'm sorry, Chaos. That information is above my pay grade. I only deliver the information I am given. The Colonel says, "She is not to be killed. Repeat those words please?"

"Arlene Petrenko is not to be killed."

"Very good. I will send over her coordinates now."

"Wait. Does the Colonel know where my sister is?"

"You will have to ask the Colonel directly. I have done what I was tasked to do. If you need additional backup dealing with Arlene Petrenko, give us a jingle."

Comms go dead. The questions keep coming folks. Chaos explodes! *"What is going on?!!! Arlene Petrenko can threaten to kill my family, but I can't kill her or hers?! You can forget about that! When I get my hands on her, I will wrap my fingers around her throat and squeeze until her eyes pop out! No one threatens my family and lives to talk about it."*

Chapter 19

Just as Chaos finishes his tirade, our cells ring. All of them. When we answer we hear, *"Hold for...!"* Then the Colonel says, *"This is bigger than Antonia Townsend. I know you want to kill Arlene Petrenko. Heck, I want to kill Arlene Petrenko. Keep in mind if you kill Arlene Petrenko, you will be declaring war on all of Russia. This is not the time to go off halfcocked! I am sitting you out on this one Chaos. You are too close to this to be trusted not to do what I explicitly told you not to do. In a word, your judgement has been compromised."*

Chaos explodes with an expletive filled *tirade.* It lasts for two full minutes. I don't think I have ever seen him this angry or this scared. The Colonel is absolutely quiet. Chaos is threatening to leave the unit if the Colonel side lines him. He will go off the reservation to find his sister. He isn't kidding. Once Chaos runs out of steam the Colonel continues as if Chaos never spoke, *"Ace, I am contemplating sitting you out on this operation as well. Give me one good reason why I shouldn't?"* Chaos is about to have a stroke. A vein is visibly throbbing in the center of his forehead. Steam is coming from his ears, and his face is a weird shade of someone who is going to die real soon burgundy. He stomps away! Cussing up a proverbial storm.

I have to convince the Colonel not to sideline me too. For one, my heart couldn't take it. Secondly, if Chaos is sidelined, I can't be sidelined too. This isn't happening! More than likely, he is going to call in additional team members for backup, anyway. But with Chaos being sidelined, I have to be on the front line of this op. Feeding Chaos every step of the way. Toni may not react well if she doesn't see either Chaos or me when she's found. So, I say to the Colonel, "Sir, if you are sidelining Chaos, then please don't pull me off this op too. We must convince Arlene Petrenko to rescind the kill order. Toni is like family to all of us. I am begging you, do not sideline me!" Then, I hold my breath waiting for the Colonel's response.

The Colonel takes his own sweet time in giving me one. Then he barks, "*Fine. You, Gravity, Thrasher, Polar, and Anchor are a go! Tell that hothead, potty mouth, he can run point from base, but when I see him, I am punching him square in the mouth.*"

"Yes, sir." The line goes dead. The Colonel was not impressed with Chaos' show of emotion. You can believe he will carry out his threat. His words are like having money in the back. Even Logic chooses his words carefully around the Colonel. I can't wait to see Logic's face when Gravity debriefs him. What will he do when he hears what Chaos said to the Colonel? I wouldn't want to be Chaos right about now.

COLONEL

I hate this gig as the Head of National Security. It's all about twenty-four-hour politics. No one in the political arena has a soul. These people lie, steal, cheat, and ruin lives like it's an Olympic sport. It's just an ordinary Monday for these people. The only reason I took this job was because the President threatened me. He is very good at getting his own way. Someone once told the President he was charming. He isn't! One evening he invited me over to the White house residence for drinks. I didn't really think anything of it. I wasn't suspicious. I should have been suspicious. This was shortly after I recovered from being kidnapped and tortured by Malik Oscega. He said to me in his most charming voice, *"Dicky, I want you as my next National Security Advisor. If you don't take the job as the Head of National Security, I will retire you. I will dishonorably discharge you and detain all eighteen of your elite soldiers. When you die, I will not give permission to bury your dead carcass at Arlington National Cemetery.*

Don't think for one second, I won't carry out the threat. I am not in a joking mood this evening. What's it going to be Dicky?" The President is the only person who dares to call me that! I stand here in complete shock. As the head of my elite squad, I falsely believed I was in control. The President is flexing his considerable might to get what he wants. He can tap one of a hundred different men who would be chomping at the bit for an opportunity like the one he's presenting me. Why is he nagging me about this? I hate politics. I hate politicians. He knows this. I have no political aspirations. I am very happy with my position on the chess board. I get to move freely whenever and wherever I want. There is no oversight. I get results and as a result the President doesn't ask me any questions.

Now, all of a sudden, he wants me out front as the Head of National Security. I am already the Head of National Security. The only difference is I work behind the scenes. I am faceless. A ghost. No one but the President knows about my elite forces, and even he is on a need to know. I make sure he always has plausible deniability. So, what am I not seeing. Why is he thrusting me out front all of a sudden? Who in his cabinet doesn't he trust. Well, he doesn't trust any of them, but he must be even more suspicious of one or two players in the arena. He is using me as a shield. A shield of a different kind. He wants to scare someone back in line. The question is who.

If you know the President as well as I do, then you will know he only tells you what he wants you to know. There is no need for me to ask additional questions. That threat he lobbed at me was just to get my attention. He didn't mean it. He needed to convey just how serious this situation is without saying it's a serious matter. Sometimes I hate my position on the chessboard. Everyone knows who I am while not knowing who I am. They have a sense of the power that I wield but are not sure who gave it to me or why I wield it. They wonder why I haven't been promoted to brigadier general. In the beginning it was seen as a smear on my military record, but with the power that I hold some people have begun to take notice. The truth is I AM COMMAND! I have no boss. It helps to make it look like I do.

I'm aware the President has knowledge of the teams, but the way he's speaking it seems he knows more than he ever let on to knowing before. My brain feels like it's been shaken and then stirred. The question is, why is the President of the United States doing this? After the coup attempt, he was shaken up. Could it be he wants me even closer? Does he not feel he can trust any of the members of his own cabinet? I barely use government funds to sustain my ultra-elite team. Everything we do is off book. They are primarily funded using the spoils we take from the evil cretins we make disappear. All very powerful, rich, and equally evil. People from all over the globe. Believe me when I say they exist everywhere. My mind is boggled. I have yet to respond. The President says, *"Don't look so surprised old chap.*

I have given you more latitude than anyone else in my cabinet. One, because you get me results. Two, because you are the sole of discretion. Three, you were almost killed to protect this country. We go back. Way back, you and me. I trust you. You know I don't trust very many people. You almost died keeping your mouth shut. Which incidentally is why they almost killed you. They were just as determined to make you talk as you were to stay silent. You're a soldier from the old guard and exactly what this country needs. You will answer to me and only me. No middleman! Come on, what do you say, Dicky?"

"I know you care for your soldiers. If your teams hadn't

gotten to you when they did, we wouldn't be having this discussion, old friend. Which would be a pity, really. Because I actually like you. There isn't a handful of people I can say that about. That's the gospel truth." The President is a sly old dog. He actually thinks he can threaten me and compliment me into doing what he wants. I would never tell him this, but I like him too. The very same people that kidnapped and tortured me was also attempting a coup. Both of our heads were on the chopping block. I had to call in some huge favors. The day was saved. My men are super-efficient. Savage. They are my right hand. They are my big guns. They are who I call when diplomacy is no longer an option.

Col. Paulson thinks he's the only one with big dogs. I'm the President of the United States. My dogs are much bigger! One day I will tell him mine is bigger than his. But today is not that day. Once the coup was discovered a call was placed. All over the DC area dead bodies started popping up. Everyone with a modicum of involvement is now taking a dirt nap. Once all the players were neutralized, I sent my dogs back to the barn. The Colonel's men are good. Mine are better. His men are growing suspicious. Asking questions. That dang Logic. He's poking his nose where it doesn't belong. My dogs are invisible. They aren't at all what they appear to be. You could pass any one of them on the street with no awareness of how lethal and efficient they are. They are quite the surprise.

They aren't at all what they appear to be. One day the Colonel and I will compare notes. I am looking forward to that day! Not even Logic knows about my team, and he finds information on just about everything. They have no idea my team has assisted them on more than one mission. It was all done from the shadows. Logic is a menace behind a computer screen. He's a menace with a weapon. He's an overall walking breathing menace. There is absolutely no digital footprint from my ultra-elite squad. My job is to make sure they remain hidden. I am the President of the United States. My job is to protect all

Americans. I also take my job very seriously. I couldn't do any of it without "Chameleon." I want so badly to introduce you to Chameleon. But not yet, reader. Not yet. Patience grasshopper. I can see the wheel turning in the Colonel's overactive brain. I have him over a barrel, and he knows it. I have to be patient too, reader.

With all the enthusiasm of a man walking to his own execution, I find myself accepting the President's offer. He doesn't even try not to look snug. Putz! He knows how much I hate politics. I have a searing hatred for politicians. The most ineffective people on the planet. A toddler could get more done in half the time. This will become my life, and I resent the President for it. The President is a tactician if nothing else. He is stationing me as his guard dog. Now the rest of his cabinet will be wary of me. The FBI has intel on the attempted coup and failed to act on it. They actually had a player or two in deep cover. That is why I refer to them as the Failed Bureau of Investigations. Even with all the intel they rarely act in a timely manner.

Unseating the President of the United States would have served the whiners of the alphabet soup agencies politically. It would have given the politicians the upper hand. Strike fear in the American people. Make them even easier to control. I say, "*Not on my watch!*" I am still gathering intel on the different agencies that assisted in the attempted coup. When all the buzz has died down, one by one the dominoes will fall. They won't even see it coming. When I'm done, they will regret the day they were ever spawned! They don't get to destroy democracy. They don't get to override the will of the American people. They are elected by the people for the people. Sometimes they forget that. It's my job to remind them. They get confused and start to believe the American people work for them. Pity.

I can no longer mislead the Alpha team into thinking this was related to Operation Thistle. Chaos and Antonia Townsend lost their parents. Their parents worked for the government. No one else knows that. Everyone who knew that is now dead. I took them under my wing to protect them. Keep my promise to their father. The longer I can keep this secret, the better. But it looks like the jig is up, and the fallout will give me nightmares for years to come. The more people know, the higher the risk of exposure becomes. I have to tread even more carefully than I normally do. Antonia has done this job for years. She's good at it. As good as anyone I've ever seen. She is the glue that holds the network together. Now I must blow her cover.

On top of that, I'm being forced to take the job as Head of National Security. It would be less painful if he'd just put an IED (improvised explosive device), under my car. I will spend most of my time not listening in boring meetings, playing pretend, and trying not to blow my own brains out. Washington politics is pure evil. If you think these narcissists care about democracy or the American people, you should just kill yourself now. It will be a lot less painful than discovering the truth. Most of the politicians are owned by lobbyists. Lobbyists are owned by the big companies that employ them. If you ever get curious about how lobbyists work; watch a movie called Miss Sloane. It will blow your mind. What I have the unfortunate opportunity to watch on a daily basis is real. It is not from a movie script.

From what I've seen, the American people are the pawns used to leverage more power, more money, more everything. Republicans and Democrats are flip sides of the same coin. Feathers on the same bird. Let's hope the public never learns of that fact. This is what will keep you up at night. It's not Al Qaeda. Our fear should be of our very own home-grown terrorists. New groups pop up just about every day. Muslim extremists have slid down on the list. Way down on the list. Home grown hate groups are now the new boogey man. They spawn Americans whose sole purpose is to kill other Americans. The country is in a mess. The politicians need the public to believe it's someone else's fault. The Muslims, the Blacks, the Democrats, or the

Republicans. Anyone will do.

So long as you never figure out who's the real culprit is. It makes the job for the enemy within just that much easier. Divide and conquer has always been an effective strategy. I digress. Enough of that dark thinking. I will keep Alpha team occupied and allow them to unravel the thread that connects to the hit and maybe a few breadcrumbs but nothing more. When Logic gets curious about something he becomes even more dangerous. That is the only concession I am willing to make. The more they know, the more danger that puts them in. I have to contain his information. There are vultures here in Washington that don't believe any government funds should be used for my elite forces. We get scraps from the government, which is why we source our funds in other ways.

No matter how minimal the funds every year I have to fight for funding to keep the ruse alive. In truth we don't need their money. To keep up the lie I go around like a beggar with my hat in hand hoping to hear a few coins jingling at the bottom of it. This gives them the illusion of power and keeps them from asking questions about where the money really comes from. They like the security the teams provide but don't want to fund them. Imagine that. They like the results but quibble about paying for them. Politicians make no sense on the best of days. Which is why more and more people disconnect themselves from the matrix every day. It's not about a red pill or a blue pill. The fact that you are fed either is what should concern you. The public will never know what the wizard is doing behind the curtain. If you knew they would have you killed.

Chapter 20

Politicians would sell their mother's souls to get their hands on my squad. I am what stands between the veils. I stand between good and evil. Between the elite forces and the politicians. Between democracy and anarchy. Between life and death. It's a dirty job. A thankless job. But someone has to do it. The President understands that. My private squad is what stands between civilization and annihilation. Everything in Washington takes time. It's called playing politics. I don't have the stomach for it! From sending out troops, to drone strikes, to full scale wars. It's a political dance. One side pitted against the other. Everyone looking to line their own pockets. There is always a mountain of red tape that must be finessed, stroked, and mounted. That takes time. I rarely have much of that. Alpha, Bravo, and Charlie teams can be mobilized 30 minutes or less depending on the situation.

They are the knives I use to cut through the mountains of red tape. Slicing through it like a hot knife through butter. While the powers that be are ensconced in committee meetings, and senate hearings, we are working hard to neutralize the threat. As covertly as possible of course. The jobs we do no one else CAN do. World leaders die. A President. Prime Minister. A Sheikh. A General. It is all well-orchestrated. It happens when it's determined they are no longer and asset to the United States of America. They die mostly of unnatural causes. We make it look natural, but it isn't. There are those who question whether the deaths are really natural, but proving they aren't, is what matters. My teams never leave evidence behind. Who knows, it could be from a snake bite or heart attack. Who's to determine these things? Once all the threads are pulled, I will make one more concession. If I don't give the team something, Logic will dig until he finds the whole lot. He is like a blood hound, that one.

ACE

Omega sends coordinates over to Me, Gravity, Thrasher, and Anchor. Anchor is Charlie's team lead. With Logic out of pocket, Anchor will ensure all the rules are followed. He will be there to take point and keep Chaos from crashing this op. This new mission is now known as Operation Inkwell. Anchor is not to be played with. I heard what Chaos said to the Colonel about leaving the unit. This is getting really ugly real fast. Chaos is not in the habit of saying things he doesn't mean. I'll wait for the Colonel to tell us what the next move is. I pray he does it soon. Chaos is on the verge of who knows what. I'm sure the Colonel understands his predicament. He's pretty good at giving the teams a little latitude. I just hope Chaos didn't push the envelope too far.

The Colonel is allowing Chaos to run point from our base of operations, i.e., the compound. That's a good sign. It's better than nothing, anyway. That means the Colonel isn't too bothered by Chaos' emotional meltdown. The Colonel in part understands the immense amount of pressure Chaos is under. The need to find his sister safe. Unharmed. If the Colonel were angry... Well, let's just say it wouldn't do well for anyone to make the Colonel angry. You would never know it to look at him, but he's a dangerous individual. With contacts in some pretty scary places. I make it a point to stay on his good side. Even Logic dares not, push too hard.

The Colonel is around six feet, dark hair with silver at his temples, average build. Not much body fat at all. Good shape for his age. He likes the ladies. I wish I didn't know that, but I do. He is unassuming. What the world doesn't know is that he has more power than the President and is more deadly than the deadliest poison. He has but to say the word and people die. It is not a position to be taken lightly. The Colonel has been around covert operations for over thirty years. He has friends, allies, enemies, and victims from every continent. Venom runs point on his whereabouts. Ever since the kidnapping he with the help of Omega have become his digital bodyguard. We will never allow that to happen again. During his surgery Logic and Venom decided to have a tracker implanted inside his body.

Outside of the team Zypher is the only other person that knows the tracker exists. The surgeon who implanted the tracker had that particular bit of information chemically extracted from his brain. He can never share that secret with another living soul. It was either the medical extraction or neutralization. The doctor is a good man. We chose the lesser of two evils. This particular doctor has come through for us more than a few times. It's nice knowing that he is out there willing to help out when needed. He is handsomely rewarded but would do the work for free. Let's just say he owes us one. More than one if I'm being honest. But who's counting.

I've received the coordinates on my phone. So does Gravity, Thrasher, and Anchor. I would like to say I don't know why the Colonel chose Anchor for this op. But I do. The Colonel's word is law. It's finite! He will not allow Chaos or anyone else on the team to do something that will cause an international incident. Anchor will ensure Chaos stays put. It seems the plan has changed. Instead of meeting us on sight, Anchor arrives here at the compound. He arrives with Optic and Sledge in tow. Two of his Charlie team members. The Colonel is not playing games.

Either Chaos sits this one out, or he is forced to sit this one out. There is nothing I can do about this. There would be nothing even Logic could do about this. I will make it my mission to find his sister for him. This is my only option.

It will go a long way to soothing his ire. Chaos looks at the Charlie team members and smiles. It is not a friendly smile. In my head I'm praying, please don't let this go left. Chaos and Optic are in a pissing contest that could last all night. No one is blinking, no one says a word, and no one will back down. I feel a dull throb beginning behind my eyes. This is an explosive game of chicken. With Chaos one can only hope he reins himself in. I'm not sure any of us present can do it for him. Let us pray, reader.

Anchor says, *"Hello, Alphas. There's been a change of plan. The Colonel sent me here instead of our previously agreed upon rendezvous point to tie up loose ends."* He looks over at Chaos and says, *"You're the loose end. Look, I get it. I understand you are worried about your sister. I promise I will do everything in my power to bring her back to you safely. What I need to know from you is how hard you're going to make this for me? Because truth be told I'm just cranky enough for a fight. So, what's it going to be Chaos? Do we do this the easy way or the hard way? You choose but understand this every moment we waste demonstrating whose is bigger is time taken away from locating your sister. Choose wisely."*

I see Chaos visibly relax. He won't say it, but he's grateful Anchor is taking this seriously. He knows Anchor is a man of his word. He also knows the Colonel won't change his mind. That is a good start. *"I was told to sit this one out. I will do as I'm told. As long as you understand my sister is my everything. Her rescue is top priority. If you understand that then we're good. I won't insult your intelligence by pretending I care about politics. Arlene Petrenko is the enemy. Period. If you are willing to stick your neck out to get my sister back, I am willing to step out of the way while you do it."*

Anchor visibly exhales. He was serious when he said he was ready for a fight. I am so glad that didn't happen. There is no way I would allow anyone to put their hands on one of my brothers. Nor would Gravity. Alpha team is just that way. We stand together, we fall together. Chaos knows that. I believe that is why he took a step down. The longer we sit here, the more time passes. The more time passes, the worse it looks for Toni. Chaos is nothing if not strategic.

Anchor says, *"Let's move out men."* As we gather our gear Anchor lays out the plan. *"Optic will stay behind to assist you here Chaos. Thrasher will meet us at a set of selected coordinates. Sledge you're with us. We are wheels up in six minutes. Flight time is ninety minutes. That will put us in DC around supper time. We will do recon on Arlene Petrenko's residence until lights out. Once the streets goes dark, we breach. In particular, Gravity, you and I will hit the residence. Ace will take up position on the roof across the street with his favorite toy rifle in hand. You know the one he caresses at night. Thrasher will be in the van on surveillance. Sledge will cover the back. As much as we would love to kill Arlene Petrenko we will wait for a more opportune time. A time when all eyes aren't scouring the globe looking for her. Any questions?"* All is quiet. It seems no one has questions.

We are loaded and off the ground in no time. We make our way to Arlene Petrenko. The flight to DC was uneventful. Gravity got us here in under ninety minutes. He's been quiet ever since we left the compound. I can't wait to find out what he's thinking. We're in a black van headed to the subject's residence. The traffic here in DC is deplorable. Even at eight pm. We move best under the cover of darkness. The windows are heavily tinted and I'm driving. My goal is to stick to the speed limits so as not to attract unwanted police attention. That is a complication we just don't need. There are enough munitions in this vehicle for a small-scale war. We don't want no smoke. We pulled up on a side street adjacent to the Petrenko brownstone.

There are two guards posted out front. Russian from the looks of them. Heavily muscled. Heavily tattooed. Heavily armed. There is one guard on the roof. I'm sure he's also Russian. In thirty seconds, we will know exactly what's happening in the back of the building. I hear a squawk on comms. Sledge says, "*We have two little birdies out back. All the shades are drawn. There is no visibility to the inside of the residence. This feels wrong.*"

Gravity asks, "*What do you mean, Sledge?*"

"*I mean the guards out back are playing cards and drinking vodka. Would you be doing either of those things if you were guarding someone with Arlene Petrenko's connections? The answer is NO! They must know people are looking for her. One would think they'd be more alert. I expected more bodies and more fire power. This does not appear to be a safe haven for Arlene Petrenko.*"

Anchor says, "*You're absolutely right. They wouldn't be relaxed. The Russians are better trained than that. We need a look inside that building. That will tell the true story. I don't want to waste time sitting out here in vain. If what you say is true, then this is a red herring. If this is a red herring, then they were expecting company. But they aren't worried because she is not in the building. Hmmm… This entire scenario is making my sac itch. This is a ploy used to throw us off Arlene Petrenko's trail. To keep us occupied. Someone knew we were coming. Who would want to and why? That same someone didn't want us asking Arlene Petrenko any questions. Which means not only were we duped, but the Colonel has been duped as well. There are way too many implications here. So many different options give me a headache just thinking about them. So, at 2100 hours we breach. We move silently. Deadly. We will neutralize all five targets at once. We can neutralize the threats and be in and out of the residence in one hundred and eighty seconds. Wait for my signal. Over.*"

I say, "*Copy.*" Gravity, Sledge, and Thrasher all say, "*Copy.*" Thrasher is in the back of the van on surveillance. Once it gets a little darker, Ace will give it the all clear then take out the guard on the roof. At the same time Gravity and Anchor will take out the guards in the front of the building. Then breach. Sledge will neutralize the guards in back. If all goes well, I can be in bed by midnight. One can only hope.

CHAOS

I'm about to lose my cool waiting for the op to begin. Waiting for answers. Where is Arlene Petrenko and where is my sister? Gravity, Anchor, Ace, Sledge, and Thrasher believe this is a red herring. They believe Arlene Petrenko has been moved. Maybe that particular birdie flew the coop. I do not believe the Colonel would deploy us here if he knew she was not in residence. Which means he didn't know. And, if he didn't know then this goes all the way up to the Presidential level. Why would someone go through all the trouble? Is it to prevent a confrontation with the not so helpless widow? Arlene Petrenko and her children aren't in that brownstone. I would bet my next paycheck on it.

So, where the heck is she? I want my sister back! I'm up pacing a hole in the floor. We won't know for sure until the team goes in. I can feel Optic watching me. We all received the same sit-rep. We are all at a loss. There is no use for senseless words. This is every team-member's worst nightmare. Having your family targeted by someone trying to get to you. I'm glad Alexei and Viktor Petrenko are dead. If they weren't I would kill them all over again! Time slows to a proverbial crawl. I can feel the stretch of my own skin. If anything happens to Toni that's on me, and I will never forgive myself. I am failing at my most important job. I will scour the earth looking for her. I will search until she is found alive and intact. Anything else is totally unacceptable.

Neutralizing them was a matter of National Security. If Arlene Petrenko hurts one hair on my sister's head, her name will be added to that list. I'll deal with the Colonel and any international incident afterward! It's now 2050. These last ten minutes feel like an eternity. Time is ticking very slowly. At 2100 they breach. I have no idea what they'll find if anything. This situation has gone from bad to worse. I will kill anyone who stands between me and my sister. That's a fact! My comms unit squawk at 2055. I hear Anchor say, *"Everyone in position. Five minutes and counting."* Comms goes silent. I am pretty sure when this is all done, I'll have an ulcer. I jump when I hear the thwack-thwack of gunfire. They're using silencers, so unless you're up close, or on comms, you wouldn't hear it. If you weren't trained, you wouldn't know that was the sound of a silencer. They will receive two bullets right between the eyes.

That is the dreadful fate for the Russian guards. They will be dead before they realize they've been hit. That is what complacency gets you. I hear Anchor say, *"Sniper!"* *Ace takes out the Russian on the roof and* says, *"Clear."* That means the guard on the roof has been deactivated and the rest of the team can breach without being spotted. Ace will stay to monitor events from his bird's eye view. Then I hear Sledge say, *"Clear!"* Thrasher is on surveillance in the van monitoring police frequencies. The last thing they need is a nosey neighbor calling 911. A relay has been established. Any 911 calls in this area will be rerouted to the van. I hear Anchor say, *"Breach!"* They go in. In my mind's eye, I can see them sweep the first level. It's like a well-orchestrated dance. Gravity speaks first, *"Clear."*

Chapter 21

The first floor has been cleared. Gravity, Anchor, and Sledge will move up to the second level. The brownstone consists of three levels. Once all the levels have been swept, we hear Anchor over comms, *"The place is empty. Not even a roll of toilet paper was left behind. There is no Arlene Petrenko in this building. We pull out now!"* How is this possible? There is no way the Colonel would give us false intel. But something fishy is afoot. I feel my tether slipping! Where is my sister? I can see Optic watching me out of the corner of my eye. He knows I am on the verge of mass destruction. I'm fighting to rein in the fury that is threatening to take over my entire being. I know I have to hold it together for Toni's sake. This almost feels like a losing battle. Almost.

ZYPHER

I handpicked Insipid as my second. Insipid will do what needs to be done without question. That's exactly what I need. It will free me up to handle the other issues at hand. Such as Operation Coin Toss. Helping Logic and Gator. I can feel my adrenaline pumping. I better pull back on the caffeine. I need to know what progress has been made, if any. How close have they've gotten. I ask Insipid, *"Do we have a lead on the Italian Death Dealer?"* I need the answer to be yes.

"I'm working on it. Give me a minute." I nod. I received my promotion as the Omega Premier after operation Thistle ended. Our former Omega premier was Sub-zero. Otherwise known as Viktor Petrenko. I never liked that guy! From the very start he was dodgy. So, I decided to keep my eye on him. Using code I invented, and only I know about, I gathered only the intel I needed to take Viktor and Alexei Petrenko down. To prevent a coup d'etat on the American government and to rescue the Colonel. This code is so effective leaders the world over would kill for it. If the American government ever discovered I've created it, it will tilt the scales of power in unimaginable ways. I have the code encrypted and hidden. When I die it dies with me.

I couldn't sleep at night imagining all the ways my code would be exploited! It could be used to cause destruction. It is much too powerful. In the wrong hands it would be catastrophic! Let's face it, there is an entire world of evil corrupt leaders who love to get their hands on something that would give them world domination. I can't have that, now can I. Sub-zero had way too many secrets for my liking. He had his hands in a plethora of illegal activity. I found myself hiding information even from him. Much like we did with Donald Trump when he was President. Never thought I'd see the day. There are just some individuals whose moral compass is simply nonexistent. These are a couple of examples.

Insipid is sitting next to me watching the monitors. I look over and say, *"Do we know where Arlene Petrenko is?"*

"Yes." I was afraid of that. I put my head in my hands. Everything I feared is coming to fruition. I am afraid to ask. If Insipid says Germany it is entirely possible, I will faint. We know she isn't in Russian, and she has ties to Germany. That would mean Germany is threatening to undo their agreement with

NATO. These people are always working on back-room deals. NATO is the one thing everyone wants. When that is no longer true there will be world chaos. I need a sip of wine. I wait several seconds, just breathing, then I ask the question I dread hearing the answer to. I know what I'm asking Santa for this year. It will be for evil to take a vacation.

I can feel Insipid watching me. Just waiting for me to ask. I really don't want to. Here goes nothing. *"Ok, I'll bite. Where is Arlene Petrenko?"*

Without missing a beat Insipid answer, *"Ukraine."* I very nearly vomited.

I can feel the bile rising in my throat. It just hovers there threatening to choke me to death. How in the world did Arlene Petrenko get to the Ukraine with everything going on between Russian and Ukraine. It seems Arlene Petrenko has gone rogue! I have an internal meltdown. The room is deathly quiet minus the low hum of the computer modems. My head feels like it wants to explode! For one entire minute I believed the worst answer I could possibly receive was Germany. Well, ha! This thing just went nuclear. Because if the Ukrainian government get their grubby little paws on uranium, this is worse than worse. They already have the capability for nuclear weapons. They are also pissed with the Russians. A war is most likely already imminent between Ukraine and Russia.

I feel my dinner threatening to resurface. I need to notify the Colonel quickly. No sooner do I discover Arlene Petrenko is meeting with Salvator Parisi (Italian Death Dealer) to supply him with uranium. Now she's also in the Ukraine? I trust the intel, so there is now another mystery to unravel. Who is she upset with more? It would seem as if Arlene Petrenko and her Russian compatriots are on the outs. That is the only plausible explanation for her to be in Ukraine. The bigger question is how much uranium does she have. It's obvious it's more than we first thought. Arlene Petrenko is now considered a heavy hitter in the major leagues. Big enough to kidnap a scientist and uranium. Big enough to put a hit out on a team member's family. Big enough to rub elbows with Ukrainian elite. She is not giving me grieving widow vibes. I say, *"Put me through to the boss."*

There is no way Arlene Petrenko escaped to the Ukraine unaided. Someone is feeding her. The only explanation for her being in the Ukraine is she's had a falling out with Petrov. That would be HUGE! He hates the Ukraine. Petrov is the head of the family. He is more Russian than Putin. Petrov and Putin are two peas in a pod. Their politics are always closely aligned. They support each other behind closed doors like blood brothers. I will notify the Colonel and wait for further instruction. There may be a way to exploit Arlene Petrenko's defection. That is if we can keep her alive. I don't care what the Colonel says, if one of the team members get their hands on her she's a dead woman. Especially given the fact that she is no longer in the states. Hmmm. Very interesting.

"Zypher, the Colonel is on the hotline."

"No?!"

"Yes!"

"If he's calling on the red phone then we are screwed."

"Sir."

"Where is Arlene Petrenko?"

"Ukraine." Dead silence. I can almost imagine the Colonel is having a stroke. *"For pete sake! I want all the details on my desk in ten minutes. I want you on a plane to Poland for extraction like yesterday. You've been burned. We might as well leak your cover now too. We can't afford to have the team digging around in this. I was duped. You know what that means. Be ready for wheels up in twenty minutes. We will work out the details enroute. It must be solid, or*

Logic will pull every thread until he finds the motherload. And until I can figure out who duped me and why, I need them occupied. Any questions?"

"None."

"Talk to you soon." The Colonel disconnects, but before he does, he's cussing up a storm. I'm so glad I'm not him. His cholesterol levels must be through the roof.

GRAVITY

I use the SAT phone to put a call in to Logic. This conversation requires delicacy. The only other person privy to this call is Polar. We need a plan. Logic will help work that out for us. *"Gravity. What's wrong?"*

"Logic. Everything. Everything is wrong. Arlene Petrenko was not at the brownstone as reported. A red herring was set up to make it look like she was though. We took out a few Russian mobsters, but other than that no sign of her. They had all the markings. We were given strict instructions not to kill Arlene Petrenko due to national security. We were to gather intel only. The assumption being she knew the whereabouts of Antonia Townsend. With Arlene Petrenko M.I.A, Antonia Townsend M.I.A, the contract hit still active, and Chaos sidelined and threatening the Colonel, my head is spinning. I know you've got your hands full, but I need directions on this one. The implications could undo our entire unit. We wonder if the Colonel sent us out on a wild goose chase. He wouldn't do that, would he Logic? Not with knowing one of our family member's is missing."

When Gravity finishes, I take a deep breath. It takes a second to digest everything he's told me. He is not one for histrionics. So, if he's calling me this isn't good. The last thing I need is for everyone to question the Colonel's allegiance. I can't tell him Gator and I are questioning a few things too concerning

Operation Coin Toss. He needs answers, not more speculation. This thing gets deeper and deeper. I will trust the Colonel until I can prove otherwise. I wouldn't put it past some unknown entity to contrive this scenario for their own nefarious ends. We are a family, and the Colonel is the head of that family. I will trust my gut once more. I pray it doesn't lead me astray. *"Gravity, it seems you have your hands full too. I doubt the Colonel would operate this way. He is more direct than that. He would never send us out on a wild goose chase. He would just make us stand down. These are not his methods. If he sent you to a particular location, it's because he believed the target was present. Or, at the very least the intel was solid at the time.*

"We both know there are always moving parts, and sometimes the parts disappear altogether! Do this. Have Omega locate Arlene Petrenko. Maybe some satellite images were captured when she vacated the premises. If she is holding Antonia Townsend in her current location, that is even better. I can formulate an extraction plan. I will call Zypher personally and find out what I can. I will get back to you in fifteen minutes."

"Roger that. Thanks."

"Don't mention it." I turned off the SAT phone. Polar is waiting for me to update him. He asks, *"What does Logic think of all of this?"*

"He doesn't believe the Colonel would betray us. He knows the Colonel better than anyone. I will trust Logic's intuition until we know otherwise. He wants me to put a call in to Omega. Maybe they can locate satellite images of Arlene Petrenko during her mad dash from the brownstone. If we are lucky, she has Antonia Townsend with her. That way we kill two birds with one stone. Because, between me and you, Arlene Petrenko is a dead woman walking. Chaos will never forgive us if we allow her to live. This was a direct attack on the family. That cannot go unanswered!"

"Roger that! I agree. If Arlene Petrenko is allowed to live

our lives may be in jeopardy. We will always be looking over our shoulders. Who knows whose family she will go after next? Chaos is serious about his last remaining relative. Between the two of us we will deal with Arlene Petrenko. Anchor need never know. That will provide him with plausible deniability. Especially if things go awry. He can tell the counsel he knows nothing about the neutralization of one Arlene Petrenko. He will be telling the truth."

I nod in agreement. I press the button on comms to signal Omega. Then I hear, *"Go, for Omega."*

"Omega, this is Gravity. I need the location for one Arlene Petrenko. Her last known location, the coordinates provided by you, were unhelpful. We need satellite images or anything you can give us on her. On her swift departure from the brownstone. The very brownstone you assured us she would be residing. Is that just a coincidence?" I am waiting for a response. What they give me is less than acceptable.

Omega says, *"I will look into it and get back to you."* Then comms goes silent. I know from experience they will not answer my questions. Even if I called them back and demanded an answer. I feel my frustration mounting like a rising volcano. I will have to find time to blow off some steam. Soon! Before it erupts.

I can't imagine what Chaos must be going through. He's worried sick. I'm sure he would be with us if he didn't have an oversized babysitter guarding him. Hopefully he won't blow Optic up. There is a distinct possibility that could happen. There are no lines we won't cross to ensure the safety of family. Please let Logic get back to me with something concrete. If not, there will be more chaos. He won't wait much longer. I find myself grinding my teeth. Everything about this feels wrong. I just wish I had some answers for him. He will reach out soon. I hope I have something for him by then.

I hear Polar say, *"Why does it always feel like we are behind the eight ball? Maybe I should have gone to college and become a physical education teacher."* All I can do is laugh at Polar. The students would take one look at him and run from the gym. He's massive. Besides, he's not fooling me. He loves his current job.

Chapter 22

COLONEL

I had to call in a few favors. Even I couldn't predict just how much worse this situation was going to become. Had I known I would have stayed in bed! We were called into a top-level war briefing at 11 p.m. last night. The President wanted countermeasures available should the inevitable happen. I've spent the last three days with an itch I couldn't scratch. That is always a sign something bad is coming down the pike. I should have known this is the direction we were headed. So, at 0100 hours I have a very important meeting. My meeting is with someone that has been dead for almost twenty years. Unfortunately for me, my hands were the ones used to pull her from the grave. If I had any other choice, I would have taken it. I am the reason the world thinks she's dead in the first place. If it is ever discovered she isn't, well, let's just say she will be and so will I.

I've done things I can never take back. Most of those things were back in my CIA days. Back before the President became the President. Back when things were easier to hide. Bodies, information, secrets. Things were a lot less complicated. What I now refer to as the good old days. Only old people refer to the good old days. Because believe me when I say compared to today, the old days seem a lot better. The days before computers it was a lot easier to make people disappear. You now have metadata, facial recognition, and fingerprinting software. Life is easier and more complicated at the same time. Talk about an oxymoron.

I haven't seen Katya Yuriyev in years upon years. Mainly because she's supposed to be dead. I had to let her go. Katya is former KGB. She and I were frenemies. We worked together to keep the lines of communication open between our two countries. To keep our countries from the brink of nuclear war. After many years of working together she was discovered to be a double agent. Her cover was blown. That was the worst day of my life. When I got the news, I rushed out. I almost didn't make it, but I got to her just in time. She was bleeding profusely from several bullet wounds. Left for dead! Barely alive. I managed to get her to an offsite doctor I knew to transfuse and stitch her up. He removed bullets, stitched her up, and cared for her until she recovered.

I was given regular updates on her condition but could never return to see her. I was under heavy surveillance. They were looking for Katya's handler. I *was* Katya's handler. The very last thing I would have done was lead them to her. Once she had sufficiently recovered, she disappeared. A body was identified as Katya Yuriyev, but it wasn't hers. I made sure to convince anyone interested that Katya Yuriyev was very dead! Everyone needed to believe it was true for her to have a life that did not include being on the run or looking over your shoulder. The goal was to give her a normal life, one she never had before because she was recruited into the KGB as a young girl. That is just the way things are done in Russia.

I knew she would recover. She's a fighter! I left the doctor with one hundred thousand dollars and Katya received a new identity card and travel documents. She disappeared and neither of us ever looked back. The doctor later informed me Katya was pregnant and lost the baby. I know the baby was mine. I throw back the tumbler of scotch and revel in the burn. Better the burn of one-hundred-year-old scotch than the burn of regret. I have a lifetime of those. We were young and in love. Neither of us planned it that way, but she was beautiful, and I had it bad. We spent most of our time in a tug-of-war of sorts. Then one day we just didn't. Eventually, all those late nights of surveillance turned into late nights of passion. We couldn't keep our hands off each other. Took unnecessary risks. Someone was watching. Someone is always watching. We got caught. They got to her first.

Things are spiraling out of control. The Russians just fired on Ukraine. The Russians say it's a practical exercise gone wrong. The Ukrainian government plans to retaliate. Reporters want you to believe it's over territory. That is what the world needs to believe. It is not over territory; it is over something a lot worse. I had to hide the true reasons from my men. Some things are above their pay grade. I am walking a tight rope. Starting to feel my age. I turn sixty next month. Maybe I should just retire. I'm getting too old for this crap! Everyone wants to kill everyone else. We should just line them all up in the street, have them face each other, and just let them go for it. Let's see who the last man standing is going to be. I grabbed my coat and my car keys. I'll be flying solo on this mission.

I sent my driver home a few hours ago. Sometimes he thinks he's more of a bodyguard than a driver. He's been with me for quite some time. He's a decent sort. The intel I wish to gather is extremely sensitive. It's for my ears and eyes only. I don't need to take the chance of someone recording our meeting, or discovering who my contact really is. I will never put her in danger again! This meeting is above top secret. I have to protect her new identity at all costs. By doing so I am ensuring she lives a long healthy life. I let myself out through the hidden door in my office. This exit has come in handy on more than one occasion. I can't afford to have anyone tail me. I am good at clinging to the shadows. My life depends on it.

The weather in D.C. is all over the place. One day it's warm and the next day it's cold. None of the elements seem to be cooperating with anything else. Not even the weather. We are meeting in an abandoned warehouse off Jefferson. It's dark and cloudy. No moon light at all. A perfect night for a covert operation. I'll arrive in under an hour. Not too much traffic this early in the morning. I find myself continuously checking my rear view-mirror. Can never be too cautious. I had to devise a plan to bring Toni in on the fly. This thing has gone south with a quickness. I've answered at least one hundred calls yesterday and about a million questions. Everyone wants answers. Especially the President. I can tell he misses being in the field. I wouldn't put it past him to dress up in disguise and come back out in the field.

Spying is not as glamorous as the movies make it out to be. There are no family dinners. The spy business is about patience. Many late nights. It's a waiting game. It's about the long game. But more importantly it's about the intel. Bits and pieces of information floating through the ether. Trying to establish reliable contacts. Using leverage to get the information needed to prevent one world disaster or another. Tying all the pieces together praying to form an accurate picture. Wanting what is best for the American people. That is always my first priority. Others not so much. Greed is what drives this world. There is absolutely nothing I can do to stop it. I prefer to expend my efforts in ways I can make a difference. A difference for the better. Stomping down corruption in my lines of influence.

The intel means something different for everyone. I pull off the highway making my way down poorly maintained side streets. I like clinging to the shadows. That's where the fun is. I park my black nondescript vehicle in the shadows on the northwest side of the building. I park parallel to the building. I don't want any passersby to pick up the reflectors on the back and front of my vehicle. I am armed to the teeth and ready for some action. Anyone looking for trouble can come find me. This meeting stays off book. Once we are done here this meeting will never have taken place. I hope she has something for me.

We've agreed to meet on the second floor of this old abandoned decrepit warehouse building. I am careful as I walk making sure to step over any debris. You never know what you could be stepping on. Old rusty nails. Crack pipes. Used needles. One can never be too careful. I take several deep breaths to center myself. I reach for the Glock 19 Gen5 9mm in my shoulder holster. Just to reassure myself it's still there. I glide my fingertips along the surface and feel the cool steel in my hand. I am prepared for whatever. Maybe shooting someone would lessen the tightness in my chest. It's that's at all possible. I can sense another presence in the warehouse walking four paces behind me. I don't panic or let on that I'm aware of their presence.

I shorten my stride. The visibility is poor. If I can't see too far ahead neither can they. I time my attack for the exact moment I pass the last window on my right. As soon as I'm in the shadows again I grab my weapon, pivot, and aim it at the head of my would-be attacker. I am in the shadows, but they are not. Not completely. I have my Glock pointed at her head. She is standing directly in front of the window. When I look down at Katya, she has her weapon pointed at my abdomen. Very little has changed about her I see. She's still in fighting shape. She says, *"You are losing your touch old man. Time is slowing you down. There was a time I would never have gotten this close."* Of course, she is correct. Time catches up to us all.

All I can do is chuckle. Some things never change. She may be presumed dead, but she still hasn't lost her touch. I pull her toward me and wrap my arms around her. A strong wave of nostalgia hits me so hard it nearly drags me to my knees. I've missed this woman. Deep down in my bones I've missed her. What would our lives have been were we just two ordinary people. Not operatives in the spy business. Just two ordinary people. What would it have been if we were allowed to marry and raise our child. I must be getting old. Waxing poetic. I released her and step back. I have to pull myself together. I force myself to take several deep breaths. "*Yeah well, time is a formidable adversary for us all. You look good, and you sound like an American. Lost your accent I see.*"

She chuckles, and my whole body tightens up. This was not one of my better ideas. Meeting Katya is harder than I thought it would be. I see her eyes are bright with unshed tears. I am not the only one affected. My pride can appreciate that. "*Yeah, well, you know. When in Rome. By the way, Katya is dead. You killed her. Remember?*"

I snort. "*Yeah, I remember. Thank you for agreeing to meet with me.*"

"*You're welcome. How did you find me?*"

"*I've been keeping tabs from time to time. You were in Switzerland for a long time. Did you enjoy it?*"

I can just imagine she's scoffing at me. "*You are a control freak, dorogaya.*"

I go still. We both do. She realizes her slip of the tongue. She called me sweetheart. Just like she did twenty plus years ago. I didn't realize how much I missed that until this very moment. I give my head a little shake. I can't do what I want to do. So, I will do what I came here to do. "*What do you have for me, Kat?*"

"*I shook a few trees. My contacts tell me Arlene Petrenko defected to Ukraine. There were three names on the shipping manifest. Her and her two children. Does she have anything to do with what I heard on the news today? Is she the reason Russia is at war with Ukraine?*"

"*It looks that way.*"

"*Ah.*"

"Arlene Petrenko is the modern-day Joan of Arc."

"Do we know why she defected, Kat?"

"She was unhappy with the fact that her comrades would not allow her to retaliate on the Americans for the death of her husband and her brother-in-law turned lover/baby daddy. She is very angry. Obviously."

"Obviously."

"There's one more thing. My people tell me she has come into contact with a scientist and has gotten her grubby little paws on uranium. It seems the scientist was an old comrade of her father's. They go way back. Anyway, her being in Ukraine is bad juju."

I am standing so still my bones could crack. My mind is blown. What is Arlene Petrenko playing at? It's all starting to make sense now. *"Do you know where the scientist is located?"*

"Yes. He's in Russia. He and Putin met three days ago. The scientist still has a daughter who lives in Russia. If I had to guess, I'd say he was coerced into absconding with the uranium. More than likely Putin threatened him using his daughter as leverage. Putin can be very persuasive!"

"Thank you for the intel, Kat. Thank you for coming out of hiding and putting yourself in danger. I really appreciate your help. Is there anything I can do for you?"

"Don't tempt me dorogaya. I should get back before I am missed."

"Are you still shacking up with that math teacher?"

She throws her head back and laughs. The sound of her laughter brings a load of unsolicited memories rushing back. *"You know very well he is no math teacher. He is a tenured professor in an Ivy League institution. What's the matter dorogaya? Are you jealous?"*

I smile. She has no idea. It's on the tip of my tongue to ask her about the baby. I wish I wasn't curious about it. I wonder if she ever planned to share that piece of news with me. I wonder if she planned to keep the baby. I wonder if she ever dreamed, we could go off to some remote island and be a family. Maybe those were my dreams alone. I don't have the right to ask her any of those questions tonight. Not ever. She deserves whatever sliver of happiness she's carved out for herself. She sacrificed a lot for her country. She sacrificed a lot for me and my country. It nearly cost her life. I will let sleeping dogs lie.

"I am jealous. More than you will ever know. We were either born at the wrong time or born in the wrong country. My heart belongs to you Kat. It always will."

"When you say these things, you make it hard for me to pretend you don't exist."

"I hope you're doing a better job of it than I am. At the moment I am failing miserably. I've missed you. Goodbye, Katya."

"I've missed you too. Goodbye, dorogaya."

Chapter 23

Before I can think better of it, I pull her into my arms and claim her mouth. Simply because I can't help myself. Add this to the mountain of bad ideas I've had in this lifetime. I pull away before I drown in this kiss. She is clinging to me. Making it almost impossible for me to walk away. But I do walk away. I did back then too. I walk away fast. Because everything in me is begging me not too. The longer I'm in her presence the more danger she will face. She has to stay dead. I will not compromise her safety. Not ever again. Her intel both simplifies and complicates things for me. I have three phone calls to make. I am not looking forward to any of them. It's moments like these that make retirement so much more appealing. I could buy a cabin in some remote location with a population of about three hundred people. I would spend my days fishing and drinking cheap beer. That's the life.

    I make it back to the office in one piece. I didn't get a chance to shoot anyone. No one was out looking for trouble. I am more wired than I was before I left. My mind is working overtime. There will be no sleep for me. Usually when I can't sleep, I call a female companion over and work off some of the stress. After seeing Katya, that just won't do. Not tonight anyway. I was tempted to invite her here for one night. I know from experience one night would not be enough. I made the right decision. My heart does not agree with my head. Some bones are better left buried. This is definitely one of those bones. I pull a secure burner from my top desk drawer. Why I ended up back in my office instead of my bedroom is beyond me. I tell myself I will not spend the remaining hours drowning my sorrows in scotch.

That is not a habit I am prepared to break a second time. My first call is to Antonia Townsend. Sometimes in order to protect big secrets we have to reveal smaller ones. The secret I have to sacrifice will piss the teams off for a bit. But eventually they will forgive me. The secret I need to safeguard, well, if the men find out about that it could be the catalyst to my untimely demise. On top of that it would unravel years and years of hard work, and hard-fought trust. This is for the greater good. I really have no other choice. Life is about choices. I have made mine. They may not always be popular, but they are always what is right at the time. I don't have the luxury of second guessing myself. There are no what ifs in this line of work. That's just the way it is!

GRAVITY

The SAT phone rings a few times. I snatch it up and bark down the line. *"Speak!"*

"I have a set of coordinates for you. I am sending them over now. Confirm when you receive them."

It takes a second for the coordinates to reach my cell. I take a quick look at the coordinates. Latitude 51.919438 degrees and Longitude 19.145136 degrees. *"I have them."*

"This is where Antonia Townsend is located. Do you need further assistance?"

"No." I disconnect the call. Chaos is staring a hole in me on one side, and Ace is staring a hole in me on the other side. It's been a long four days. Neither of them has slept for more than an hour or two. They look like crap! *"The Colonel just sent over the coordinates of Toni's location."*

Chaos says, "Then *why are we still standing here? Let's go!*" He has not been cleared for this rescue mission.

Anchor steps forward. Before he can speak Ace says, *"He's going. I will shoot whoever I need to shoot to ensure he does. It's been four days. This is his sister we are going to rescue. I dare anyone to try and stop him."* Ace has his hand on his trusty dusty Beretta 92X. I don't know a man faster than Ace. All I can do is pray no one tries to stop them. There will be bloodshed!

Before anyone is shot my cellphone goes through a series of beeps. Actually, all of our cell phones do. Then an encrypted message comes through. It's from the Colonel. The message reads: The coordinates you have just received are for a small town in Poland. From the intel I've received Antonia Townsend is being held in a cabin on the outskirts of town. Follow those coordinates and you will find her. Chaos is cleared to travel. It looks like the Colonel came through, again. I kinda feel bad I suspected him of betrayal a few days ago. Up until now time has been ticking by slowly.

Ace says, *"Let's go fellas. One man. One might. One mission."*

We all yell, *"Oorah!"*

I tell the group *"We are wheels up in two minutes. Grab your gear and meet me at the bird."* I run to the X34A to go through a quick preflight checklist. It doesn't take more than two minutes. I know Ace and Chaos will bring my gear. It's been locked and loaded for almost a week now. I start her up just as Ace and Chaos load up. Right on their heels is Anchor, Optic, Dome, Polar, and Thrasher. Pyro will take up the command position from base. We are looking at a twelve-hour flight and will need to refuel, possibly twice. I will need to refuel in the air as I will be flying under radar range for a large portion of the flight. Lower altitudes require the use of more fuel. Fewer air streams to ride. Pyro will work out the logistics for that from his location.

Anchor joins me in the cockpit. He is sitting in as copilot. That's usually where Logic sits. I kinda miss him.

Anchor asks, *"You good, Gravity. We are all working on fumes. Let me know when you are ready for me to take over."* I'm about to respond when I hear a squawk on comms.

"Hello, fellas. My name is Insipid. I have been instructed to assist you with transport. So, in exactly twenty-six minutes I will be taking over piloting your aircraft. Sleep tight gentlemen."

Comms go silent before I can respond. There is no way I am giving over control of my aircraft to a total stranger. Anchor is cussing up a blue streak. Everything he's saying goes double for me! Those Omegas have some boulder sized stones. I see why Logic is always threatening to shoot them. They rub him raw! Right now, they are rubbing me raw too! I tap on my comms unit to activate it. I will let this Insipid person know in no uncertain terms that at no point will I be giving over control of my aircraft. That's just stupid. It squawks once, and the Colonel comes on the line.

He says, *"Look here soldiers, it's a twelve-hour thirty-minute flight. None of you have slept. I am not taking the chance of you flying into the side of a mountain. You can either allow Insipid to pilot, or you can turn around and I will send someone else."* Then silence.

Chaos says, *"Yes, Sir. We're on it."* Comms go dead. I hear Chaos say, *"Sorry, Gravity. I just want my sister back."*

I respond, *"Roger that!"* I sit back in my seat and sigh. A very heavy sigh. One thing I know for sure is, whoever this Insipid person is, I have a bullet with their name on it.

The team and I take up position on all four sides of a medium sized log cabin. This is where the coordinates sent us, but there are no guards posted in the woods. There are no guards posted around the cabin. There is no electronic security feed visible. It would appear as if Antonia Townsend has been abandoned if she's present at all. The cabin looks empty. Chaos and Ace are chomping at the bit to breach. I sent them to do some forward recon. This area is densely populated with trees and bushes. From the size of these trees, they've been here for centuries. It's a cloudy night. Which means it's perfect. The darkness provides cover. The current temperature is fifteen degrees below zero. We are wearing masks to hide the condensation from our breaths. Don't want breathing to be the reason we are shot dead. I hear a squawk in my left ear.

It's Chaos. *"I got a look inside. I don't see anything."*

Ace says, *"I don't see anything from my side either."*

"We need to get inside this cabin."

"Ok. We breach in 10, 9, 8, 7, 6, 5, 4, 3, 2." Doors are kicked in, and windows are blown out. Ace and Chaos enter first. Followed by the rest of us. There is no security anywhere. Hmmm. No men posted guarding the prisoner. No security system. No external cameras. Nothing. The cabin isn't very big. It doesn't take long to clear it.

I hear Chaos yell, *"She's in here."* We all rush to find Antonia Townsend tied to a chair. She's sitting on a chair in the middle of the small bathroom. It looks like she was just dumped here and left to die.

I hear her screaming. *"Please, don't hurt me."* She's hysterical. We leave Chaos to soothe her. While Ace stays behind to hover.

The rest of us file outside the cabin and take up defensive positions. This just gets weirder and weirder. Was she left here to die? I feel a headache crawling up the back of my neck. I slept for six hours. I really had no choice. Insipid took control of the aircraft. I get so mad every time I think about it. Over comms I hear Chaos say, *"We are coming out."* I answer, *"Roger."* The sooner we leave Poland the better. The bitter cold is putting me in a bad mood. Chaos has his sister dressed in a snow suit and wrapped up in a blanket. He and Ace are supporting her body weight from either side. She looks weak. But other than that, not too bad. We follow the exfiltration plan.

Again, I didn't get to shoot anybody. What is the world coming to? Our return to the aircraft was uneventful. I have so many questions I don't know where to begin. Before I could get the bird in flight Antonia Townsend had already passed out. There is no telling what she's been through. I'm just glad to have her back. Chaos and Ace are watching her like a hawk. She was taken to the back of the aircraft. There's a bedroom back there. Chaos is with her, and Ace is pulling sentry duty. He was pacing a whole in the floor last I checked. We are headed home. I expect to hear from Insipid, but I don't. They would be pushing their luck with me right about now!

We make it to the halfway mark before we have to refuel. Another aircraft pulls up beside me. In my headset I hear, "Alpha, this is Tango. We are here to juice you up, over."

"Tango, this is Alpha. Commence with aerial refueling." I insert my retractable probe into the basket. Now all we have to do is latch. A seal has been established between the basket and the retractable probe. It's pumping about 300 gallons per minute. I can thank Alexander de Seversky for this technology. Makes my life a whole lot easier. Flying out of Polish airspace was a little hairy. We made it out without having the authorities alerted. Would hate to have rescued Chaos' sister only to be shot down from the sky. That would ruin everyone's day. Anchor and I take turns piloting the aircraft in two-hour shifts. I for one will be happy to be back in the United States.

Chaos is going to insist Toni be given time to rest before the debrief. Although I can understand that, if we are going to find Arlene Petrenko, and put her out of her misery, time is of the essence. I would love to know why Toni was dumped off in the woods. Add to that who took her and why was there no security. I want to know what happened to Arlene Petrenko. I have about a million and one questions. I'm sure I'm not the only one. Getting home seems to take a lot longer. We make it back to the compound. I pull out the SAT phone. I need to call Logic and tell him Antonia Townsend is safe. He came up blank too. He was not able to provide us with any information. We were all stumped. The Colonel came through. As usual, though. Again, I have questions.

Chapter 24

COLONEL

When Zypher told me Arlene Petrenko was in the Ukraine I couldn't believe it. I had to verify the intel. Not that I would ever doubt the Omega. It's just like WOW! Which is why I met with Katya. It may not be the only reason, but I am not going down that road. Sure, enough the coordinates were accurate. It's obvious Katya still has a few viable contacts. She came through. On top of that this is just one more reason why I'm glad Zypher works for me. I would never have guessed Arlene Petrenko would defect to the Ukraine. Yesterday's enemy is today's friend. That is how it is in the spy business. Information is ever changing. Ivan Yuriyev would be turning over in his grave if he knew his daughter ran to the enemy.

Petrov, the head of the Russian mafia, won't stop looking until her head is brought to him on a platter. That must have been one huge falling out he and Arlene had to make her defect. Petrov is Russian mafia, born and bred. They don't come much meaner than him. There is no place in this world where Arlene Petrenko and her children can hide and continue to breathe. It is just a matter of time. She signed her own death warrant. Hers and that of her children. She is attempting to arm the Ukrainians with nuclear weapons. That is the very last thing the Russians will allow. I am going home and going to bed. If I'm lucky I will fall asleep. If not… Well, I don't even want to think about it. More and more I am feeling my age.

LOGIC

Just as expected the chess pieces arrived. A luxury sedan and two black non-descript vans pulled up outside of the Musee d'orsay. Out comes Arlene Petrenko. Yep, the defector herself. Only that makes no sense. Our latest intel puts Arlene Petrenko square in the middle of Ukraine. Unless she has discovered teleportation abilities how is it possible that she is in two places at one time? My spidey senses are going haywire. I say over comms, *"Men, can anyone tell me how I am looking at Arlene Petrenko when she's supposed to be in the Ukraine? Has she been cloned? Anybody! Tell me...!"* Before I start to believe I've lost my mind.

Razor says, *"No idea. Maybe this is a body double. She is on everyone's most wanted list. I would stay hidden if I were her. If it is her, she is traveling with her very own personal army. I am filled to the brim with mirth. I can scarcely contain it."*

Thrasher says, *"Y'all seeing what I'm seeing? By my counts she has twelve heavily armed meat heads in tow, plus the driver."*

I say, *"Indeed we do my friends."*

"This is one happening scene. We actually get to shoot people, yippee!"

Gator asks, *"Razor, how old are you exactly? Happening scene. Were you born in the sixties?"* Everyone chuckles.

We have our eyes glued to the warehouse. We've all taken up tactical positions around all the warehouse entrances and exits. Thrasher is in the van running surveillance. Once she is out of the sedan, we notice Arlene Petrenko is carrying a silver case. That must be where the uranium is being stored. I didn't see Salvatore Parisi carrying anything, so this must be a cryptocurrency transaction. For what he must be paying for the uranium carrying around that amount in cash is not feasible. Arlene Petrenko saunters into the warehouse filled with confidence. Once they are both inside men from both vehicles post up outside. There are forty-two men in all. Parisi and Petrenko each took a guard in the building with them. And they each have guards posted up around the building.

I arm all ten drones to kill phase. I set the coordinates and then deploy them. Each drone carries twenty rounds of ammo. Once they run out, they will automatically switch to surveillance mode. Once each drone is in place, I hit the button on the remote to fire. The first twenty guards drop like dominoes. Then we go in hot. We don't want to attract attention from inside the building. We count as we go. I start the count twenty-one. We hear twenty-two, twenty-three, twenty-four in quick succession. Then twenty-five, and so on and so on till we reach thirty-eight. When I heard thirty-eight, I make my way over to the driver still in the vehicle with earbuds in, and I quickly slit his throat. I say, *"Thirty-nine."* Gator takes out the other driver as well, and says, *"Forty."*

Thrasher does a thorough sweep then says, *"Gentlemen, you are now cleared to move about the cabin."*

I say, *"On three, we breach the warehouse. One. Two. Three."* I turn the knob and push the door open. I am so glad we didn't have to blow this door. I enter with Dolphin on my heels.

We turn the corner to find Arlene Petrenko is about to hand over the case to Salvatore Parisi. Her guard spotted me a second before I put a bullet through his skull. Dolphin takes out Salvatore's guard. He is in his element. Their options are quickly dwindling. Arlene stumbles back and almost drops the case. She seems surprised to see us. Salvatore snatches the case just in time. He has quick hands for a dead guy. Would hate to spill even a drop of what's inside. Dolphin and I step out of the shadows in full hazmat gear, with our weapons locked and loaded.

Salvatore says, "*Careful where you point that thing, gentlemen. You wouldn't want to hit this case now, would you?*"

While he's asking questions Gator manages to put a bullet into Arlene Petrenko's head. The blood is pooling around the Italian Death Dealer's expensive footwear. There was just no way she was leaving this building alive. It couldn't happen! The Italian Death Dealer looks down and takes a step back. He is feeling too full of himself. He says, "*I have every intention of leaving here with this case. Unless you came here prepared to die today, there is nothing you can do about it.*"

I say, "*Well, that is one hypothesis. I have a counteroffer for you, Parisi. I am willing to make your death painful and quick. I will also take the case off your hands in exchange for a little intel. How does that sound?*"

"*There is nothing you have to say that I'd want to hear. I don't plan on telling you anything! Nothing at all. Go home to that sweet little family of yours while they still breathe.*"

"*Parisi, it's quite obvious to me you hate life. You mention my family and what, do you imagine you left here in anything other than a body bag. I hope you don't have plans for later this evening. You will not make it. Let me ask you, the person that just handed you that case of uranium is not Arlene Petrenko. Who is she?*" For a second he looks confused. Then he says, "*You won't pull that one over Ion me. Of course, she's Arlene Petrenko. I've been in the game a long time. I've had her under surveillance for over a week. She is definitely* Arlene Petrenko." I say, "*Ok. If you insist. But there is a good chance there is no uranium in that case. Don't be shocked when I'm right.*"

"*What are you talking about? I came prepared. I tested the case. The Geiger counter picked up high levels of uranium. You can't put one over on me.*"

"*Did you actually open the case and put your eyes on the

uranium, or did you just scan the case?"

He looks positively flummoxed! He's at a loss for words. "Maybe, you should open the case. Make sure you're getting your money's worth. Would hate for you to be double crossed."

The thought of someone double crossing him has made him careless. He sets the case down on the ground, uses a key attached to his wrist to unlock it, and slowly opens it. Whatever he sees has him cussing up a blue streak in Russian. I give him five seconds to realize he's been made a fool of before also putting a bullet between his eyes. The look on his face is priceless. This was all too easy. I wanted to smack some sense into him first. I am faced with the fact that we have uranium out there somewhere, and Arlene Petrenko is on the loose. The only bright spot in my day is knowing I killed the Italian Death Dealer.

Once Salvatore Parisi (The Italian Death Dealer) topples over, Dolphin walks over to look inside the case. He laughs and shakes his head. Inside the case is a bottle of Russian vodka. I can't wait to find out how much Salvatore paid for it. By this time the rest of the team had filed into the building. They are enjoying this a little too much. From the van Thrasher says, *"Bring the bottle. We've earned it."* The Colonel is also watching the live feed and is not happy. Gator walks over to the dead woman, squats down, and removes her wig. Underneath her wig is a brunette who looks eerily similar to Arlene Petrenko. Arlene is blond.

Over comms the Colonel says, *"Omega, run her through facial recognition. I want to know who she is within the hour. Gentlemen, go back to the compound and rest up. You are wheels up in twenty-four hours. I want the uranium and the real Arlene Petrenko in my hands pronto."* The Colonel doesn't stay on the line long enough to hear a response.

There's a squawk over comms and Omega says, *"A clean-up crew is in route. ETA three minutes."*

I say, *"Men, mount up!"* I turned away but saw Dolphin snatch the bottle of vodka out of the case. Otherwise, this would just be a big old waste of time. We loaded it up in the van and took off back to the compound. From the looks of things, I ain't ever going home.

TONI

We're back in the compound, and I've been allowed to rest. This is on me now. Ace is hovering, and Chaos is playing nurse maid. I can see it in their eyes every time they ask me if I'm ok, that they have so many questions. Out of respect for my "ordeal", they are being patient and gentle with me. I haven't been updated since being "rescued", so I'm not sure what else has developed. It's been about eighteen hours and on a cellular level I know my time is running out. They will want to debrief me. I never imagined my vacation would turn out like this. It's the worst! Ace asks, *"How you holding up? You know you're safe, right! We've got you. Do you want to try and eat something? We can get you whatever you like."*

"Sure, that sounds good. Something light would be nice." My brother jumps up so fast you would think the seat was on fire. *"On it! Mom once told me you liked eating breakfast for dinner. Is that still the case?"*

I have to smile at that. *"It is definitely still the case."* *"French toast coming right up!"* My brother isn't fooling me. He's just relieved to have something to do. Sitting around is not his thing.

He's left the room before I can even thank him. I'm left alone with Ace. I feel the air getting thick. I begin fidgeting with the covers. I don't have what needs to be said planned out, so I'm praying for a little more time. This is going to be the hardest thing I've ever done. Ace says, *"You'll feel more like your old self* once you eat something. So, breakfast for dinner, huh?"

"Yeah. Most of my favorite foods are breakfast foods. There is no rule that says you can't eat them when you want."

"That's true. There isn't."

"It looks like your face took a beating. My brother didn't break anything did he?"

"No, he took it easy on me. I wasn't fighting back, so that made me a soft target. He did NOT like that!"

"Thank you for trying to protect me. I'm so sorry you took a beating. Why did you tell him about the events of seven years ago? He didn't have to know about that."

"Toni, I know it doesn't seem like it right now, but maybe in time you will see it is better that he does know. It has been weighing on me for a long time. I was serious when I said we don't keep secrets on this team. And having this secret was killing me. The only reason I held onto it this long was to protect you. If it were up to me, I would have laid it all out on the line a long time ago. All of it including how I feel about you. If you were my sister, I would want to know."

I won't address the elephant in the room no matter how badly I may want to. I am still keeping secrets of my own, so the last thing I should do is delve into his feelings for me. I don't have the right to do that knowing those feelings will change in the very near future. This suck! The best response is a diversion. "Did my brother threaten to kill you once I was found? Maybe he still plans to go back and break something while using you as a human punching bag?"

"No. Even in his fury he was careful not to. He was pulling his punches. One of your brother's superpowers is his ability to see through the fog. Even though he was furious with me he never intended to kill me. Not without allowing me a chance to defend myself. That was just him telling me what I did was dead wrong, *and he was not pleased about it. Believe me, if he wanted me dead, I would be." "You guys are insane! You know that right?"*

"It may seem that way on the outside, but we are a highly functioning cohesive unit. One that understands the bylaws. Those bylaws allow us to make decisions on the fly. So, from the outside we may seem insane, but we understand that trust is what keeps us alive out in the field. There is never any time for questions. So, doubt and confusion will be the death of you. Possibly the death of men who are brothers to you. If doubt creeps in, people die. It's not rocket science."

"Sounds like you have it all figured out."

"That's a good thing, believe me."

Chaos enters the room sometime later with a tray filled with enough food to feed an ogre. We must be having company. He says, *"I figured you would appreciate eating in here without the prying eyes of the group, micro-assessing you. Once you're done, we need to ask you a few questions. Let me know when you're feeling up to it?"*

"Ok." He leaves the room. Ace takes the tray and sits it on my lap. I look down and my mouth begins to water. I love my brother. There's French toast, crispy bacon, eggs with cheese, fruit, orange juice and coffee. Two of each. I guess Ace is staying. *"My brother thinks of everything."*

"He's very thorough."

"Are you hungry, Ace?"

I chuckle at that and shake my head. *"Doll, I am always hungry. I'm a growing boy. My body requires a lot of calories. Eat what you want, and I will take care of the rest."*

"We can eat together. There is silverware here, too."

"I see that. I am going to leave and give you a few minutes alone. I will be back shortly to clear up whatever you didn't. I'll be

right back."

"Ok." Ace leaves and for the first time in a long time I take a deep breath. He has been by my side ever since my rescue. I eat as quickly as I can from one side of the plates leaving a huge portion for him. I set the tray on the dresser and jumped up and run into the bathroom. I need a shower so bad! I'm sure I smell myself. I start the shower and brush my teeth. I take a long hot shower. I'm almost afraid to get out. Once I'm done here the interrogation will begin. I haven't spoken to the boss, so I have no idea what the next move is. Once the debriefing starts, I am on my own. I need to be ready for that!

I exited the bathroom to find Ace sitting in a chair with an empty tray in his lap. He looks up at me and the air shifts. It never occurred to me he would be back in the room. Although I was in the shower for quite some time. He does a slow perusal of my person. He starts at my head and works his way down to the chipped blue nail polish on my toes. I doubt he missed one single thing. I see his nostrils flare before he says, *"I'll take this empty tray to the kitchen. I'll be back in fifteen minutes."* All I can do is nod. He walks to the door with the empty tray in hand. Before leaving he says, *"I'm all in for exploring the feelings we share."* Then he's gone. Taking all the air out of the room with him. I am aware of the elephant in the room. Things are always evolving, and this too must change. I don't have the right to even have that conversation. Not until I come clean.

Chapter 25

LOGIC

We've been held up in this compound for almost thirty-six hours. We are waiting for further orders. Everyone is ready to be home. But none so more than me. I sent Samar a few heavily encrypted texts, but that is not enough. I am always careful about contacting home when I'm out in the field. I never want to send danger to my front door. Our house sits on thirty acres of land. We have several structures filled with farming equipment and the like. One of those structures is where Venom is running his base of operations. Venom has relayed a signal that allows me to tap into the cameras in our home. So, I can watch Samar and Ty whenever an opportunity presents itself. This just makes me even more homesick.

Her belly has definitely grown bigger since I last saw her. My mom is taking good care of both her and Ty. Samar continues her telenursing job. It keeps her busy and she prefers to work. You have no idea how thrilled I am about that. I didn't say a word either way. It was all her decision. I'm not crazy. My wife is stubborn. Telling her what to do is her number one pet peeve. Once she made up her mind and announced it, I sent up a silent prayer of thanks. Her pregnancy hormones make for interesting emotional displays. I love my wife and am ready to go home. The SAT phone finally rings. Please let this be an order to kill someone. I answer and hear, *"Hold."* It's the Colonel. He must have a target for us.

The Colonel comes down the line and says, "*So, here's what we know. You were right. The handler was not Arlene Petrenko. It's a long twisted idiotic story but the abbreviated version is she had a twin. They were separated at birth due to some superstitious crap about the mark of the devil. Her sister was placed in an orphanage. Anyway, they found each other and kept in contact. Her sister lived in the Ukraine and helped Arlene defect with her children. According to the latest intel Arlene is still in the Ukraine, and Petrov is closing in quick. Her days are numbered. Long story short, the President wants us to stand down on this mission.*"

"*What about the scientist and the missing uranium still floating about?*"

"*You've recovered the missing artifacts. The country owes you and the team a great debt. The President has gone into talks with Ukraine. We will continue to search for the uranium Arlene promised Salvatore Parisi. This has become a political issue now. It's about national safety. We could never be seen giving nuclear capability to the Ukrainians. That would violate our NATO agreement. Russia is still a part of the NATO alliance. There is now a way for Ukraine to keep them in line. With the threat of nuclear war. We didn't have that opportunity before. Even with the NATO alliance Russia is an unpredictable piece on the chest board.*"

"*Colonel, are you saying this plot was orchestrated to arm the Ukrainians with nuclear weapon's capability to be used as a not-so-subtle threat by the U.S. government against Russia? To keep Russia in line. Releasing us from all blame by using Tibetan artifacts and kidnapped scientists operating in the US. Making it look like the Chinese betrayed their close ally Putin by reaching out to the Americans for assistance. Thus, weakening the Chinese/Russian alliance.*"

"*What I'm saying is you can go home now soldier. Your family needs you.*" The connection goes dead. I am sitting here in stunned silence. On one hand I can appreciate the brilliance behind the design. I would love to know who the designer is. Sheer mastery! On the other hand, this is just another reason to hate politics. Once I'm stateside I will gather all three teams and we will have a debrief. What I've discovered is politicians never take a break. They start plotting and scheming before they open their eyes in the morning. The scheming lasts until well after they hit REM sleep. They are still plotting in their dreams. It's exhausting!

I round up the men for a quick debrief. Everyone gathers in the master suite closet. I say, *"I have good news and bad news. Which do you prefer first?"*

Coup says, *"Hit us with some good news for a change."*

I smile at him. *"The good news is we can go home now. And you my wayward friend can go back to your unscrupulous ways!"*

"Wow. Really? That cut deep, pops. You have become so judgey since being domesticated." The team gets a good chuckle out of that.

"I'll show you domesticated."

Coups not done. *"Samar, has you wrapped around her little finger. What happened to you? You were one of my idols. I think married life is making you soft. Maybe it's time to challenge for a new team lead."* The guffaws coming from the men are over the top. I'm sure the neighbors hear it.

"Once we're stateside I will see you in the ring, son. My goal is to change your mind about me being soft. It's the least I can do. I promised you a whooping. I will keep my word."

"Didn't you also promise me a raise in my allowance?" I crack up. This man is certifiable. I may just pack up and leave Coup in France.

He's been very busy the last three days. When I ask,

he tells me he's brushing up on his French. Coup's French is impeccable. Which means there's a woman involved. Work hard, play harder is our motto. The team is laughing and shaking their heads. They know he's certifiable too.

We get a squawk on comms. *"Men, the cleanup crew set to arrive in one hour."*

"Roger that!" Comms go dead. I say, *"Let's go men. Wheels up in fifteen."* The men know the drill we take all munitions with us. The rest is handled by the cleaners.

Gator says, *"What's the bad news?"*

"The bad news is we leave an incomplete mission. We won't be looking for the uranium Arlene Petrenko promised the Italian Death Dealer."

Thrasher says, *"That's politics for ya!"* We nod our heads in agreement.

The bottle of vodka we confiscated from this op is completely empty. We enjoyed it immensely! I got to cross the Italian Death Dealer off my to-do list. So that's a plus, and we got our hands on the Tibetan artifacts. So, I guess that's something. The men got to blow off steam with some target practice. Reducing the number of bad guys on the planet is always a plus. I'm always thankful when we get to do that. Why do I feel an itch like leaving our mission incomplete will have repercussions? I'll tell you why. No uranium. No scientist. No Arlene Petrenko. In case I haven't made myself clear I hate politics. Nothing is ever what it seems with politicians. I know once we have the full debrief, I am going to have to answer a million questions. They will be valid questions, and I may not have all the answers. I try very hard to give the men complete answers. They risk their lives daily for this country. The least I can do is give them a reason to believe their sacrifices are all worth it.

Sometimes I wonder. All eighteen of these men were

handpicked by me. Including the team leads. We function separately while at the same time as one overall unit. The team leaders I've chosen have to follow a very strict set of guidelines. Gator and Anchor were thoroughly vetted, by me. As were the seconds on each team. Gravity, Razor, and Optic. It was a stringent process. I went over every detail of their lives with a fine-tooth comb. They even managed to pass the psych evaluations I created just for them. I needed to know they were capable of excelling in highly stressful situations and sustaining extreme conditions for long periods of time. The lives of the men that follow us depend on it. I will stow my personal feelings away for a later time when I can analyze all the new data.

Our flight home is noisy. The men are coming down off an adrenaline high. They are going at it back there. They have me laughing so hard I may have broken a rib. I have to cut comms to focus on piloting this aircraft. All I can do is shake my head. I appreciate our joint missions. It gives me an opportunity to look everyone in the eye. To reassure myself that everyone's holding up under the stress. These men were chosen because they thrive in stressful situations. That is a rare breed. Some of them I don't get to see very often. So, when I do, I pay close attention. We have become a well-oiled machine. None of us are likely to discuss our feelings, but I can tell when something is off. Then I sit back and watch to see if I will need to intervene. My leads are very good at wrangling in their own men. I can appreciate that.

I hear Gator say, *"I feel the same way."*

"What do you mean?"

"I can tell by your expression you feel this op is incomplete." Sometimes I really believe he is psychic. He scored off the charts in intuition on my psych eval. I just chuckle and shake my head. The men all accuse him of reading minds. If you ever sit across from him at a poker table just know you will leave empty handed. You are better off just giving him your money before

the game starts. Reader, remind me to tell you about the time we went on an op to Vegas. Fun times.

"Aside from removing Salvatore Parisi from the board, it doesn't feel as if we accomplished our mission at all."

"No, it doesn't. Although, we did recover the Tibetan artifacts. That is something anyway. Gator, my Cajun friend, you are a very wise man."

ACE

Chaos and I went to Gravity and asked him to speak to the Colonel on Toni's behalf. We felt it would be beneficial to give her one more day to rest before the debrief. It seemed like a good idea at the time, but now I wonder. Mainly because the Colonel is flying in, and Logic and the remainder of the men will be in attendance also. Everyone except Venom. He's on babysitting detail but will be linked in via a secure network. The debrief is scheduled for today at 1500 hours. The guys are starting to filter in a couple at a time. Logic, Gator, and Coup show up first. Chaos is in the kitchen whipping up something that makes my mouth water. As soon as he arrives, Logic makes a beeline for the kitchen. I'm not sure if it's to have a quiet word with Chaos or to grab a bite of whatever smells so darn good.

Everyone else is putting space between themselves and the kitchen for the time being. Smart men. Then Razor and Dolphin show up. They are in a heated debate about the life expectancy of LeBron James' basketball career. Razor thinks he has three to five good years left. Dolphin is only willing to give him one more good run at a championship ring. Thus, the heated debate. Polar, Thrasher, Reaper, and Dome are on weapons cleaning duty. I did it after the last op. It's tough work. We use a lot of different weapons! Optic, Sledge, Crucible and Pyro are in the gym. I've been posted up wherever Toni is. Chaos hasn't been too far away. Once Logic leaves the kitchen, Gravity, Gator, and Anchor disappear behind closed doors. They will update Logic on all he's missed to bring him up to speed before the debrief with the Colonel. I pray things go well for Gravity. He's had his hands full with this op. By now Logic knows I'm with Toni. I will have my turn in the hot seat too. I am dreading it.

I spend as much time with Toni as I can before the debrief begins. She's very nervous about the meeting. I've tried telling her there isn't much to be nervous about, but she isn't convinced. Chaos and I will be by her side the whole time. That knowledge has done her little good. When she isn't wringing her hands, she is pacing the floor. Both Chaos and I tried everything to get her to calm down. Chaos even made her a cup of chamomile tea. She only drank half a cup, and it did not have the desired effect. At this point I just want to get this over with. Chaos rings the bell indicating the food is ready. Toni says, *"You should go eat. Get it before it disappears."*

"You're not hungry?"

"No. I had a large breakfast."

"You hardly ate much at all."

"It felt as if I had. You go ahead. I will wait for you here."

I leave to go to the kitchen. I get the feeling Toni needs space. We are in the middle of our shrimp etouffee when the Colonel strides in. He looks tired. He takes the only empty seat at the table. Chaos has yet to sit and eat. Chaos serves the Colonel a steaming plate of food. The table is completely quiet. The Colonel says, *"At ease, gentlemen."* Everyone goes back to what they were doing. Mainly eating, laughing, and talking crap. Every now and then the Colonel smiles at something someone says. I get the impression he misses these times. I'm sure they conjure up memories from his past assignments. You know what they say, heavy is the head that wears the crown, and it's lonely at the top.

A. C. GREGORY

Chapter 26

The Colonel looks at Chaos and says, *"I would like a private word with you and then your sister, if I may."* Chaos hesitates for a second. He is weighing his options. He knows this meeting is inevitable but after what Toni has gone through, he doesn't want to stress her out any more than she already is. Chaos nods. The Colonel finishes his meal and exits the room with Chaos on his heels. It's almost time for the debrief so I doubt this will take long. The debrief will start at 1500 hours on the dot. That's a given. I go into the room to see how Toni is holding up. I have a small bowl of etouffee and a spoon with me. Maybe I can convince her to take a few bites. For the record, she is as stubborn as her brother. I knock on the door a few times before entering the room. Toni is laid across the bed with her head in her hands. She barely acknowledges me.

"Hey, how are you feeling? I brought you a bowl of shrimp etouffee just in case. It's delicious of course."

"Thanks." She takes the bowl and spoon from my hands and begins to nibble. I inform her the Colonel wants to have a word with her before the debrief. All she says is, *"Ok."* I don't know what to make of her response. I was expecting a little more, I guess. Her tacit agreement catches me off guard. I just hope this ordeal doesn't leave lasting scars behind.

There's a knock-on Toni's bedroom door. Chaos peeks his head in and glances in my direction before addressing Toni. I noticed a few drops of blood leaking from a busted lip. I guess that came courtesy of you know who. It looks like the Colonel made good on his promise. It's obvious he was not happy when

Chaos cussed him out and threatened to leave the team. It looks painful. He doesn't come close enough for Toni to notice though. She seems mesmerized by the bowl in her hand. I give him an imperceptible shrug. I'm just not sure.

Chaos says, *"Toni, Colonel Paulson would like a word with you in private. Are you up to it?"*

"Am I in trouble?" The Colonel steps around Chaos and enters the room.

He says, *"Not at all. This is more of an informal visit. To introduce myself and to make sure you're ok. I want you to feel at ease before the formal debrief. Is it ok if we speak briefly?"*

"Yes, Sir."

"You can call me Colonel." Toni looks at Chaos and smiles. We leave the room. I promise myself I am not going to hover, so I go to the kitchen for a bottle of water. The debrief will start in three minutes. All of a sudden, I feel nervous. I never get nervous.

Chaos finds me in the kitchen. *"Hey, you good?"*

I respond, *"I wish I could say yes. I just don't get a good feeling about this. That lip looks painful."*

"It'll heal. You know the Colonel."

"Yeah. It's like you're reading my mind, bro. Something huge is coming." We shake our heads while making our way to the conference room. Everyone is seated when we arrive. I notice Toni is sitting to the left of the Colonel who is at the head of the table. Logic is seated to his right. The seat next to Toni has been left vacant. Chaos takes that seat. I am on the opposite side of the table with a clear view of Toni's face. She looks nervous. I would love to have been a fly on the wall for the conversation between Toni and the Colonel.

Once everyone is seated the Colonel stands. He walks to the podium in the corner of the room and stands behind it. Hmmm. The debrief begins with a bombshell. *"Let's begin. Normally I would start this debrief with a question-and-answer session. Today I am going to do things a little differently. I want to make an announcement. I will give ten minutes to address it then we will move on to the business at hand. Any questions?"* The room is silent. Logic has a look on his face that is hard to describe. It's almost like he's drawn a conclusion and is not happy with the conclusion he's drawn. What does he know that we don't? I glance around the table and everyone else looks equal parts wary, baffled, and interested. Everyone but Logic. The look on his face makes me want to laugh out loud. This is going to be bad. At the very least, not good.

COLONEL

My presence here is telling. Normally we would have our debriefs over a secure teleconference network. But because of the news I have to share I felt my presence would be best. I need to contain this situation as much as possible. This also gives me a chance to speak to Antonia Townsend. Once this debrief is over, I will be looking at eighteen very angry men. This news has been about eight years in the making. I might as well get on with it. Here goes my peace of mind! *"I thought it best to come and tell you in person that Antonia Townsend works for the United States Government."* The room erupts in literal chaos. For whatever reason I am compelled to glance in Logic's direction. He doesn't so much as flinch. Yep, he knew! Everyone is talking over everyone else, and Logic is just as calm as a cucumber.

I have a good reason for not telling Logic Antonia Townsend works for me, but he knows. As sure as I'm breathing, he knows. He worked it out on his own, but it must have been recently. Too recently for him to have confronted me about it. I am busy studying him for a reaction when I see him raise his hand. The room becomes instantly quiet. Everyone takes their seats again. He looks at me as if to say, you may continue. The stones on this guy. Loathe as I am to admit it, I am also proud. His men respect him. That is everything. I can't help but smile. I notice Antonia Townsend is sitting quietly as if nothing is happening. That is what makes her irreplaceable!

I say, *"Now that you've got that out of your system are there any questions?"* Chaos, looking positively murderous, is the first to speak. I just may have to punch him in the mouth again.

"How long have you had my sister on your payroll? How long has she been risking her life? It's obvious one Townsend risking their life for the sake of this country wasn't enough?"

"It's been seven years, six months, and twenty-two days. Zypher, would you like to explain, or should I?" At the sound of Miss Townsend's handle, the room erupts again. I don't have all day, so I've decided to fill them with intel on the quick.

Logic looks at Toni and says, *"I'm glad I didn't shoot you. Chaos would be so mad at me."*

Chaos sits in stunned disbelief. He says, *"Toni, I have no words."* He looks hurt. She glances at me, and I just shake my head. I have no words either.

Toni says, *"Please, let me explain. Shortly after our parents died, I was feeling restless."* I noticed Miss Townsend glancing at Ace. There's a story there I just know it. *"That restlessness caused me to poke around in places I should never have been. Into things that were not my concern. Classified things. Highly classified things! The next thing I know is there are two FBI agents on my doorstep. They were talking about National Security breach, and federal prison. I was scared out of my mind. Then the phone rang. I am handed that phone. On the other line of the phone is a voice telling me I can either go to federal prison or work for the United States government in data collection. As you see I opted for option number two."*

Chaos looks at the Colonel and says, *"You knew she was my sister. Why have you never mentioned this?"*

"I was given the intel just in time to save her. She was on her way to Guantanamo Bay when I made that call. Your brilliant sister hacked into our mainframe and extracted the names of half the covert operatives around the world. Including everyone at this table. The government believed she was working as a spy. They were going to waterboard her for the names of her handlers. I was livid when I found out we were breached. We were supposed to be impenetrable. So in lieu of the worst, I recruited Miss Townsend and convinced her to use her powers for good. She fixed our system too. Your sister is very important as an Omega. The work she's done is remarkable.

You men are safer because of it. I'm alive today because of it. She suspected Viktor Petrenko from the beginning. She began investigating him and gathered the intel to bring him down. She came to me with all kinds of goodies. She single handedly revealed the plot to take down the President of the United States. Her work speaks for itself. It isn't that she didn't want to tell you. She couldn't tell you. And now that you know you all need to just forget that you know. We all have jobs to do. The world is evil. You all know just how evil. Her role in fighting that evil is just as important as yours. So, if you're going to be mad at anyone be mad at me. If she blew her cover she was going to prison. Period! That was non-negotiable." I hope this helps to take the heat off Miss Townsend. She really is a God send.

Miss Townsend looks each man in the eye and apologizes. She says, *"Because I've been keeping this secret, I've worked extra hard to make amends. It's been eating me alive, Chance. You have no idea. I never wanted to lie to you or to Ace. Any of you really. I consider you family and went above and beyond to bring you home safely. Please forgive me big bro. Please forgive me Ace. I couldn't* handle it if you were disappointed in me. I will quit my job if you tell me to." The entire room goes silent. *Whatever you want me to do just say it. You are the only family I have left. It would kill me if you are angry with me!*

I never told Miss Townsend quitting was an option. What is she up to? Chaos says, *"I need time to think. We will discuss this later."*

Logic says, *"Zypher, I am an admirer of your work. The next time you take command of my aircraft we are going to have a problem. Being Chaos' sister won't save you. Are we clear?"* He's only half kidding. I think.

Zypher says, *"No offense, boy wonder, but I out rank you."* The room erupts in laughter. No one talks to Logic that way. But he's smiling so he must be ok. I think he just wanted to diffuse the tension in the room. He is primed to take over my spot one day. I need to get everyone back on track. I have things to do. *"Ok. That is all regarding Antonia Townsend being an Omega, so we can move on to other business."* I won't tell him she's not just an Omega. She's The Omega Prime. Which means she only answers to me and the President. So, yes, she does outrank him. She outranks her brother too, but let's not throw salt on the wound. I chuckle to myself. One day they will find this out as well.

"You men were instrumental in neutralizing the Italian Death Dealer, in recovering the stolen Tibetan artifacts, and in recovering Zypher." That's not technically true, but... She technically rescued herself, but we'll give them the win. *"As of this morning Arlene Petrenko is still in the Ukraine with her children. I'm not sure for how much longer. Petrov wants her head on a pike. Putin wants her head on a tray, and I want her head in a bag so I can toss it out to sea. Omega discovered the handler tasked to hand over the uranium to Salvatore Parisi was Arlene Petrenko's twin sister. They were separated at birth and Anya was sent to an orphanage to be raise by catholic nuns. When the girls were born the family believed they were*

cursed. The father wanted sons. One daughter he could abide. Two was unthinkable. He never had a son."

"Arlene Petrenko began looking for her twin after hearing time and again she looked like someone people knew. She asked enough questions and found intel leading to a twin. And the rest, as they say, is history. The President wanted me to thank you personally for your service. He says he's grateful. He wants you to stand down on Arlene Petrenko, the scientist, and the uranium. I have assured him that you would. See to it that you do. I am looking into the person responsible for the bogus intel we were given. We wasted a lot of time going around in circles. Believe me when I say heads will roll. I just want to be sure I have the right people before chopping off heads. We also stumbled across intel on Alpha team. It seems Viktor Petrenko was compiling a file and that is how he knew you had a sister named Antonia Townsend, Chaos.

Try as he could he was never able to find a corresponding photo before he died. The Omegas use Monikers only, so he had no idea Antonia Townsend worked under him. Sometimes in the same spaces. After his death, Arlene wanted to get back at the team, so she put the hit out on Miss Townsend. We don't know who provided a photo of Toni, but I have my suspicions. Once confirmed, that person will be forced into an early permanent retirement. I am with you Chaos family is to be protected at all times. So, I will see to this personally. I would never leave a situation like the kidnapping of your sister to go unanswered for. There are times when a little finesse is required. This is one of those times."

Logic asks, "Can you tell us who was being tasked out to find the missing scientist and his portion of the uranium? It's burning a hole in my brain!"

"Logic, you know what I know. I was told to tell you it was handled, and you're to stand down. I haven't heard one word about another set of elite covert operatives. Nor have I heard of anyone commanding a set of elite covert operatives. I will admit to some curiosity. I will investigate discreetly. This requires a delicate touch." He looks Logic right in the eye and says, "*I am telling you to stand down. I know how you can be with unanswered questions. If you disobey me on this the consequences will be dire. This isn't just about gathering intel. This could very well jeopardize the life of everyone in this room. There is only one person I can think of who has the power to move in the deepest of deep shadows, and he's untouchable. I want to hear it from your own lips that you will stand down Logic!*"

Everyone is waiting to hear what Logic has to say. He looks the Colonel in the eye and says, "*You have my word I will not go poking my nose into another group's covert ops. But I'll be honest with you, I am more than curious to meet them.*"

"*That makes all of us. Logic, you just want to know how good they are. If those men are better trained than your men.*"

"*I have no doubt in my mind that those men are NOT better trained than my men. I trained these men personally. They've worked hard to exceed even my expectations. They are better than good!*" Logic is dead serious, and everyone finds that hilarious.

The Colonel says, "*Shut the ship down and go home. Oh, and by the way, the compound that was destroyed was filled with twelve dead bodies armed to the teeth. You did good Ace! The cleaners removed any traces of evidence and made it look like a gas line explosion. Everyone is satisfied with that explanation. Omega made sure to keep it off the news cycle. Good work men. Have a safe trip home. I am proud of the work you've done. You're dismissed.*"

Chapter 27

LOGIC

The Colonel leaves just as quickly as he appears. With very little fanfare. Everyone huddles around the room. No one is leaving. They know the real debrief is just about to begin. I will leave it up to Chaos to decide whether his sister stays or not. Everyone is talking at once.

I hear Toni say, *"I need to rest, if that's ok?"*

Chaos says, *"Sure, go ahead."* Toni leaves the room. I glance at Ace, he looks troubled. Everyone reclaims their seats.

Gator says, *"I don't know what that was, but..."*

Coup pipes in with, *"That was a cluster... And to think I dressed up in a monkey suit and for what?"*

Polar says, *"This is the first time I've come away from an op feeling unfulfilled, and I don't like it."*

Dome agrees, *"You can say that again. There is no closure!"*

Sledge hits us with the mother load by saying, *"If there's another group of covert operatives out there, I want to know who they are. I can't be the only curious one in the bunch!"* A wave of nods goes around the room. *"I'm sure we all want that particular information. If for no other reason than to compare notes. We know we are better. We want to know how much better."* I just smile and nod. If nothing else, I love a riddle.

Chaos says, "Wait! Logic. We are going with the assumption that there is a group or team out there somewhere that functions like Alpha, Bravo, and Charlie squad, and we don't know about them. How is that possible?"

"Think about it for a sec, Gator. All of us. Alpha, Bravo, and Charlie teams were being hunted during operation Thistle. When we finally got the Colonel back, and neutralized the Petrenko's, we were being told not to worry about the players responsible for the coup in Washington. We were told they were already neutralized. If neither of us, did it, then who did?"

"Wow! Ok. You have a very valid point. Thank you for the headache this riddle is likely to cause me. Because, if what you suggest is accurate, and it usually is, then who are these people? Where are these people? Why would they be kept secret? Even from us. More importantly, who leads this super elite killing squad? Alpha, Bravo, and Charlie were formed around the same time. We all knew the others existed from the beginning. Why would this squad have been kept secret?"

"I don't have all the answers yet. But I will. There are two possibilities. Either they were formed before us, or they were formed after we were. What I find most puzzling is to wonder who's qualified to lead the squad of super elite killing soldiers? I highly doubt it's the Colonel. He has his hands full already. What with us and being the Head of National Security. There is no way he could also be leading another group of covert operatives. That is way too many irons in the fire. Even for the Colonel."

"You're right Logic. There is no way he could juggle all of that and stay sane."

"Nope!"

Pyro says, "*I have a question.*"

I say, "*Shoot.*"

"No offense Chaos, Ace, but if Arlene Petrenko had her hands on Toni why would she just dump her out in the middle of the woods in Poland? Why not kill her?"

This is how I know my men are better. They have been trained to think outside the box. That was not explained by the Colonel, and it wasn't touched on by Toni.

Chaos responds, "No offense taken. That is a very valid question. One that has been whipping my butt since we rescued Toni. I don't have an answer. Toni claims she was being held by four men with Russian accents. After a brief phone call they left, and not too long after that we swooped in. So, the question is who called and why did they leave her alive?" There was an operational kill order still active on Toni at that time. There was no rescind order until after the rescue. The only thing that makes sense to my brain is either Arlene Petrenko didn't have her hands on Toni, or the rescue op was used to throw us off another lead. Which raises even more questions."

I groaned inside because I was hoping no one brought this up. Knowing Antonia Townsend is Zypher should put this entire situation to bed, but it raises more questions than it answers.

All eyes turn to me. Great! I respond, "I believe Arlene Petrenko put the hit out on your sister, but I don't believe she ever had her in her clutches. Toni locked you guys in the compound and took off. We are out in the middle of nowhere. There is no way she hiked out of here. Someone came in and whisked her away. The question is who? I can tell you now from the looks of it none of this is what it seems. The Colonel gave us Zypher to withhold something else. If we approach her directly, she will notify the Colonel we are asking questions.

Zypher outranks everyone in this room. There are things she can't share with us. I believe we were made to believe we rescued Chaos' sister. I don't get the impression she was ever in danger while in Poland. Not unless assassins had tracked her down to that cabin. Which would be highly unlikely. Chaos, your sister is an Omega. She can never get out. So don't go suggesting it. She has powerful *connections and power of her very own. There is no out for her. We'll have to shake the trees with her in the dark. The Colonel will skin us alive if he discovers we are still asking questions. We have to be very careful in the way we approach this. So, in the meantime, you go about as you normally do. Your sister will need a new place to live. You might as well get started with that. We are wheels up in one hundred and twenty minutes. I miss my family. You're dismissed!"*

ACE

I make my way outside and burst out laughing. I don't know what else to do. I should probably look for Toni, and have a word, but I have no idea what I would even say to her. Toni is living her life in the way she sees fit. Out of all the things I could have guessed it was not this. How is any of this possible? Antonia Townsend is an Omega. Not just any Omega but Zypher. THE Zypher! I believe it and don't believe it all at the same time. My mind is blown. All this time I've been treating her with kid gloves. She must have been laughing her head off. I can't imagine what Chaos must be feeling. Mostly because I don't know what I'm feeling. I just need time to process this. I will go back inside and pack up my gear to head home. I'm too tired for a conversation of this magnitude.

Hopefully Gravity is ready to leave too. I am hit with an overwhelming desire to just lay down. It's not that I'm angry about this new bit of intel. The truth is I don't know how I feel. Until I can figure it out, I will keep my distance. We all have a job to do, and the last thing Toni needs is me interfering with hers. It's obvious she's very good at what she does. I can respect that. I go back inside and go right into helping to shut down the compound. With so many of us present it doesn't take long. I haven't seen Toni or Chaos since I came back in. That is probably for the best. They have a lot to work out. I do see Gravity though. I ask, *"If you're leaving soon can I hitch a ride?"*

He studies me for a few seconds then says. *"Sure. Wheels up in ten."*

"*Roger that.*" I grab all my belongings and go right to the bird. Three other team members are also hitching a ride. Thrasher, Dolphin, and Optic are already waiting.

Of course, the entire ride the conversation is centered around Antonia Townsend working for the Colonel. She's Zypher. My mind is still blown. It's going to take some getting used to. Zypher has saved our butts too many times over the years to count. To think all this time, it was Toni. I remained silent the entire flight. In truth, I have nothing to say. Once we land, I make my way to my ride. My black tricked out Ducati is right where I left it. Off to the right side of the hangar.

Once the team deplanes, Gravity approaches me and asks, "*You wanna grab a beer?*" He has something he wants to say.

"*Sure.*"

"*Let's go to Joe's.*"

"*I'll meet you there.*"

Joe's is a sports bar located nine miles from here. As badly as I want to go home, I will hear the man out. I want to shower and sleep. That is all. It doesn't take long to make it to Joe's. We enter at the same time and find an empty table way off in the back. As soon as we enter the bar the atmosphere shifts. It happens every time. We command attention when we are alone; it gets worse when we are in a group. The big bad bikers used to test us. They caught us on a bad day. Let's just say that never happened again. Everyone lived to tell the story. All things considered that was a good day for the bikers. They just may not know it.

Kelly Ann sashays over. She's a cute blond that's begging for trouble. So far, I've been able to avoid it. She winks at me and says, "*What will it be, boys?*"

"The usual for me."

"A Guinness for me."

"Coming right up." She sashays away with a little extra in her swing. Like I said, she is begging for trouble.

Gravity asks, *"Is that you?"*

"Nah."

"Do you mind? I need to blow off some steam."

"All yours, bro." I'm thinking to myself I hope he knows what he's getting himself into. He's a grown man after all.

He looks at me and says, *"You know she loves you right?"*

"What's your point?"

"Maybe, you should have spoken to her before you left. She must be feeling a sense of déjà vu."

That stops me in my tracks. I never thought of that. I shake my head and put it in my hands. I am a complete idiot! I left without saying a word. I left without making a path forward for us to... I don't know to anything really. The magnitude of my stupidity is choking me out. The waitress delivers our drinks.

Gravity says, *"This one's on me."* He slides Kelly Anne a fifty and his phone number. Yeah, he's that sure of himself.

She smiles at the fifty-dollar bill, and it brightens when she sees he's slipped her his number. She addresses Gravity, *"My shift ends at eleven."*

"I'll be waiting to hear from you by 11:05." She giggles and sashays away. She's twenty-eight years old and ready to settle down and have kids. I will keep that bit of information to myself. That is the very reason I haven't taken her up on her offer. If Gravity isn't careful, he's about to have a baby momma. I chuckle

at the idea while sipping my beer. I glance at the door and nearly choke when I see who enters the bar. Oh crap! The moment our eyes meet I chug my beer down to the bottom of the bottle. I am going to need all the courage I can get. This does not bode well for me. Every eye in this joint is on her. Both men and women. She's gorgeous!

Toni stops in front of the table and stares me down. She says hi to Gravity without even glancing in his direction. Gravity picks up his beer and leaves the table. He disappears to parts unknown. Thanks for having my back bro.

Toni asks, *"May I have a word with you in private?"*

She's not really asking. For some reason I feel real fear. I'm man enough to admit that. I get up from the table and follow Toni out the bar door. Her backside will make your mouth water. I follow her to an all-black Escalade. She unlocks the doors and gets in on the driver's side. Yeah, I guess she's driving this train. I get the feeling I am in so much trouble right now. I get in on the passenger side and turn to face her. She isn't looking at me. This is bad. Very bad.

So, I throw myself on the mercy of the court. *"Toni, I'm sorry. I shouldn't have left without at least speaking to you first. I didn't know what to say. I still don't. I am trying to process this. But I should have stayed to tell you that much. Tell you I needed time. I didn't do that, I'm sorry."*

When she looks at me, I see tears sliding down her cheeks. I want to kick my own butt. I go to touch her, but she pulls away. Yeah, very bad. She doesn't say anything for a very long time and when she does, I think I die inside. *"I'm sorry I couldn't tell you about my job. I know that hurt you. I mistakenly believed maybe we could talk about it and come to an understanding. You've made it very clear that isn't an option. I came to say goodbye. I figure it's the least I can do."*

"What do you mean, goodbye?"

"I am leaving the states."

"Wait. What? I don't understand."

"I can't go back to my house. It's been compromised. So, I've decided to take a post out of the country. There is nothing holding me here. I discussed this with my brother. I think its best."

"So, let me get this straight. You aren't here to discuss this with me. You are coming to inform me. The decision has already been made."

"From your lack of a response, I didn't think it mattered."

"Toni, it matters. It matters a lot. I was afraid of saying the wrong thing, so I left."

"Yeah, I noticed. That's seems to be a pattern of yours. For the record, it hurts like a son-of-a-gun when you do that. Maybe work on that for your next relationship. No woman I know will tolerate that behavior. Just a bit of friendly advice. Take care of yourself."

"So, this is it? You have nothing else to say to me."

"I had a lot to say, but you weren't interested in hearing it. So, now all I'll say is goodbye."

Chapter 28

I take several deep breaths to keep my head from exploding. My chest also feels like it will explode. I don't know how to fix this, and it scares me. *"Toni, I love you. I have always loved you. I will always love you."* I'm not sure what's going on, but it feels like my heart is breaking. This isn't how I picture this would go.

"I love you too. You know that."

"Then give us a chance."

"I did that, and you walked away! Again. It hurts too much to allow you to continue to do that. I won't continue to take risks with my heart. You don't seem to want to protect it. So, I have to. It's getting late, and I have a few loose ends to tie up before I leave tomorrow."

"Tomorrow! You're leaving as soon as tomorrow. So that's what I am to you, a loose end? You're leaving tomorrow?"

"Yes. I'm leaving tomorrow." I notice she doesn't answer my other question. Her mind is made up. I don't know what else to say. *"Toni. Please?"*

"Please what, Adam. Do you even know what you want?"

Whoa! She sounds angry. *"Yes. I want a life with you."*

"Let me tell you what I see Adam. Maybe you do want a life with me, and that's debatable, but you walk away like you're the only person with something invested. With something to lose. That does not make for good boyfriend-husband material. When you love

someone, you fight for them. You refused to fight for me! I want a man that is willing to fight for me. Not someone who walks away when a difficult situation arises. Not someone who will bail on me. You may want to work on your interpersonal skills. I can't be in a relationship and be afraid that if I make one mistake things will fall apart. I have to know that you will be there for me no matter what. I would be there for you no matter what. You know that don't you?"

"Yes. I do. I admit I need some work, and I am all about progress. I am asking you to reconsider. Please, give me another chance to make this right between us. I know I messed up and I'm sorry. Don't walk away from what we have here."

LOGIC

When I walk through the door my very pregnant wife is waiting for me. I never get tired of how that makes me feel! I say, *"Hello, wife."* She says, *"Hello, husband. We've missed you."*

"You have no idea, Princess." I wrap my very pregnant wife in a tight embrace. She is everything I ever dreamed of. She's, my anchor. I love this woman with everything in me. I nuzzle her neck and she squeals. I lift my head and ask, *"Where's Ty?"*

"He just went down for the night. If you hurry, you can still catch him before he falls asleep. He had an adventurous day."

"Let me kiss him goodnight. You coming?"

"Nah. By the time I make it back up those stairs he'll be in REM sleep. You go ahead. I'll be waiting down here for your return."

"Sounds good. I won't be long." I take the stairs two at a time to get to my little man. I have missed my family like crazy. I hate being gone this long. It always feels like I've missed so much when I return. I walk into his bedroom. He must have heard me coming. He's standing up in the middle of the bed. I scoop him up and hold him close. We just stand there holding each other. I wouldn't trade this for anything in the world. I don't know how long I hold him, but he lets me do it without fussing. After a few minutes I pull back and look at his sweet face. He says, *"Dada. Home."* More like "dada 'ome", but I get the picture. The sweetest sound I've ever heard. *"Yes. Dada home. I've missed you son."* He is smiling and nodding his head. Everything he needs to say has been said. I just stand here breathing him in. This is my life and I'm so lucky to have them. Nothing is better than this.

After a hundred kisses and a few bedtime stories my son gives way to sleep. He fought it for as long as he could. My wife sent me a text saying she would be waiting in our bedroom. I can only imagine she's eager for me. Samar says you've been with Ty for an hour and wiggles her eyebrows at me. Yeah, we are definitely on the same page. Thank God for pregnancy hormones. They are the best. I am home. Finally. I tell her. *"Let me take a quick shower. Don't fall asleep on me. I need you."* She says, *"Not a chance big guy."*

PRESIDENT

"Thank you for stopping by on such short notice, Dicky." Whenever the President calls me Dicky, I am not going to like what he has to say. I remember the last time he called me Dicky. I was strong armed into becoming the Head of National Security. What can it possibly be this time? I think I prefer it better when he calls me Colonel. I try hard not to tense up at the sound of his moniker for me. I don't want or need anything else on my plate at the moment. I feel tired.

We have company so I refrain from saying the first thing that pops into my head, and instead respond with, *"I serve at the pleasure of the President."* I noticed him fighting hard to hide his smile. He knows better. We are both full of crap! I don't so much as twitch. Any other time I would be howling with laughter after uttering such drivel. He has Howard Montcrief, his Chief of Staff, in attendance. Something about him seems slimy to me. So, I refrain from misbehaving. We try to play nicely when others are in the sandbox with us. I don't like this guy. I have my eye on him for several reasons.

"Have a seat, Colonel. Can I get you anything?" That's code for I need a minute. *"Howard, Emma is away from her desk, would you mind rustling a cup of coffee up for the Colonel."* Of course, he'd mind. But when the President of the United States tells you to make a cup of coffee, you very well make the darned coffee. That doesn't mean I'm going to drink it though. I don't happen to like coffee. Once Montcrief leaves the room the President says, *"There will be a package waiting on your desk when you get back to your office. Another package will be delivered to your men. Tell your pack of rabid dogs the President of the United States says to stand the freak down! That is an order. Dicky, so help me if they continue to poke their noses in matters that don't concern them, I will hack their noses off. Are we clear?"*

"Yes, Mr. President."

I knew Logic wasn't going to let this one go. I may just have to shoot him myself one day soon. Why can't he ever let anything go? He is one of the best to be in the business ever. Even better than I was when I had his position. I am hoping to turn the throne over to him one day, but I can't do that if he's dead. What a rock head! I barely have time to smile and say, *"When's the last time you were fishing, Mr. President?"* Before Montcrief returns, coffee in hand. This is done to make Montcrief believe we've been shooting the breeze waiting for his return. He's a self-serving piece of work! Filled with his own self-importance. I can hear his whiney voice in my head saying, I work directly for the President. He relies heavily on my sound judgement. I'm the sole of discretion. Blah, blah, blah.

What he doesn't know is the President keeps him close because he can't be trusted. He is kept out of the loop on most matters. It's comical really. Howard passes me the cup of coffee. I would be insane to drink from this cup. I wouldn't be surprised if he put cyanide in it. I thanked him graciously and set the cup down on the table. I use the spoon to stir it and pretend I'm about to lift it again for a sip before conveniently responding to something the President asks me. Back in the saucer the cup goes. Where it will remain untouched. Howard smiles real pretty, but he doesn't like me much. He tries to hide it behind his horn-rimmed glasses. But I see more than he would like to reveal. He sees me as a threat. He may be right. I am currently investigating him.

He better hope he's squeaky clean! If not, well… A syringe to the back of the neck with an untraceable cocktail will be my gift to him. With a major coronary being the end result. The President is up for re-election soon. Once that is shored up a dirt nap may very well be in Howard's future. His connections will no longer be necessary. He's a puny pale little fellow. More than likely he was bullied in school. He's intelligent enough one could say. But there is nothing really impressive about him exactly. It's his connections that give him value. His connections have come in handy a time or two. He is greasy and slimy. The connections he has are of the same ilk. These people are more likely to stab you in the back in a dark alley than meet you face to face on a battlefield. There is no honor in them!

I'm holed up with the President for over an hour before making it back to my office. True to his word there is a large square box sitting in the center of my desk. I don't see the name of the messenger service that delivered it. I am curious about what's inside. I sniff and feel around the box just to be safe. I take a letter opener and slice up the outer wrapping. I peel it away to find a beautiful mahogany box inside. I wouldn't mind if POTUS saw fit to gift me with a box of Cuban cigars. I deserve them after all. The bottom of the box is cold to the touch. Hmmm. Could very well be cigars. I lift the lid to peek inside. When I glance inside, I throw my head back and laugh and laugh. I laugh so long my eyes leak. This is way better than Cuban cigars!

Chapter 29

ACE

The Colonel decided we should get together and kick back as a team. So, we decided to have a BBQ. The Colonel's paying for everything, so we took him up on his offer. We got the most expensive cuts of meat. The most expensive alcohol. We didn't bother to cut any corners. We deserve the best. All eighteen of us are in attendance. We are still reeling from the tongue lashing the Colonel gave us two days ago. He was pissed! He knows we've been looking into the whereabouts of Arlene Petrenko. We've also been trying to figure out who the other covert operatives are. Logic feels he may be on to something. He stumbled across an acronym. C.E.N.T.A.U.R., we have no idea who or what that is. A person or a group. Could be just about anything.

But from the reaction we got from the Colonel it appears we stumbled onto something important. According to the Colonel, POTUS is ordering us to stand down, or he will stand us down. Logic stumbled across something huge. Someone knows something, and if I know Logic, and I do, he ain't standing down. So, there's that. He will just go about his doings a lot more discreetly. He's very good at getting information. Especially the kind of information people tell him not to touch. That is his way. I doubt even the Colonel can stop him. He loves and respects the Colonel. So, the president ordering him to stand down. I just don't see it happening.

We are just about to clear the table when the doorbell

rings. We're in the middle of nowhere, and everyone that knows about this place is sitting around a monstrous table. So, who can possibly be ringing the doorbell? Before you could say boo, there are eighteen heavily armed men with various weapons at the ready, and we begin to fan out in all different directions. It's done so quickly and smoothly you would think it was choreographed. Logic goes to the door, and I follow. The others are fanned out around the backyard. Expecting trouble. Logic has his sidearm down by his side. He checks the peephole. He looks back and shakes his head, then proceeds to open the door. Just a little. I come to stand on the other side of the door.

There's a tall thin person dressed in all black, including a helmet with a large square package in hand. Logic says, *"Remove the helmet."* The delivery person sits the package on the ground in front of the door and then proceeds to remove the helmet. Standing before us is a woman. One of the most beautiful women I've ever seen. Her skin is the color of midnight. Her eyes are almond shaped. A piercing blue in color. Her hair is almost platinum blond, but not quite. It slides down her back in a long braid. Her features are ethereal. She is the most exotic creature I've certainly ever seen.

Logic inquires, *"May I help you?"*

"Yes, sir. I have a special delivery."

"From whom?" She has no discernible accent. She could be from anywhere on the planet. Before she responds our phones buzz. All eighteen of them. I pull mine from my back pocket and scan the text. The text reads: A gift from POTUS. Enjoy your evening, xoxo Colonel. The Colonel thinks he's funny. I accept the package from the messenger. I look out to the driveway. She is riding a scooter, but it has no logo on it. I ask, *"Which messenger service are you with?"*

"I don't work for a messenger service."

"Who do you work for?"

She says, *"Enjoy your evening, sirs."* She turns around and walks away. I go to grab her arm. In two moves she has me on my back. She moved so fast I barely recognized what was happening. I jump up and grab her by the throat. She throws her hands up in mock surrender. Then she smiles and winks at me. She doesn't seem the least bit fazed. I apply a little pressure and she blows a kiss at me. Logic is studying her in stunned silence. I too am stunned, but I can't show it. This thin slip of a woman put me on my back. There are men who weigh three times what she does that can't do that. If I wasn't already in love, I would be falling hard and fast for this sublime creature. We are in a standoff. She doesn't look the least bit afraid. Unless I missed my guess, she is enjoying this. After a couple tense minutes, Logic says, *"Please release the fairy."*

By this time several of the guys have come outside and gathered around to watch the show. I am so happy none of them were present when she took me down. I couldn't live with them if that happened. I would never hear the end of it. I take my time and remove my hand. She puts her hands down by her side. Her stance is anything but casual. This one is trained. It takes one to know one.

Coup says, *"Dad, can I have her for Christmas?"* She smiles, and so do the men.

Logic says, *"Afraid not, son. This one's poisonous."*

Gator says, *"Yum."* She saunters over and grabs her helmet. She winks at Logic. Then sits on her scooter and replaces her helmet. Before starting the scooter, she takes a look at each of our faces. It's almost like she's cataloguing us. She smiles. Her teeth are so white they look fake. This woman is drop dead gorgeous! Before replacing her helmet, she blows the group a kiss. Then rides off into the night. We are stuck in place long after she leaves. It's like being hit with a bolt of lightning.

Gator says, "*I want one of those for my birthday.*" We all nod in agreement. We go back to the backyard. After seeing perfection this party feels anticlimactic.

Logic pushes used disposable plates to the side and sits the box directly in front of his seat. Pyro says, "*Let me have it, boss.*" He literally body blocks Logic to the side. Logic stares down at his six-foot four-inch frame but doesn't utter a sound. Sometimes we are protective of Logic. He gets it and gives us a little latitude. Just a little. Pyro unwraps the package and opens it slowly. Very slowly. We are all waiting on bated breath. Once Pyro gets a glimpse inside, he throws the lid back and smiles. We all huddle around the box. We move back to give Chaos a better look. Sitting in the center of the box on a bed of black satin is a severed head. Not just any severed head. It's Arlene Petrenko's blond severed head. Attached to the lid of the box is a note. The note reads: Compliments of the United States government. Chaos throws his head back and laughs. We all do. This is the gift that keeps on giving.

Epilogue: Ace

A few months have passed since our last op, and I'm feeling restless. Logic's wife Samar gave birth to another baby boy. So, Logic has taken a leave of absence. He's as happy as a man can be. Our family is growing. Venom is sticking close by for added security. Gravity had a pregnancy scare of his own. He was shaking in his boots thinking he may have knocked up his barmaid. He caught a lucky break. She got her period. I wonder if she's disappointed. He won't be drinking from that well again. I crack up every time I think about it. Gravity as a baby daddy. Gravity and Thrasher got back into the ring. We had to declare a draw. They were both bloody, and neither of them would stand down. They resembled mincemeat. It was an ugly bloody mess. No winner declared, so the money rolls over to the next cage match. The pile is getting higher and higher.

We haven't found an answer to the question of our unknown elite operatives. Once we received the severed head, we knew without a shadow of a doubt they existed. Not only do they exist, but they went into the Ukraine during an active war situation and decapitated Arlene Petrenko. Then served her severed head to us on a platter. That was cold blooded. I for one love it! Whoever these people are, our paths are sure to cross. There aren't a lot of people out there who do what we can do. At some point our paths will cross. Logic and the rest of the team members can't wait for that day! I am looking forward to introducing myself. What fun!

I have decided to take matters into my own hands. I have been on the sidelines long enough. I can't accept the decision

Toni made to end things between us and move across the globe. I just can't. I am hitching a ride to Switzerland. I need to see her, and now is the perfect time. I will admit I'm a little nervous, but I love her. That won't change. Chaos has been giving me these weird looks, but he hasn't addressed the situation. I know he wants to, but he's giving us room to work this out between the two of us. I can appreciate that. After a long eight-hour flight I am ready to be on terra firma. I feel restless and a little cranky. I was able to finagle Toni's address from Chaos and make him promise not to tell her I was coming. After an hour's drive, I stopped in the middle of the road. I can see her cottage sitting off in the distance. I don't really have a plan. I am going to wing it, I guess. I put the car back in drive and finished the last leg of my journey. Standing outside her cottage door, I feel my palms sweat. I wipe my hands on my jean leg and ring the doorbell.

I hear some rustling around right before the door opens. Toni opens the door with a smile that is quickly replaced by confusion. *"Ace, what's wrong? Is Chaos, ok?"* She called me Ace. She gives a quick glance over her shoulder. I step into her personal space, but don't see anyone else in the room.

I say, *"Hi, doll."* I do this while perusing the room. Toni hasn't invited me in and is blocking the door. Something feels off. She doesn't look scared, so maybe she isn't in danger. I ask, *"May I come in. It's cold out here."* She doesn't move right away. After a few tense seconds she takes a step back to allow me to enter. Needless to say, I am not prepared for what greets me.

FIN!

About The Author

A. C. Gregory

I am a disabled Army Veteran, retired nurse, and aspiring author. I am the mother of seven, and the grandmother of eight. My husband of one hundred years and I are empty nesters. We share our home  with our fur baby, Rebel. I enjoy reading, riding my ATV around our land, and traveling (pre-Covid), and more reading. Some of my favorite authors are: L.A. Banks, Brenda Jackson, Rochelle Alers, Mika Jolie, Christine Feehan, and many others.

Books By This Author

New Beginnings: Montgomery Clan Series Book 1:

Taming the Alpha Male… Ambitious. Determined. Resolute. Edward Montgomery has been trained to take over the family business. Walking in his father's footsteps is a plus. Walking down the aisle was never in his plans. Having a woman on his arm is one thing, putting a ring on it, something else entirely! When Edward Montgomery says he has no plans to marry he is to be believed. Since taking over the family business their stock has soared. It has taken all of Edward's time and energy. Montgomery Mergers and Acquisitions is his lady love. She is the only lady he makes time for. Sheila Waters just wants to save the world. One person at a time. She's chosen a path that will allow her to make her dreams come true. After a lot of hard work and sacrifice the last thing Sheila expected was to be accused of prostitution. The events that follow has her plotting a certain someone's murder. She will get back to saving the world later. After losing her soul mate Sheila put all of her time and energy into making her department more efficient. Bringing smiles to the faces of those in need. Now is not the time to lose focus.

Started With A Kiss: Montgomery Clan Series Book 2:

DIGITECH CEO Derek Montgomery shared a steamy stolen moment with a total stranger. He's so thrown off balance that when she is standing in front of him, he's rendered speechless. Derek has always been confident and self-assured, but this moment causes doubt. Does love at first sight truly exist? Should you believe in fate? Raven Sinclair has vowed never to enter into another relationship, ever again! Her marriage to an evil narcissist crashed and burned! The experience left enough scars behind to cause her to run far and fast. She's a travel nurse and doesn't stay in one place long enough to worry about a relationship. The universe has other plans! One dance leads to an unforgettable encounter. Try as she might, she cannot outrun her destiny!

Denying Logic: Men Of Honor Series Book 1:

There are people in this world whose sole purpose in life is to keep evil at bay. Putting their lives on the line so the common man can sleep safely at night. Men and women whose first thought is to defend their country. Logic is such a man. He takes pride in his country. His list of priorities are as follows: God. Country. Duty. Logic is an elite level soldier. He has honed his skill as a Navy seal, and was handpicked to lead Alpha team. His genius IQ and his size puts him head and shoulders above the enemy. The terror he faces on a daily basis has made him jaded. Logic has vowed to rid the world of the evil that lurks in the shadows, and to do it without a spouse. He cannot cope with the idea of bringing kids into this messed up world. For every evil human he removes from the earth another three steps forward to take its place. The question is: Is it possible to win the war on terror? With Alpha team on the job and Logic leading them the answer is a resounding YES! I sleep a lot better knowing they are on the job!

Second Chances:

Cache McCabe: Widow. Father. Horse ranch owner. Has only ever loved one woman. His late wife, Susan McCabe. When he finds his eyes and his mind wandering to a certain someone, he feels guilty. He knows Pamela Bennet is much too young for him. Like twenty years too young. And if that wasn't bad enough, he also feels like he's betraying his wife's memory. For the first time in many years his body is starting to respond to the sight, sound, and smell of a woman that isn't Susan. Pamela is younger than two of his three sons. Will he walk away, or run head long into a love like he's never known? What's a man to do?

Pamela Bennet: Single. Scarred. Teacher. She ran away from Chicago after a disastrous relationship almost turns deadly. All she wants now is a fresh start, and to heal. She finds herself on a ranch in Oklahoma. Life takes unexpected turns, and takes you along for the ride, whether you're willing or not. She buries her pain deep, and her emotional scars even deeper. The mere thought of a relationship causes her to break out in hives. When she finds her eyes searching, and her imagination wandering to a certain ranch owner, she knows trouble is brewing. Some situations can't be avoided. Will one night of passion lead to a lifetime of regret?

FACING THE EARL:

The Earl of Sussex is set to marry in one weeks' time, to Lady Arabella. The whole world will be watching. The last thing the Royal family needs is a SCANDAL! William, Earl of Sussex is playing with fire. This particular flame has a name, and it's not Lady Arabella. Her kisses send the Earl up in flames. Will he resist the temptation for the sake of duty and honor? Piper McAllister is a journalist for the London Times. She goes undercover to get photos and write and article for their social column. The very last thing Piper needs is to make the front page of the very newspaper she works for. Piper is keeping a secret. Her secret leads to an explosive confrontation, and an extensive hospital stay.

Burning Desire

Rose Marie Warren has tried just about every conventional method available to her to aide in her finding a man suitable for dating. Barring a male-ordered-groom, of course. Her professional life is sown up tight. The only thing missing is a husband. Rose has her demons. One of her demon's has a name. Angela Marie Warren. Angela is Rose's mother, and the example she set for her daughter to follow is less than exemplary.

Rose wants to be nothing like her mother. in order to ensure that never happens she has set into place a set of complexed, iron clad rules. Her rules are non-negotiable! But every once in a while, life has other plans. How will Rose navigate her complexed system of rules when tall, handsome, sexy Eric Chambers enters the scene? Eric's nearness makes it difficult to adhere to her rules.

Eric Chambers is the very definition of tall, dark, and handsome. He is also so much more than that. His parents raised their five boys with equal parts love, discipline, and respect. Eric's is used to following rules. His father is a retired marine. Discipline is his backbone. He will give Rose exactly what she's asking for. Right? Eric had dedicated his life to public safety. He has decided that thirty-six is the perfect age to settle down and have children. He has decided Rose is perfect. Eric will need patience and perseverance to navigate the rules.

Eric is on a blind date when he spots Rose sitting at a table nearby. When their eyes connect every fiber of his being responds. His reaction to Rose is visceral! The chemistry is palpable. His reaction to their brief interaction throws Eric off guard. There is nothing he can do about it, but fate has it's own plans. Fate won't allow the two of them to leave the restaurant without some form of contact. That contact shakes both of them to the core. It scares the living daylights out of Rose.

Her response to Eric and the chemistry between them is to run all the way to Paris. Rose imagines she can outrun her destiny. She won't answer his calls. She won't return his texts, but all is not lost. Eric has three unsuspecting guardian angels. His guardian angels know Rose as well as she knows herself. They've decided to step in. She can run away, but Iris, Lily, and Daisy will yank her coattails so hard, it will stop her right in her tracks.

What's a girl to do?

Worth The Wait

Tara Reeves married Paul Reeves believing love conquers all. She was not prepared for the I Do's to include multiple affairs. Paul's sex life could be a spectator sport. He is doing every in N.C., but his wife.   Tara finally decides enough is enough. She never expected to come home and find Paul had beaten her to the punch. He took his belongings and some of hers. After all Tara has suffered this is her undoing. Thank God for best friends. Tara's best friend Staci is part southern charm, and equal parts Pitbull. Paul Reeves better watch his back.

 James Caldwell was left at the alter eight months ago, by a woman who ran off with a friend of his. Little did he know they were sneaking around behind his back. James is smart enough to realize someone up above has his back. When he meets Tara he acknowledges the instant attraction, but his morals will not allow him to even consider Tara as a viable candidate for a relationship.   James Caldwell is firmly in the I don't have time for a relationship category. There are times when things just don't go the way we plan them, and some things are well Worth the Wait!

Made in United States
Orlando, FL
16 June 2023